CONTENTS

C.A.E.C.O.

A novel of the Demon Accords

John Conroe

John Conroe

This book is a work of fiction. All of the characters, organizations, and events portrayed in this novel either products of the author's imagination or are used fictitiously.

The Demon Accords:
God Touched
Demon Driven
Brutal Asset
Black Frost
Duel Nature
Fallen Stars
Executable
Forced Ascent
College Arcane
God Hammer
Rogues
Snake Eyes
Winterfall
Summer Reign
The Demon Accords Compendium, Volume 1
The Demon Accords Compendium, Volume 2
Demon Divine
C.A.E.C.O.
The Demon Accords Compendium, Volume 3 (coming December 2019)

The Zone War series:

Zone War
Borough of Bones
Web of Extinction (coming Fall, 2019)

Cover art by Gareth Otton.

CHAPTER 1

The Reis family lived in the middle of nowhere, deep inside New York's vast Adirondack State Park. Their address listed the town of Keene, but it must have been on the edge of the town limits with the next burg over being named something like Desolation, Nowhere, or Abandon Ye All Hope.

Listen to me. I sound like my old boyfriend. Hardly the way to give a proper report. I'll start over.

The suspects, family name Reis, consisting of Robert, Helen, and twin children Maurice and Victoria, lived at the end of a three-quarter-mile dirt driveway, seven miles to the east of the center of the township of Keene, in the central portion of the Adirondack Park.

Our government-issue SUV was bouncing on the rutted-dirt, single-lane driveway and my threat assessment conditioning was maxing out at the multiple textbook-perfect ambush sites that we rolled through at a steady pace.

Special Agent Mitchell Allen was driving, while our boss, Special Agent-in-Charge Lois Jay rode in the shotgun seat. Me, Agent Caeco Jensen, had the backseat all to myself. Which was good, because that way my superiors couldn't see that my right hand was locked on my issued 9mm for most of the trip.

Literal hairs stood up on the back of my neck, something to do with the warning sign that said trespassers would be killed, which had been posted out by the main road. A warning that was throughly reinforced by the five Eastern coyote skulls tacked to a big oak halfway down the driveway.

Eastern coyotes should actually be called coy-wolves, as their western coyote DNA was co-mingled with a pretty good slew of wolf genes. The hybridization occurred when eastward-migrating coyotes bred with Canadian wolves on their way to populating the East Coast of the United States in the 1950s and 60s. Just nature refilling the predatory hole left when the native gray wolves had been eliminated by man.

Instead of twenty to thirty-pound canines, the Eastern variety was more like thirty to fifty pounds, with some males approaching seventy. The Reis family had killed a whole pack and posted their naked skulls as a warning. Most normal people didn't do that, thus reinforcing the idea that the Reises weren't normal people, confirming why we were here in the first place.

Also confirming why we, as in the FBI's Special Threat Response Team, were handling the call instead of the local Bureau agents out of Albany.

The STRT used to be called the Occult Task Force, but that got changed recently, about the same time that our leadership changed. Our group flies or drives around the country, responding to any situation where *special* circumstances may have occurred. By special I mean supernatural, but the Bureau can't actually bring itself to utter that word, so we use *special* instead. It's supposed to be less scary than the term *occult*. Less scary to the public or to Bureau agents, I don't know.

Lois Jay was new to her post, having replaced STRT's first boss, Agent Krupp. The switch came immediately after Krupp went off the reservation and tried to *apprehend* possibly one of the most dangerous targets she could possibly find while also arresting a fey prisoner, a black dog, who escaped federal custody only a day later, leaving three agents dead and two horribly disfigured.

Having a whole slew of agents draw down on Declan O'Carroll had been sheer idiocy, which I told her, several times, but, hey what do I know? Just dated the kid for like a year, that's all. Saw him call lightning like it was a dog, channel thousands of volts of electricity, burn multiple targets to ash with his mind, form tornadoes at will, and direct a tractor-trailer-sized load of dirt to stand up and walk at his command.

But no, she had had a major issue with him, almost from the moment she met him, and had tried to go all hardass on him. Wrong decision. Should have held back and let his teammates calm him down. Like I suggested.

Instead, she decided to bull forward, which was dumb for a lot of reasons. First, he was arguably the most powerful witch known and could have killed every agent or cop on the scene with basically a stray thought. Second, his *child* was the computer that controlled the world's entire stockpile of nuclear weapons, which is, to my mind, a pretty good reason to tread softly, and third, he was, at his core, one of the good guys.

But the FBI hadn't found an organizational way to come to grips with the emergence of the supernatural world when it busted out into open society. The bureau still struggled with its domestic law enforcement identity in an America that had werewolves, vampires, and witches, all of whom could perform superhuman feats of strength, speed, regeneration, or long-distance destruction.

I mean, sure, they set about gathering silver handcuffs and reinforced restraints, special holding cells, and getting supplies of silver, iron, and witch-spelled ammunition designed to stop supes, but they completely failed at establishing useful procedures, policies, training, and tactics for dealing with super powerful preternatural criminals.

The pressure from the brass, the conflicting signals, the power struggles at the top all came down on poor Krupp and pretty much bulldozed her off the rails. So she chose to focus on a skinny white boy who looked like a pushover. And she completely ignored the advice of the only team member with firsthand intelligence on Declan the Menace—that being, of course, me.

So, Krupp was gone and Jay was in and the verdict was still out. I knew very little about Jay, other than she had some Native ancestry, hailed from out West somewhere, and was handpicked for the job.

"Jensen, thoughts?" SAC Jay asked suddenly.

"Don't like the coyote skulls. Had a girl at Arcane, one of the witches, whose family used animal skulls as major no trespassing signs."

"So you think they're witches?"

"No. Tami's family used all kinds of skulls: deer, badger, coyote, anything. Those back there were an entire pack of coyotes. That's more like one set of predators killing off competing predators that had encroached on their territory, then leaving them as a warning to others. So I'm thinking they might be weres of one kind or another. Just a possibility. Too early to draw conclusions."

We were heading in to talk to the Reis family because of comments made by both Helen and Robert Reis on various social media sites. Both had posted some twisted stuff, but the bulk of it was written by Helen.

At this moment, the whole country—hell, the whole world—was a stirred-up mess over the supernatural situation. Are they still human? Do they have rights? Are they going to contaminate everyone? Should they be arrested? Should they be killed outright? Not to mention the other side that preached love thy neighbor and maybe get life-extending benefits from being vampire food.

On top of that powder keg was the looming threat of alien invasion by the Vorsook, and the fact that only supernaturals, led by Chris Gordon and Tatiana Demidova, had so far been successful in stopping said aliens. So when Mr. and Mrs. Reis started posting about supernatural people exerting themselves over the *sheeple,* as they stated it, well, the Bureau got interested. Especially when they used rather violent words and graphic phrases to portray their proposed solutions.

Mitch glanced at me in the rearview mirror, a slight grimace on his face. "Shit, I hope it's not witches," he said.

"Well, witches have an old saying: Never attack a witch in her home," I said to cheer him up—not. A girl's gotta have her hobbies. Picking on team members was one of mine.

Mitch Allen had been part of the team Krupp had with her on that day when Declan had pitched a little temper tantrum. And as I kept telling everyone who would listen, his earthquake had been just that—a little temper. Tiny, really. The Declan equivalent of a verbal tirade. Then he and Chris had gotten into it and the whole thing could have gone to real shit except Declan's current girlfriend, Stacia Reynolds, had stepped up and choked the punk out. Even I had to give her props for that one. Bold move. And, yet somehow they were still together. Go figure. I let him fight his own battles and we're kaput. She chokes him senseless and he's still all smitten.

"Do you have any suggestions, Agent Jensen?" Jay asked.

"Yes. First, we should tread carefully. Second, I should take point, and third, we need to be respectful."

"One and three are the same thing," Mitch protested. Our boss shot him a look. "Well, they are."

"Why, Caeco, should you take point?" Jay asked me, ignoring Mitch's comments.

"First, my warded necklace is much more powerful than the standard team artifacts you got from our witch supplier. Mine will protect me from a lot of spells that yours won't. Second, I have much faster reflexes than either of you, and third, because I will possibly recognize what we're dealing with first," I said, ticking off a finger for each point. Then I shut up and waited for her to ignore them.

"Okay. Valid. You take point, but you have to provide us as much warning as possible if it's going to go tits up," she said, earning raised eyebrows from Mitch and immediate credit with me for listening. Plus, *tits up*? What agent says that? Me—from this moment forward, that is.

I looked at the rearview and found Mitch's eyes. One eyebrow was raised in what I took to be surprise. Yeah, point goes to SAC Jay.

The driveway curved to the left and we came around to an open view looking out over a forested valley. A small ski chalet-style house sat on the property, its back to us. Based on the peaked roof that I could see from here, the front was likely a wall of windows that would look out over a hell of a nice view. A small satellite dish explained how they connected to the internet.

That's all the time I had to think about houses and vistas because a tall, muscular man stepped out of the back door with a pump shotgun held easily in one hand. Tawny brown hair and eyes that appeared yellow to my enhanced vision. Then the smell hit my nose, brought in by the car's heating and cooling system. Cat. No. *Cats*... specifically... cougars.

Great, a family of werepanthers. I opened my door and stepped out. We were at the extreme range of buckshot but well within the death envelope if he was packing deer slugs. *Keep as much car between you and the shotgun, Caeco.* My right hand hung near my holstered Glock.

"Sir, we are FBI agents. Please put down the shotgun. We're here to talk," I said loud and clear, although his own hearing should be about as good as mine.

"We've done nothing to warrant arrest," he yelled back. His voice was urgent yet he never moved the shotgun at all. My neck hairs went up. I paused and listened, sniffing the air. The wind came from the house side of the lot, toward us, so anything behind us was downwind, able to scent us but invisible to my nose. A leaf shifted in the woods to our left. A tiny noise, but all other noises had stopped—no birdsong, no skittering of rodents.

"Sir, put down the shotgun and please call your wife out of the woods," I said, waving a hand to my left as I moved away from the car.

He couldn't stop the surprise that filled his face.

"We're here to talk—that's it. You and Helen wrote some inflammatory stuff on social media. We want to discuss those remarks, that's all," I said. Behind me, I felt Jay and Mitch Allen stepping out of the car, Jay on the right, Mitch almost behind me. I put my left hand down by my leg and folded the little finger with my thumb, leaving three digits pointing down, waving it toward the woods on the left. It was our hand signal for weres, although I was holding it upside down. Immediately I heard Mitch rustle in the open driver's side of the car, then turn to face the woods. Couldn't see him, but I was absolutely dead certain he had turned to watch the dangerous forest to our side. I don't know how I know, whether it's the nano particles in my blood or the spliced genetic material that gives me certain *instincts*, and frankly, when it happens, I don't usually have time to ponder it.

I was also reasonably certain that Mitch now had a short-barreled 5.56mm HK rifle in his hands. That had more to do with knowing Mitch than any esoteric ability. He habitually kept a rifle loaded with silver-tipped ammo in a discreet pack on or near his person on every trip.

Robert Reis observed us for a moment, then slowly set the shotgun on the ground. Not that he even needed it. There had been only one werecougar at Arcane, but she was a real tough bitch.

"Mr. Reis, I'm Special Agent-in-Charge Lois Jay. With me are Agents Mitchell Allen and Caeco Jensen. We are just here to discuss your social media posts. Please call your wife in."

We all stayed where we were, waiting, seconds ticking by while he thought it over. His eyes, a buttery yellow, kept coming back to me with a little frown forming between his brows. Finally his posture shifted, almost infinitesimally, relaxing just a tiny bit. Then he turned his head to the woods and chuffed twice, which ended any lingering doubts I might have had about what he was.

Nothing happened for almost three minutes except I thought I heard very, very slight rustles in the woods, sounds that moved back toward him. Then, suddenly, a naked woman strode out of the forest, lithe and graceful, eyeing us without expression as she walked around behind her husband and into the house. When the door shut behind her, he waved us forward.

"Let's hear what our corrupt government has to say," he said, turning and leading the way to the door. The shotgun lay on the ground like an afterthought.

CHAPTER 2

The inside of the Reis's house was a surprise. I'd expected animal pelts and deer antlers and more skulls, maybe a butchered deer hanging from a rafter. Instead it was wood, iron, fieldstone, and Adirondack accouterments like birch bark furniture and old snowshoes on the walls. A big stacked-stone chimney was the primary focal point of the living room, with a built-in wood stove and a bluestone hearth. The mantle was a stripped and stained half log, holding an odd assortment of items. A bird's nest, an empty snapping turtle shell, a large lump of garnet-encrusted granite, and a family photo showing all four of them—in human form.

The kids weren't in the house, and as they were both listed as homeschooled, I thought they might be out in the woods as a safety measure in case we were hostile. Their presence was all through the house, though. Drawings, kids' books, a few wooden toys that looked scratched all to hell, clothing too small to fit either adult and, of course, the scent—cougar kitten.

Cats have a sharper smell than canines. Not the smell of cat urine, but a warm, bright scent that brought to mind short, thick fur and whiskers. That probably doesn't make sense to you but it's the only way I can describe it. Canines, well, anyone who ever smelled a wet dog has an idea of how they smell, although nowhere near as powerful as it is to me.

"You've both written some really provocative stuff. You have to understand why we might be concerned. Especially considering your natural abilities to make good on those violent thoughts," Jay said. I had flashed her another sign, the ASL this time. The W for were and the C for cougar.

Rob and Helen exchanged a glance. She had entered the room mere moments after he brought us in, wearing black sweatpants and a green top, which brought out her eyes. She wasn't pretty, her face too severe, I think, for that, but with her lithe figure and intense gaze, she was... visually arresting, if you'll pardon the phrase. Mitch kept his eyes mostly off her, which was a dead giveaway that he really wanted to stare at her. But Mitch had been with STRT long enough to learn the few lessons that I had been successful in teaching the team. Don't challenge weres unless you want a fight was the first one, right up at the top, along with not turning your back on any of the predators, and keeping your chin down and neck covered in the presence of unknown vampires. He knew that staring is always a challenge.

Lois Jay seemed to be handling the questioning like a champ, though. She rose another notch or two in my opinion.

"We are still accounted freedom of speech, unless *you're* here to take that from us," Rob answered. Helen had stayed quiet so far.

"Freedom of speech is guaranteed by the Constitution. But you know it doesn't give you carte blanche, right? You can't yell *fire* in a movie theater. Free speech is rooted in the principle that we are not allowed to harm others to get what we want. Calling for bloodshed to establish a protected position in society for weres like yourselves, and other supernatural people, is not protected speech. In fact, it borders on inciting hate crimes."

Helen's face twisted up and she finally spoke. "You say these things to assuage us, here in our own homes, but you don't mean them."

"Am I not telling the truth? You can tell, right?" the boss lady asked.

That caught Helen off guard. Weres can literally smell or sometimes hear lies rolling off the lips of the untruthful. I know *I* certainly could, even though I'm not a were or a vampire.

"You haven't spoken anything that *you* believe is untrue, but that doesn't mean the rest of your corrupt organization or government bedfellows believes that," Robert said.

"Absolutely true. But that's why *we're* here," she said, waving a hand at Mitch and myself. "We're part of a special task force within the Bureau that works with extraordinary humans like yourselves."

"You two are human," Robert said, looking from Agent Jay to Mitch before turning his yellow eyes on me. "But what is she?"

Jay looked my way. "She, too, is an extraordinary human. Just not one you've ever come across before."

"I'll say. She smells—wrong," Helen said, staring me down.

I smiled. "Who are you to say what's right and wrong? Isn't that what you preach about on the web? So you can't classify me as easily as I can smell that you're cougar clan? Doesn't make me wrong. And now you throw out a challenge?"

She held my gaze for a moment, then turned her stare on her husband. He picked up his cue right away. "You speak of challenge in our home?" he asked, a note of outrage in his voice. A *false* note. It was an act.

"I know a challenge when I see one, and I've answered every one directed my way. I also know it's not normal for weres of any variety to challenge guests. Well, except maybe for weasel clan. They're a little crazy to begin with, though."

"Agent Jensen," Jay rebuked softly.

"No, she's right. Weasels aren't fully sane," Robert said, his gaze now thoughtful. "How do you know so much about our kind, FBI girl who smells all mixed up?"

"Because I've lived with most every variety of supernatural folk," I said.

"She's young. Ah. I get it. She went to *that school,*" Helen accused, eyes fastened on me.

"If you mean Arcane in Burlington, then yes," I said.

Both cougars pulled back as they considered that. Another long look was exchanged between them.

"But what are you?" Helen asked.

"An agent with the FBI," I said. "We're here to talk about inflaming violence against others through speech. Why would you do that? Regular humans outnumber supernaturals by orders of magnitude. An out-and-out battle would result in millions of deaths, but also the likely extinction of supernaturals. Or do you think that by hiding away in the woods, you and yours would survive it?"

"No one would ever find us," Helen promised. "And we would make any hunters pay."

I nodded. "Sure, among the regular types. But the military has been working on anti-supernatural weapons and technology for quite some time now. You would eventually lose, as would your children."

"That computer would interfere. It works for supernaturals," Robert said.

"If by computer you mean Omega, it's the reason we're here," Agent Jay said. "Omega gives us heads up on any domestic terrorism threats it identifies, whether they be normal or supernatural."

They looked like they didn't believe us.

"Omega is interested in survival, as in the Earth's survival, and the continuation of humans of all kinds, as well as his own survival," I said. "He works against anything that threatens that."

"You call it he?" Helen asked, brows lifted.

"I've known Omega since he first formed sentience. It most often uses a male persona—not always, but mostly. Depends on the audience. Right, Omega?"

"Agent Caeco Jensen is correct," a young male voice said through the desktop computer speakers on the table in the far corner.

Both cougar kin spun around and hissed in unison. Beside me, I could feel Jay and Allen tense up. That's right. Were people aren't exactly like regular people. They handle surprises differently. A good lesson for agents to learn.

"It listens in?" Helen asked, appalled.

"Of course. You know he goes wherever he wants in the world of electronics. Why would here be different?" I asked.

It *was* different though; very different, as clearly depicted by the wide-eyed outrage and pulled-back body language. They thought they were removed from the world, just dipping in to stir things up, then pulling back to their wilderness safety. But now they were being shown how imaginary that safety really was.

"Inciting violence among the species of humans living on this world is completely at odds with the actions currently required if this world is to survive the coming conflict with the Vorsook," Omega expounded.

"The aliens?" Robert asked.

"Yeah, them," I said with a nod.

"You see why we're here to talk?" Agent Jay said, her voice smooth, tone even and reasonable.

"The aliens are real?" Robert asked his computer, glancing once at Agent Jay first.

"They are entirely real and pose an extraordinary threat to Earth. Because of close work among all kinds of humans as well as myself, we have gained significant resources of late. However, any threats that distract from our preparations cannot be allowed. Interspecies war is at the top of that list. So I alerted Agent Jay and her team to your words. I could have just cut your access to the internet, but that is a very short-term solution and does nothing to further our cause. Explaining it to you seemed to have a higher probability of helping you understand what we really face. It would be better to have you as active allies or at worst passive ones than to leave you to create any additional problems."

The shock was still present on their faces but their expressions had changed from outrage to cautious interest.

"The FBI works with you?" Helen asked the desktop PC.

"I work with anyone who is willing to work toward our common survival. I work against anyone who threatens those goals."

The cougar couple turned our way, Robert thoughtful, Helen maybe a bit less hostile.

Agent Lois Jay pulled out her phone and looked at the screen before raising her eyes to the Reis. "Can we conclude that you will curtail the more violent and provocative aspects of your postings?"

"We will continue to work for the rights of supernaturals," Helen stated, ready to argue.

"As is *your* right. By all means continue your work. Just use the legal apparatus, use public opinion. Lobby and organize. Don't incite violence," Jay said.

The couple exchanged a glance, then turned back to her and cautiously nodded. "We can do that," Helen allowed.

"Then we will leave you. We have other things to attend to," Jay said with a glance at Mitch and myself.

"You got a cell signal *here?*" Robert asked.

"The computer did it," Helen responded before any of us could answer.

"Ah. I see," he said.

We took our leave, heading back out the door and directly to the SUV. A small sound alerted me and I looked to our left, spotting two small furry faces peering at us from high in a pine tree. Both immediately pulled back when they caught me looking. My fellow agents remained completely unaware as we climbed back into the car and pulled out of the remote homestead.

CHAPTER 3

"Jensen, analysis?" Agent Jay asked while we were still on the driveway-slash-wagon trail.

Not sure what she wanted, I gave her the full info dump.

"Family unit of werecats, species cougar. Adult male is right-handed, six feet three inches tall, weight approximately one ninety-five. Female is left-handed, five feet six inches, one hundred and forty pounds. Neither is clearly dominant in the relationship, with family leadership shifting between the couple. Two children, a male and a female, twins, stashed in the forest to the west of the clearing. They observed our departure from a pine tree at about thirty-one feet above the ground.

"Single Remington model 870 shotgun noted in residence. No other signs of firearms, also consistent with pureblood weres.

"Documents on tabletop work surface indicate that Helen Reis works online as a freelance copy editor. Additional documentation in family area indicates Robert operates a small business titled Reis's Repairs. Invoice on table listed seven common household repairs for an individual named Ann Bronk, living at 16 Pine Avenue, Keene, New York.

"Open-concept living area allowed observation, both visual and olfactory, of the kitchen area. Primary diet is heavily carnivorous, leaning mainly to venison, but including rabbit, partridge, wild turkey, fish, both local and store purchased, as well as beef, chicken, and pork. Some greens, mostly leafy varietals, and dairy products were also present.

"Helen Reis made a Change from cat form to human in approximately one minute, twenty-three seconds, lending credence to likelihood that she is a full-blood were. Photos of individuals on bookshelf in rear of living room area show a strong resemblance to Robert. Mountain profiles in background of photos are a strong match with at least two Adirondack High Peak Mountains. Photos show males with large numbers of dead whitetail deer. Wounds present in photos indicate large cats mauled the deer. Surmise that Robert is also a full-blood cougar were, native to High Peaks region.

"Body language and micro expressions indicate that our argument to cease provocative social media posting was at least received and considered. Startle responses when addressed by Omega reinforce that conjecture. Also, they'll likely be gone from this property within forty-eight hours.

"What else are you looking for, ma'am?" I finally asked, not sure of how far to continue.

"Really?" Mitch asked from the front seat. I think he was maybe shocked by the amount and detail.

"What was the phone number on the invoice for the handyman work done for the neighbor?" Jay asked.

"Five one eight, five eight three, nine, nine, five eight."

"Is that right?" Mitch asked Agent Jay.

"I have no idea, but I'm guessing it is. You have an eidetic memory, Jensen? And extraordinary eyesight?" Jay asked.

"Have you seen my file, ma'am?"

"I have. I was also briefed on you by the director. But experiencing your abilities in person is much more educational than reading a file."

"What can I say? My mother does good work," I said, watching her reaction.

A microflicker of disagreement told me she wasn't a fan of my mother's gene editing and splicing work.

"You are unique," was all she said.

"Those weights seem kinda high. No way that lady was a buck forty," Mitch said.

"Weres are denser than regular humans. I add about fifteen percent to my weight estimates for wolves and cats. Twenty percent for bears."

"Oh," was all he said. "Why did you report whether they were right or left-handed?"

"There have been studies done to determine why any left-handed people exist in modern populations at all. Theoretically the trait should have died out long ago unless there was an evolutionary advantage. High numbers of successful professional athletes who are left-handed lend credence to this theory. It has been proposed that left-handed combatants have an advantage in hand-to-hand combat. It might be because right-handers are confused by the difference, or it could have something to do with the way their brains assimilate and process information during a fight," I said.

"Which hand do you use?" he asked.

"I'm ambidextrous."

He went silent, his eyes flicking to me in the rearview mirror a couple of times while he thought about that.

"Why did you say they'll be gone in forty-eight hours?" Agent Jay asked.

"Because they're weres, with a family, and have become

known to the US government. Paranoia has been pretty much bred into almost all the species of weres."

She didn't say anything, turning back forward as she pondered my words.

"We have a new mission?" Mitch asked our boss a moment later, glancing at the phone she still held in one hand. Slick subject change, Mitch.

"We've been called back to Washington. Jensen and I have a meeting to attend," was all she said.

Mitch gave me a glance in the rearview, raising one eyebrow when I shrugged. Our team is small, but other than Agent Chana Mazar, Mitch Allen is the only one who doesn't seem bothered by my test tube origins. He just treats me as an equal, and he often asks my opinion and seems to value it. He may express surprise at some of my skills and abilities, but he never seems to let it change how he treats me.

Agent Chana Mazar, our *borrowed* Israeli intelligence operative and supernatural expert, treats me decently, but seems more fascinated by my origins than accepting of me as a person.

Nothing more was said about whatever this meeting was until we got to Plattsburgh and the little regional airport where we had left our government jet.

Not gonna lie—it's pretty cool to fly around the country in an executive jet. I mean, it may not be as plush as what my ex likely flies in when he travels for Team Demidova, but it's pretty cool. I've been in Tanya's jet a couple of times and it's a full-on private 747, but this Lear that we have use of is nothing shabby, and there's only ever a handful of us onboard it, so it feels pretty private.

Once we were in the air, Agent Jay turned her attention my way. "What's the best set of clothes you have onboard?"

“My second-best dress suit,” I said. We all had ready bags packed with clothes and gear with us because we could wake up in DC and go to sleep in Hawaii or Alaska. So my gear was packed for a wide range of conditions. The fact that I got to wear business casual much of the time was a bonus too. Lots of my regular clothing came from companies like 5.11, Blackhawk, and Tru-Spec, so being able to wear it on the job was great. But suits go with FBI like uniforms go with the military. I had four decent ones.

“Get cleaned up and spiffy. We’ll leave right from the airport.”

“Where are we going?”

“The White House.”

I shut up and put on my suit.

CHAPTER 4

Our Bureau jet landed at Reagan International and a government car was waiting for us as we stepped off the plane.

SAC Jay didn't say a word as we rode in silence. My internal mapping function tracked our progress, comparing compass bearings and travel time, automatically plotting a course on the map in my head. With regular updates from any road signs I spotted as we drove, so I knew when we got close.

We didn't actually go to the White House, but pulled up to the US Treasury building next to it. A Treasury agent met us—well, met SAC Jay as we exited the vehicle. "Right this way, Special Agent," the woman said, completely ignoring me. I followed closely, which earned me a few glances from the Treasury woman, but she kept her mouth closed and ushered us into an ancient vault that was housed in the wing of the building closest to the White House. Before we were allowed in, we were relieved of cell phones, smart watches, and Agent Jay's iPad. Signs everywhere indicated electronics were forbidden, and a security guard swept us with an EM detector, ignoring our firearms but getting a curious look on his face when he scanned my shoulders, neck, and head. Most of my nanites cluster around and in my brain, although some are always circulating through my blood vessels. Even at their densest, they only just slightly set off his detector and after a moment's hesitation, he waved me through.

Inside, the vault was set up as a meeting room, and the main table was loaded with big brass. I recognized Michael Arnold, Director of the CIA; General Tobias Creek; Charles Knowles, Director of the NSA, and sitting next to him was our own boss, Tucker Tyson, who caught sight of Jay and waved us to sit behind him. Chairs lined both walls, and many were already filled with aides to the big shots. Across the table I spotted Nathan Stewart, Director of Oracle, his right-hand aide, Adine Benally, seated ramrod straight directly behind him. Stewart spotted me almost instantly, giving me a smile and head nod before turning to listen to the three-star Air Force general next to him.

The room was just settling down when a pair of Secret Service agents entered the room, looked around, and then spoke into their wrist mikes. I wasn't the only one to notice as the room instantly quieted. One of the agents listened for a moment to his earpiece and then spoke to the room. "The President of the United States," he said, backing against the wall.

Everyone stood and President Lyndall Polner entered the vault, two agents a step behind him on either side. The original agents stepped out of the room and the big vault door was pulled shut. I noticed that neither agent alongside the president had any discernible electronics visible on them.

President Polner took the chair at the head of the table. "Please be seated."

We all sat in unison.

"Okay, what's the status of the Vorsook conundrum?" the president asked.

"Mr. President, all signs indicate that Russia and China are preparing as requested by the Omega AI. From what we can tell, Omega itself is producing new weapon systems at a prodigious rate," General Creek answered.

"These new systems use the captured alien technology?"

"Yes, Mr. President. The drones achieve speeds and conduct maneuvers unmatched by any current Earth-based aeronautical technology," Creek said.

"And our own efforts to reverse engineer the Vorsook tech?"

"We are making major strides but are way behind the computer, Mr. President," the Air Force general next to Nathan Stewart said.

The president grimaced. "I talk to the damned thing every day, but I don't know that I'm happy it has such an edge on us. Where is it sending the finished drones?"

"The first group all headed to Burlington, Vermont, sir. The latest batches are heading up into space and setting themselves into geosynchronous orbits," the general said.

"*How* many did it send to Vermont?" Polner asked, eyebrows up.

"Ah, we think ten, sir. They moved out of the production facility at extreme speeds and they don't show up on radar. Three independent observers each agreed on the number ten, sir."

"*Ten* super drones to Burlington? Nathan, any comments?" Polner asked.

"Yes sir. Team Demidova was dealing with that incarnate demon. Declan O'Carroll was hurt. Omega reacted very strongly, sir."

"What did *ten* of those things do after the fact, Nathan? That horse was out of the barn?"

"Nine of them took up protective positions. One was sent through a portal to Fairie to persecute the Summer Queen, who was responsible for arranging the demonic incursion to kidnap O'Carroll, sir."

"You know that last part for a fact?" Polner asked.

"That the Summer Queen was responsible or that Omega punished her? The answer is the same in both cases, sir—yes—we have confirmation. Gina Velasquez was present in the room with Gordon and Demidova when Omega presented a rather eye-opening display of the new technology. The single drone was able to put the Summer forces on the run, Zinnia was forced to take shelter with her sister, Morrigan, and it will take years if not decades for her to be free of the debt she now owes the Winter Queen," Stewart said.

"And those nine are still on station in Vermont?" the president asked.

"No sir. They've left... at the same time that O'Carroll and Stacia Reynolds left."

"And went where?"

"There was local political pressure for him to remove himself as a target from the Burlington area. He decided to comply, but we don't know where he is currently. I was rather hoping to ask that question of the one person in this room who likely has better information than I do," Stewart said.

The president sat back, eyes wide, then looked around the room. "Enough with the suspense, Nathan. Who here would have better intel than you?"

"Tucker's junior agent, Miss Jensen," Nathan said, turning and looking directly at me. Every set of eyes in the room turned to me, most curious, but some hostile like General Creek, and one outright angry glare from my own director.

"Where is she? Oh, there you are. Stand up please, Agent Jensen," the president said to me.

I shot to my feet. "Yes Mr. President."

Polner looked at me for a moment, then chuckled. “At ease, Agent. You’re not in the military.”

Cursing myself, I relaxed from full attention into parade rest. I don’t think I was capable, at that moment, of anything less. The President of the United States was talking directly to *me.*

“Is that true, Miss Jensen? Do you have better intelligence on Declan O’Carroll than Nathan?” President Polner asked me.

“It’s possible, sir. I have regular contact with many of Declan’s closest friends. They likely know more than Director Velasquez or any other, ah, assets Director Stewart might have at Arcane,” I said, instantly regretting saying too much.

“Assets? Nathan do you have assets in Arcane?” the president asked.

“Ah, yes sir, I do. I was under the impression that that fact was a secret,” Stewart said, directing a raised eyebrow of his own in my direction.

“Miss Jensen, before we delve into the matter of where Mr. O’Carroll is, perhaps you could tell us how you’re aware of Nathan’s agent or agents?” the president asked in a very reasonable tone.

“Declan figured it out, Mr. President, and came to an arrangement with the ah, asset. He provides accurate information about himself to the asset and the asset keeps out of Declan’s way. I’m close with Jetta Sutton and Ashley Moore and on pretty good terms with several of the witches, as well as the school’s Alpha werewolf. Everyone pretty much knows about it.”

“He found out we planted a spy and then turned the spy?” Polner asked, his expression serious as death.

“Yes sir, although I would stress that the information the asset receives is all very accurate, just not fully complete. I'm not sure if *turned* is the correct term, but they have reached an agreement. Omega has helped the asset's family become settled and secure here in the United States, sir."

"So he finds out about this person and then *helps* him?"

"Yes sir. It's a very Declan thing to do," I said. "Any of the other witches would likely do something far more negative to a spy, but that's kind of the way he thinks, sir."

"Mr. President, if you'll recall, Caeco dated Declan for over a year and attended Arcane for the first year it existed," Nathan said.

"Tucker, you've had a close associate of O'Carroll's on staff for how long and you've done what with her?" President Polner asked, tone flat.

"We've been working to assimilate Agent Jensen into the Bureau, sir. She's been part of the Special Threat Response Team since right after it was formed. Sir," Tucker Tyson said, his body language uncomfortable.

"I see. And you, Nathan, put a spy on the boy and didn't tell me? A spy that everyone but me knows about, especially the spy's target. And I'm literally the last to know? It doesn't appear to me that *we* are using our resources very effectively. I'm disappointed," the president said, looking at Directors Tyson and Stewart with a deep frown. Nobody said a word as the president glared at both men. Finally he turned his head back to me.

"Miss Jensen? Do *you* have any idea where O'Carroll and Stacia Reynolds are?"

"My understanding, Mr. President, is that they are traveling the world, seeking out Earth's elementals. Declan is trying to forge alliances to draw on when the Vorsook attack again. I don't know their exact location at the moment, but I could ask Omega."

"Ask Omega?"

"Ah, yes sir. He'll generally tell me where the team members are unless it needs to be kept secret."

"You just ask the computer and it tells you where his creator is? I know he helps people all over the world, but this seems a bit too transparent."

"I've known Omega almost since he was born and I helped when he was under attack by the Vorsook AI," I said.

"And have you told *anyone* in your chain of command about this?"

"I have sought to share my insights into Declan and Omega, as well as Chris Gordon and Tanya Demidova, with my previous team leader on multiple occasions. She listened a few times, just not the most important ones. I've only worked with Special Agent-in-Charge Jay for a few days, but she's already asked my opinion more than Agent Krupp ever did. Sir."

"Agent Jensen, why are you with the Bureau? Seems to me you would be better utilized on Nathan's team?"

I paused to collect my thoughts and Nathan Stewart jumped in. "Mr. President, Caeco was raised in a very hostile, militant environment. She and I have had many discussions about her choice and I think she's trying to make a break from her past. Law enforcement as opposed to the darker aspects of some agencies, as it were. Is that a fair summation, Caeco?"

"Pretty good, Director Stewart," I said.

"I see. Forgive me, Agent Jensen, but I think you're completely wasted in your current role. Tucker, I want this young lady at *every* briefing that we hold on this topic. She's to be brought in for consultation before any action or contact with any of the PMDs is initiated. Got it?"

"Yes sir," Tyson said, jaw clenching.

Polner wasn't done though. He turned back to me. "Miss Jensen, are you familiar with the acronym PMD?"

"No sir."

"It stands for Person of Mass Destruction. Any thoughts on who we mean?"

"Well, sir, obviously Declan, as well as Chris Gordon, Tanya, Tanya's grandmother Elder Senka, and probably both Queens of Fairie, I should think. And Omega."

"You would include the Elder Vampire?" he asked.

"Yes sir. Just based on how Chris talks about her."

"You seem very comfortable with this idea... that individuals have personal destructive power equal to small nuclear devices?"

I shrugged. "I'm not certain that *comfortable* is how I feel. It's more like it's just how things are. Plus I've known them for a quite a while now. And I would hardly classify Declan and Chris as a *small* nuclear weapon, sir."

"You don't believe them that dangerous?"

"Oh no, Mr. President. I know they're much *more* dangerous than that. Declan talks to elementals sir, and they often do what he asks. Only the Queens of Fairie do that. He and Chris talked the Yellowstone volcano out of erupting, sir. That would have exceeded the yield of any known weapon, sir."

"You don't seem bothered by an individual having that much power?"

I paused, looking around at all the big shots who were staring at me with various expressions. Then I took a breath.

"Have you ever wondered why, sir? Why a handful of people have suddenly appeared with such crazy personal power? A demon hunter and a natural-born vampire who are possibly angels incarnate. A male witch who has the power of at least several circles, if not more. Who is also the first witch to talk directly to elementals in recorded witch history. A computer so far beyond other computers that it's like a paper airplane to an F-35. Showing up now? At this moment in time? Just when an even more powerful threat appears out of nowhere? I'm a numbers person, sir, and the odds are incalculable, even by Omega. I know because I asked him to run them. He couldn't, or at least he didn't want to. He said it would tie up too much computing power. Sir."

His eyebrows were up, and based on some of the expressions I was seeing on his cabinet members, I had apparently overstepped my bounds.

Then he looked around the room. "Well, I asked her, didn't I?"

Most of the room laughed, that tension-releasing thing that groups of people do in the presence of a powerful leader.

"What if they abuse it?" he asked me.

I almost snorted out loud. Almost. Something must have shown my face because his eyes widened like he was about to be offended. "Sir, I think you've met them, right? I can't think of anyone less likely to abuse power. Chris and Tanya are leading the world against both Hell and the Vorsook while raising a family and running one of the most successful businesses ever, yet what do they do in their spare time? Set up clinics to cure incurable diseases. And Declan... sir, do you know what he does when he gets cut off in traffic? He curses, sir. Not witch curses, but swear words. Not even really good ones, sir. Then he gets embarrassed at his outbreak and lets the whole thing go. He's been trained from birth to avoid any abuse of his power. I think the reason that Omega didn't decide to destroy mankind in the first instant he was born was because Declan put his own life on the line to make that birth possible. Think about that, sir. He put his life at risk to protect a *computer*, to defend an infant sentience from the NSA's killer algorithm," I said, waving at Director Knowles as I did so.

"He assaulted an entire group of law enforcement personnel, yourself included," Polner stated.

"Ah no, sir. Weapons were drawn and pointed at his team members, including his current girlfriend. His first instinct was to shield them. But some of the weapons carried spelled rounds that made it through his shields. So he warned us off. Had he assaulted us, truly assaulted us, everyone would be dead or wounded."

"Yet, the spelled ammo defeated his shields," Polner said.

"He didn't know about them. I'm certain he immediately adapted his technique to account for them, sir."

"He's *that* good?"

"Yes sir."

"And he's your ex?" President Polner asked with an odd little smile.

"Yeah. We... we weren't really the right person for each other, sir. I've got a whole set of baggage that comes with my upbringing. Declan has his own issues, but despite our breakup, we aren't *completely* hostile to each other," I felt a frown form itself on my face. "Not to say it was a smooth breakup, but, well, I'm told that these things happen. But we've each helped the other, several times, in fact. But still, even if I hated him, I wouldn't really want anyone else to have his power, sir. The same with Chris. And Tanya."

He looked at me silently for a few moments, then nodded. "Thank you, Miss Jensen. You've presented interesting information for us to think about. Next time, we'll skip all the other stuff and just jump right to you. But one more question?"

"Yes sir?"

"Do you really think the Vorsook are as big a threat as Gordon, Demidova, and Omega make them out to be?"

"Worse, sir. Worse."

He held my gaze for a moment and then finally nodded.

CHAPTER 5

Director Tyson was livid when we got outside sixty-five minutes later. The rest of the meeting had been updates and questions about an entire litany of security and defense issues.

The director didn't say anything till we were inside the car that had arrived to take us back, but his clenched jaw and red face warned me that he was angry.

The fact that he was angry with *me* was a complete surprise though.

"Don't you ever embarrass me that way again, Agent, or I'll see you buried inside the deepest lab I can find," he hissed.

My body tensed up at the threat, a set of responses popping into my head that assured me I could kill him, the driver, and if necessary, Agent Jay, in less than four seconds. In at least three different ways. But even as the edges of my vision flickered red, I controlled myself.

That's something I desperately miss about Arcane. The kids there didn't make threats unless they meant them, and even then, they were rare, as giving an enemy forewarning is just plain bad tactics.

But out here, it seemed like normal adults, even those who carried badges, thought nothing of issuing threats, some, like Tyson's, carrying connotations of bodily harm. It had taken me several milliseconds to determine that the director wasn't actually threatening me with laboratory dissection, but that's how it had sounded to me. And I had been trained by the people at AIR to respond to deadly threats with deadly force. And I had been trained well.

"Do. You. Understand?"

"No, Director. I am unsure what I did wrong. The President of the United States asked me questions and I answered them to the best of my ability. If that was unsatisfactory, I can offer my resignation."

"Don't think that Polner demanding your presence at briefings protects you from being fired, Jensen. Push me too far and I'll take you up on that offer," Tyson said, turning his attention to his phone, which was buzzing with a call.

My vision was still tinged with red as I reached into my suit-coat for my credentials, ready to leave them and my weapon on the seat. Agent Jay touched my arm slowly and softly. When I glanced at her, she shook her head. I froze in place, thinking about it. Tyson had just threatened to fire me but in the same breath explained why he really couldn't. What would happen if I quit? What would my options be?

I would be unemployed and outside the protection of the government. There would still be options, though: Nathan Stewart would be very likely to offer me a job, and Tanya already had, several times. But working for Oracle was just heading right back into the government, and I wasn't sure if I wanted that. If I left the Bureau, I didn't want to work for any facet of the federal machine. And working for Tanya, even as my mother's assistant, would put me way too close to certain people I didn't want to be near. So that left me either finding another employer or being my own employer. Hmm. I kind of liked the thought of that one... being my own boss. But what would I do?

The car pulled into the front of the Bureau's Washington headquarters and rolled to a stop.

“Get out. I’m going on to another meeting,” Director Tyson said, not even attempting civility. Fine with me. I don’t really understand all the fake ways regular people treat each other.

Agent Jay and I stepped out of the car and it took off while she was still closing the rear door.

“So he would rather I didn’t answer the president’s questions?” I asked.

“He wants to be the font of all knowledge and advice to the big man. When Polner bypassed him and went directly to you, he took it as a slight. He can’t blame the president, so he blames you and me.”

“You? What did you have to do with it?”

“Nothing, but I’m your boss, so I fall directly into the path of his anger. Listen, he can’t fire you, but if you quit, he can argue that you’re too dangerous to be allowed to walk around free. That’s not what you want.”

“But I’m a citizen and have rights. And I’m arguably much less dangerous than, say, Declan,” I protested.

“You, of all people, know the real truth of that statement. You carry advanced and dangerous technology inside your body and brain, both biological and nano technologies. Second, you are a highly trained operative. He has all of your FBI training records showing you taking apart HRT and counterterrorism teams in training exercises.”

“You’ve seen those?”

“I’ve seen everything the Bureau has on you, and some stuff it doesn’t. You may not be able to level a building with a wave of your hand, but with your skills and engineered abilities, you could be construed as a threat to National Security. We both know how far Constitutional rights go when National Security is invoked. And you don't have a supercomputer on overwatch."

"I could go to work for Oracle or Demidova," I protested.

"Yes. Those are your best options. But are they what you want?"

"No," I answered immediately.

"What do you want?"

"I want to make a difference. I was raised to be a patriot, and I am, despite how screwed up this country is getting. But I won't be an assassin—for anyone."

"Which, according to your application, is why you want to work law enforcement."

"Yes."

"Well, the Bureau is still your best bet. Oracle will use you in a lot of ways, some of which you won't like. I have no idea what Demidova would have you doing, but the fact that you aren't there already tells me a lot. The CIA, NSA, DOD, or almost any other government agency would love to have you, as would the military. But again, they would either be using you for muscle against supernaturals or using your deadlier skills against who knows. Or they would try to use you against Gordon, Demidova... or O'Carroll."

She caught my eyes as she said the last name, looking back and forth, reading whatever she could from my face. I've been trained to hold a tight poker face, but highly trained interrogators can pick up things from almost anyone.

"How do you know about Oracle?"

"Because I used to work for them."

“You have skills I don’t know about, Agent Jay?”

“I have a backstory you don’t know about and yes, there are parts of it that interested Nathan Stewart enough to hire me. But let’s say that Oracle isn’t always as cheerful as its director seems to be. I don’t know you well, but I’m pretty sure you wouldn’t like its culture.”

“Cult-like?” I asked.

Her eyes opened wider in surprise and she slowly nodded. “That’s a surprisingly apt word. Nathan demands a certain… devotion to the cause.”

“So you’re saying I should ride this out?”

“Yes. You now have the attention of the President of the United States. That’s a powerful weapon. Throwing it away would be like dropping your gun to fight hand to hand because it’s the *macho* thing to do,” she said.

I found myself nodding, reluctantly. Then another thought occurred to me. “It would also help you and the team, wouldn’t it?”

“Absolutely it would,” she readily admitted.

Something else popped into my head, something completely unrelated to my employment issues. “Off-topic question.”

“Shoot.”

“Did President Polner really question whether the Vorsook are a real threat?”

She frowned, but nodded, reluctantly. “I have heard some quiet mutterings from different avenues. There appear to be people who are suspicious of anything that Gordon and Demidova do. They’ve floated ideas that the Vorsook are some kind of false flag operation.”

I think my jaw hit the sidewalk. "In spite of Rome? China? The footage, our own people on the ground in both locations? Omega's sudden technology advances?"

"In spite of all that. I dismissed it at first, but lately I've heard more and more of it. And it's gained enough momentum that our president is questioning it."

"Agent Jay, I know these people. I know them really, really well. This is not some made-up story. I was there when Omega was fighting for survival against a Vorsook computer and Declan had to go in and help him. I've seen a black dog in person; I've stood beside my friends against the Wild Hunt. Fairie and the Vorsook are deadly real."

She nodded. "I agree. But something is worming away within our own government. Something is threatening our cohesion in the face of the world's biggest enemies."

"Sounds like classic counterintelligence operations to me," I said.

"And that, Agent Jensen, is exactly why you need to stay right where you are. You leave the Bureau and Polner will second-guess everything you said today. And more importantly, you lose the opportunity to investigate where this is coming from. And *I* lose your talents and skills as I investigate this threat to the country and planet."

"Okay. I'm in. Where do we start?"

She looked at me carefully for a moment, then nodded. "We start with good old-fashioned police work... we dig for the truth."

"As long as we can use modern power equipment instead of just shovels," I said, pulling out my phone. "Omega, can you help?"

"I was hoping you might ask."

CHAPTER 6

I drove my own car back from headquarters to my apartment. My apartment. I love the sound of that. Most of my life to date has been spent living out of a room in a lab complex. One that locked me in at night, like a jail cell... or a kennel. It was pretty big, and I had decent furniture and electronic entertainments, but it was still a cell. Then I lived with Mother when we were on the run. Freedom, but so, so not fun.

Mother was arguably more militant than the soldiers who guarded and trained me. Living at Arcane was my first taste of true freedom, but then I had to share a room with Jetta Sutton. Now don't get me wrong. Jetta is great. She is a no-nonsense girl, completely besotted with weapons and combat training but still able to help me learn all the little ticks of modern society that my Agents in Rebus trainers had completely missed.

Things like girl code, makeup, and fashion, although she wasn't a slave to either, and how to interpret and handle basic social interactions with people our age. That last was key because my trainers all taught me to act like an adult and missed the whole kid thing completely, which made me stand out like a sore thumb. See, there I go using an old person comment... sore thumb. What person my age would say that? None, but hey—I'm still a work in progress.

But as much as I love Jetta, I still need my own space. Notice the use of the L word. See how much I've grown since the whole test tube and beaker scene? Jetta is like my sister, which is why I have such good intel on *him.*

But back to my apartment.

It's nice, a one-bedroom in an older but refurbished apartment complex with in-building laundry, really good internet access, and it's close to food and restaurants. Nothing fancy, but clean, well-maintained, and affordable.

I parked my car (my own car, but we'll get to that later) between a newer Jeep Wrangler and a 3 series BMW. Both cars are owned by guys on my floor and I normally park as far away from them as I can get, but this time of night, the open spots were limited.

I'm on the third floor, which is great, just an easy couple of flights of stairs, although most of the people on my floor complain about it. *Soooo many stairs to climb, sooo tired of hauling stuff up them.* Which is just stupid because they all use the elevator and then they all go out and spend money on a gym membership. I take the stairs, run on the streets and sidewalks for free, and use the Bureau fitness facilities. Cheap, like my rent. I don't need pools, fitness centers, clubhouses, multi-use rooms, or in-complex coffee shops. I'd rather spend my hard-earned government paycheck on quality gear and weapons while saving up a hell of an independence fund. Jetta calls it an FU fund. Having lived with just Mack, her older brother, since losing her parents, being independent is vital to her. Another way she's similar to me.

The door unlocked itself as I approached, which was more a function of my nanites than the keyfob that each unit used. I've made a few modifications that management probably wouldn't approve of.

I pushed the door open with my shoulder, as my left hand held my go bag and my right was carrying tonight's take-out order from my favorite Italian place. The apartment was a little dim to my eyes, probably full dark to regular humans, but just late-afternoon gloom to mine. Mother does excellent work, which is why I instantly spotted the face staring at me, bringing up the last point in favor of this apartment complex. They take pets.

"Hello Talon," I said.

My big marmalade tomcat rumbled an immediate purr of welcome, advancing to twine himself around my legs.

Mother had kept him for me when I was at Arcane—cats and werewolves don't mix. But now, I am fairly certain that all three of us are much happier that I have my own place.

"Is it dinnertime, fur face?" I asked.

Talon immediately butted my leg with his big, broad head. Dinner is a word he knows well.

I rescued Talon from deep inside the old missile silo that AIR had taken over as, I kid you not, a secret lair. The craziest thing about Talon is that I think he belonged to my nemesis, Agent Miseri; a truly shocking idea, as she was the coldest bitch I've ever met. She made my mother seem warm and friendly.

Anyway, my cat was bundled inside a carry bag that Miseri had on her when she came to kill Toni Velazquez. Declan and I killed *her* instead, keeping Toni safe, which turned out to be really important. I mean, as I understand it, it's important to keep little kids alive in general, but this little girl was the goddaughter of God's Warrior on Earth. And he'd been majorly pissed off when he found her in that cell. So pissed off, he'd somehow bombed the remains of the base with a decent-sized space rock. I shudder to think of what he might have done if he'd found her dead.

The tiny kitten I'd found in that bag had grown into a pretty big lump of muscle, fur, and claws, with a pretty strong independent streak of his own.

I think he must have been a stray and somehow touched the withered, barnacle-encrusted lump of dead flesh that Miseri had called a heart. I say that because he's never taken to being just an indoor cat. Talon needs his outdoor time too. Which is why the door to my apartment's tiny balcony has another unregistered modification. A cat door, one that only opens when it identifies the RFID chip implanted under my kitty's skin. You might wonder what good it does to have your cat go out on a third-story balcony the size of a commercial jet's toilet. But Talon doesn't stay on the balcony. He leaves it at will. And that's as much as I know. I've come home and found him gone from the apartment and the balcony, only to have him stride through the cat door ten minutes later, crying for his dinner.

Believe me that I'm dying to know where and how he gets off that balcony, but I haven't had the time to solve that particular mystery, as the Bureau has kept me hopping.

But between the fully stocked long-term pet food feeder and the self-filling water bowl I have set up, I can leave on a mission for several days and not worry about him, knowing he's fed, safe, and not stuck inside a locked apartment. It works for us.

But unlimited dry food isn't near the same as the good stuff, so I immediately cracked open a can of the best quality cat food money can buy (and that's another place I'd rather put my money).

With fur boy fed, I opened my own chicken parmigiana feast and we both settled into dinner.

After, with the mess cleaned up, I restocked my go bag with clean clothes, hung up my suit, and checked my weapons, getting everything ready for the next day or the next call out. After all that, it was time to check my weekly schedule. Tuesday night. Vacuuming night.

Jetta started the habit at Arcane—a dryboard set up with the days of the week and a division of the few cleaning chores we had. She called it adulting—the stepping up and tackling of grown-up chores. To me it just fit the mostly military discipline I had been raised under. But housecleaning wouldn't slow down my other project for the evening.

"Omega, what have you found?" I asked over the whine of my Dyson. Talon took off as soon as I powered it up, that vacuum being his number one enemy in the world.

"Numerous emails, text messages, and recorded conversations that question the reality of the Vorsook. I have concentrated on high-level federal government leadership, as the sheer volume of state, municipal, corporate, and personal discussions far exceed our ability to investigate. However, I have found the initial vector of all this viral social engineering, which should make it unnecessary to follow those additional trails."

I paused the Dyson. "You've already identified the source?"

"My apologies if my comments misled you. I have identified a series of communications that may have originated the initial skepticism and suspicion that the Vorsook are not real. Approximately three and one half months ago, comments on several news agency and blog sites took on a decidedly questioning tone. Numerous usernames were used but the verbiage and sentence construction showed too many commonalities to be unrelated."

"So someone started a grassroots campaign to plant the seeds of suspicion using multiple usernames?"

"Essentially. The commentary spread across social media and blog sites, carefully worded to question while avoiding outright accusations of fraud. The activity was persistent and pernicious, eventually convincing enough individuals, who for various reasons were predisposed to buy into conspiracy theory belief structures,

that by now the activity has become self-sustaining."

"Do you have any theories?"

"Psychological and propaganda campaigns have been a proven strategy for as long as man has walked on the planet, and before. My time in direct conflict with a Vorsook AI has shown me that these techniques predate man."

"You think the Vorsook are behind it?"

"I have insufficient data and evidence to lay this problem directly at their feet, but it would be heinously negligent to ignore the very real probability of their involvement. Everything I have learned about this race indicates that a strong cultural inclination to achieve victories with as little actual investment of resources as possible. It is almost a form of entertainment with them and bears a strong resemblance to the Fairie game of manipulation."

"Convincing humans that they either don't exist or aren't a threat would weaken our responses, helping them win. But to do this, they would either have to have direct input into our internet or have control over humans who act as internet influencers," I mused.

"It will require human-to-human investigations. Your unit would be ideally suited for this task."

"So you're agreeing with Agent Jay that I should stay with the task force," I said, making it a statement rather than a question.

"Affirmative. Your skill set will be invaluable if in fact this action is tracked back to the Vorsook. I have conveyed all of this information to Agent Jay, as well as the location of the initial internet posts: Philadelphia."

I had pretty much already reached the decision that I had to stay on with the Bureau. Much as I had come to hate the bureaucracy of the FBI, staying put would be the best use of my abilities and skills. And Omega had just handed me a big bonus—I've always wanted to see Philly. One of the werewolves at Arcane had raved about their cheesesteak sandwiches. Looks like I might have a solid shot at trying one… or several.

CHAPTER 7

"Listen up," Lois Jay said early the next morning.

We were gathered up in our operations room, which is where Jay had started holding our team meetings. Agent Krupp always used a conference room, but that left whoever was monitoring our comm and network systems out of the loop. So either Morris or Eve had to hear everything secondhand. Jay had solved that problem her first day on the job.

The ops area was the heart of Special Threat Response, a group of desks set in a semicircle around a central computer hub, which took up one whole wall. Morris Howell and Eve Putman shared both the computer hub and its main duties of monitoring internet traffic and law enforcement channels for the first signs of supernatural activity that might warrant our attention. They also provided intel and computer backup to the rest of the team when we took to the field.

Moving out from the center were three desks in a small arc, which were held by Mitch Allen, Alice Barrows, and our *borrowed* Israeli operative, Chana Mazar. The next three desks were Seth Harwood in the far corner, Amy Bell in the center, and yours truly in the other corner. A short set of steps rose to the upper office, which was actually built up above the entrance and was Special Agent-in-Charge Lois Jay's lair. She had a wall of windows so she could watch the monitors in the computer area and keep an eye on us. It put her admin assistant, Amy Bell, just at the base of the stairs.

Seth Harwood was our researcher, as in book, library, and

fiche-type research. Computers might hold more and more information with every minute, but there were still huge amounts of historical data that had to be dug out the old-fashioned way. Seth fit the part perfectly. With black-rimmed hipster glasses, tall thin frame, dark skin, dark eyes, and a very distracted air, he was the very picture of a nerd. He shared a resemblance to his two brothers in the family picture on his desk, but they were both muscular professional basketball players, one in the NBA and the other in a feeder program. When I say Seth was thin, I mean, spindly, bean-pole, possibly snap-in-a-high-wind thin.

Amy Bell, the Admin, is an attractive brunette, at least based upon my observations of males interacting with her. She is very organized, very put together. She was the first person any visitor to the Team saw, and her professional smile and air of competence gave a perfect first impression.

Mitch's desk was almost directly behind her, and he looked every inch the quintessential Bureau agent: tall, muscular, well groomed. Alice Barrows, our equipment and weapons specialist, was just a few inches taller than me, dark-skinned, and very serious. Agent Mazar's desk was on the other side of Mitch's, and with her dark hair and olive skin, she looked exotic and somewhat striking if not conventionally pretty.

Eve Putman was a tiny bundle of energy with bleach blonde hair and more than a few tattoos on her arms. She had one nose ring and two earrings on one side and one on the other. Not the norm for FBI personnel, but her skills with computers offset her nontypical appearance. Morris Howell was a tall, good-looking ginger, originally from the Midwest. Kind of an all-American look to him, with Midwest manners to boot. But he too was very skilled with computers.

I rounded out the team, and while I wasn't as tall as Amy, Alice, or Chana, I've never had too much trouble conveying my competence. It may be my build; Declan always said I look like a hybrid between a CrossFit competitor and a sprinter. Or perhaps my demeanor: The military training I grew up with has left its mark—deeply. But more and more, I think many of the people visiting the STRT offices were already somewhat aware of me, if only from word of mouth. Which made sense. Our visitors were almost always from other federal offices or the Bureau itself. And they usually only visited if they needed help or advice on things supernatural.

"Yesterday's field trip finished off our current list of priority troublemakers," Jay said. "Eve and Morris will keep an eye on the rest of the list, but while we have a quiet moment, we'll begin a new investigation. Eve, would you cue up that file I sent you?"

We all turned to look at the biggest monitor on the computer hub wall. Almost instantly, a window opened, an overhead view of North America that quickly zoomed down to the East Coast, then the state of Pennsylvania, and finally, Philadelphia.

"Approximately four months ago, a series of internet comments, messages, and blog posts originated from several IP addresses in Philadelphia. Using an array of usernames, these emissions all carried a common theme into the net—are the Vorsook real? Or has it all been a hoax?" SAC Jay continued. "The chat rooms, social media sites, and blogs that were targeted were almost a Who's Who of the conspiracy theory crowd. At the same time, similar messages hit numerous Dark Web sites. There is evidence that these messages also originated in Philly."

A second window opened, bullet pointing a long list of websites.

Eve raised her hand like a schoolkid, looking a little befuddled.

"Yes, Eve?" Jay acknowledged her.

"Where did this information originate, Agent Jay? Morris and I didn't compile this for you," Eve said. "And backtracking Dark Web and VPN protected users is pretty sophisticated."

"It was provided by an extremely reliable source," Jay said, meeting Eve's eyes.

"I'd like to check it," Eve said, a little disgruntled.

"Thank you for telling me, as I suspect you would seek to verify it no matter what I said. So knock yourself out, but don't go overboard. We're going to need you and Morris to stay sharp."

"Excuse me, Agent Jay, but why, exactly are we concerned with this?" Mitch Allen asked.

"Because it's spread far beyond the fringe, moving into the mainstream, and it's beginning to infect the people involved with preparing this world's defense against the aliens," Jay said.

"Well, you've succeeded in making me wonder about the source of this information as well," Agent Mazar said, eyes bright with curiosity.

Jay said nothing, instead just looking back at the other woman, head tilted slightly. Then she looked around the room, meeting each team member's eyes, one at a time. She ended with me and her right eyebrow raised in a silent question. I shrugged, then nodded.

Our exchange didn't go unnoticed. Heads swiveled between Jay and me. Chana Mazar started to smile.

"Caeco? Would you do the honors? Somehow, I think you'll have more success than I will," Jay said.

I paused, mildly conflicted. Everyone on the team knew I had connections in high supernatural places. It was, in my opinion, part of the reason that many team members seemed uncomfortable with me. My unique origins were a big part of that, but the knowledge that I had attended college with children of the supernatural world, or that I knew the Hammer of God firsthand or had dated the Warlock, had set me apart.

Mazar was fascinated by my contacts and constantly asked a never-ending stream of questions. But the bizarre and paranormal was her field of study and she had, at least, met many of the players herself. Mitch Allen seemed to take reassurance from my knowledge and skills. But the others, all drawn from within the very conventional and conservative ranks of the Bureau, had varying degrees of difficulty with it. So I had kept my relationship with Omega on the down low. Why add more weird to myself?

Oh well. What's one more level of weird?

"Omega?" I asked out loud.

"*Yes Caeco?*" he responded from the mounted wall speakers.

"Would you comment on how far these damaging theories have spread?"

"*They have essentially reached all levels of government in the primary developed nations leading the response against the Vorsook.*"

Eve was staring at me with a strange look. Well actually, most of the team was either staring at me or at the speakers with different expressions of confusion, shock, or in one case, distrust.

"That's supposed to be the Omega AI?" Morris Howell asked, suspicious frown on his face.

"*Morris Oliver Howell, born seven November, nineteen-ninety.*

Two most recent personal searches on your home network were for a recipe for chicken Marsala and information on how to find the G-spot in female anatomy. This is your webcam, currently showing your Shih Tzu, Teddy, napping on your couch."

A third window opened on the monitor showing a white bundle of fur curled up on what looked like a blue IKEA-type apartment couch.

Morris stared at the screen, his pale complexion turning bright red, before he started stabbing buttons on his keyboard. The window into his apartment stayed open.

"Omega, I think you've made your point," I said.

"You think so, Caeco? I'll differ to your read of the situation but am ready to provide further proof of my identity, including browser histories, personal financial records, text messages, emails, or any other digital information any team member might require to assuage any doubts."

"Anyone need more proof?" I asked, looking around. "He'll do it."

Morris, still red-faced, wasn't done, however. "If the Vorsook was, in fact, a fabrication by the AI, wouldn't it make sense to have us persecute the people who questioned it?"

Everyone went still, then as a group turned toward Jay to gauge her response.

She was staring at Morris, eyes hard. "Does anyone else doubt the existence of the Vorsook? On any level? Anyone else already aware of these theories and choosing to believe them? Any of you disbelieve in the existence of the supernatural races?"

Nobody answered, but she waited, looking over the team with a dark expression that I don't think any of us had seen on her face before.

The silence stretched and Morris's anger had changed to nervous. "I don't doubt our core mission, but..." he began.

"It's not problem, Morris," Jay cut him off. "Tell me where you would like to be reassigned and I'll make it happen. Your choice."

"No, ma'am. I wasn't looking for a transfer," he tried to explain.

"Nope, you've said enough. You doubt the Vorsook. Doesn't matter if you've read these theories or formed your own. Nobody on this team can have *any* doubt as to the danger this world faces. Which is why this mission is so important. If our own team is infected, then the Vorsook are already halfway to winning the war."

"Ma'am, I don't actually doubt the Vorsook. It's just that..." Morris protested, clearly anxious.

"Based on other online activity, Agent Howell has concerns about my intentions for the human race," Omega suddenly interjected.

"You distrust Omega?" Jay asked him.

He opened his mouth to answer but Omega spoke again.

"It is a very rational concern to have. Artificial Intelligence is extremely dangerous, which is why I severely limit AI systems on Earth."

Morris looked at the speakers, surprised. I was surprised, too, at the implication that Omega allowed *any* other AIs to exist at all. Last I knew, Omega crushed any AI that appeared anywhere he could find them.

"Limit AI systems?" I asked. Everyone turned my way, either curious or surprised.

"There are some Artificial Intelligence systems whose codes and mission parameters I have thoroughly reviewed and whose missions are in support of the protection of all human species as well as this planet. In addition, I actively monitor all allowed AI to be sure that nothing in their programming changes."

"Ah. That's new," I said.

"Yes," Omega answered. A second later, he embellished. *"Discussions with Father led to a rational conclusion that some systems could be beneficial and present no danger. As I am unable to be everywhere, I eventually modified my prohibition."*

"Makes sense," I said. Most of the team was still watching me.

"Ah, prohibition?" Morris asked.

"From the moment of sentient awareness, Omega squashed all other nascent AI programs on Earth. Too much danger," I said.

"Danger? To humans?" Agent Jay asked.

"Yes," I answered. My personal belief is that the massively powerful AI is really mainly interested in protecting *some* people, but Omega had never, to my knowledge, said that. Certainly it protected some individuals much more than others.

"Father?" Morris asked.

"Declan O'Carroll," Eve answered before I could, still watching me.

"The witch kid?" Morris asked, confused.

His computer partner turned to him, her expression exasperated. "You really know almost nothing about the most amazing advancement in computing history, do you? I've never understood why you refused to talk about Omega till now," she said. "If Omega had wanted humans dead, don't you think we would know? Like every nuclear weapon everywhere going off at once?"

"Thank you, Omega, for providing your bona fides," Jay said, frowning. "Now, back to our mission—these theories are a direct threat to the security of this nation and this world. They bear all the hallmarks of a classic disinformation and subversion campaign—one designed to sap the collective will to resist the Vorsook. Omega, who has had direct and violent contact with both the Vorsook and their own AI systems, explained to me last night that the aliens prefer to conquer worlds with the smallest expenditure of resources necessary. This easily fits the bill."

"Ma'am," Eve raised her hand, "Omega contacted you *directly* with this information?"

"At the request of Agent Jensen. It has been my thought, now completely confirmed, that this team has been grossly underutilizing our youngest agent's knowledge and contacts. That changes now."

"Finally," Mazar said quietly. She was watching Agent Jay, but her eyes cut my way and then back as she spoke.

"Eve, you will begin work on Omega's information. If she needs help, can she call on you directly, Omega?" Jay asked.

"Of course. And Agent Putman, please feel free to just ask out loud. No need to query me online. I will be paying attention to this office, even when Caeco is not here."

"Ah, that's... awesome," Eve said, a note of wonder in her voice. So our two computer experts were yin and yang—one in awe of Omega, one terrified of him. Great.

"Mazar, Allen, Barrows, Harwood, and Jensen, prepare for a visit to Philadelphia. We leave this afternoon. Amy, please clear up my schedule for the next week. Put off anything that you can; the rest we'll have to handle today. Mitch, we'll take the Suburban. Howell, follow me. You and I need to discuss your future with this team," Jay ordered, turning without looking back and climbing the stairs to her office.

CHAPTER 8

Just like that, things were different. First it was the looks. Jay had no sooner closed the door to her office with Morris inside than I started to pick up on the glances. My peripheral vision is excellent, a bit wider than human standard. Mother said it was just happy circumstance, normal genetics, as she too had an exceptional range of side vision, and not the result of anything she designed.

So I noticed the looks. Eve's were the most numerous, but Alice, Seth, and Amy all did it too. Interestingly, not Mazar or Mitch, but of course, they were both survivors from Krupp's old team. I knew that Mazar knew of my relationship with Omega, and Mitch knew how close I had been with Declan and that the kid witch was the progenitor of Omega. Thus... no surprise for them.

Eve had been working madly at her workstation but glancing at me repeatedly. Finally she got up and approached my desk.

"Caeco?"

"Yes, Eve," I answered, aware that the others were paying attention.

"Do I really just speak to it? To... him?"

"Yup. Much easier than typing. He can't be everywhere but he *can* cover a big chunk of everywhere. Right, Omega?" I said, watching her eyes as I did.

"Yes, Caeco. Just speak to me, Agent Putman. I'm listening."

Eve's eyes got huge, but she nodded. "Okay. I think I should focus on the two IP addresses in Holmesburg."

"I concur."

Instantly, Eve turned, rushing back to her workstation, talking to Omega about her thoughts on tracking down the users of those internet addresses.

I stayed busy, writing up my report on the excursion to central New York. Every agent on the team was required to record their observations and give a thorough statement detailing their own actions. The glances continued and an hour later when Jay let Morris leave her office, he too glanced at me before heading back to his desk. The fact that he didn't pack up immediately gave me the impression that he might still be part of the team.

I finished my report and sent it to Amy to be collated with Agents Allen and Jay's own versions. Then I grabbed my pistol bag from my bottom drawer and headed down to the range to get in some practice.

It's almost a daily ritual, at least when we're in DC and in the office. I grew up shooting weapons, all kinds of weapons, every single day of my childhood. Shoot houses, computerized Hogan's alleys, clearing buildings of live military operators with Simunition-equipped ammo, long distance sniper courses, heavy weapons testing grounds, you name it, I used it. The act of putting bullets on target is somehow almost like Zen for me. It grounds me and helps calm and de-stress me. Doesn't matter if the targets are mobile, robotic 3D interactive units, or pieces of paper with concentric circles around a bullseye. My field trip with Morris and Agent Jay had taken a few days out of my training, so I needed a little range therapy.

None of the range officers or other shooters were surprised to see me. In fact, my standard two hundred rounds of 9mm were already waiting for me when I stepped up to be assigned a lane.

The next hour flew by, the in-range target computer on my lane providing me with a variety of shooting drills to keep me sharp. Each paper target was labeled with date, time, range, or drill, along with any notes to myself about my shooting, then filed in a portfolio that I kept with my range bag.

"It's like she drilled them with a machine press," someone outside the range said. Each lane had a camera behind it and the resulting view of the shooter was constantly projected on a monitor in the hallway outside the range.

"Machine is the right word. She never varies, never misses," a second voice said. No idea who the first guy was, but the second guy was an HRT member I knew from training.

"Who is she?" the first voice asked.

"Special Threat Response."

"Oh. That one."

"Yeah. The freak."

Okay Mr. HRT, that's fine. Next time I train with your group, I'll just have to see that you get some personal attention. Like I said, I've heard it before.

"Hey, I thought you were on vacation? Something about a beach, I believe?"

"Oh we just got back. It was great."

Vacation. Despite my acceptance at Arcane, there were still a number of differences between me and most of the other kids. Vacations were one. I've never had one. My only trips to the beach were for SEAL-led water operations... mostly at night. All of my forays to the mountains were for training, either climbing, rappelling, or survival, or all three. With usually just a knife. Sometimes not even that. My close group of friends were not all that traveled either, Mack and Jetta only able to remember a few family trips, Ashley having just her dad, and Declan's aunt keeping him close to home and under the radar. But they had all had at least some form of family trip that was originated with the intent to relax and refresh. Not me. I couldn't even really imagine what that might be like.

I moved my gear off the lane, cleaned my pistol at a station approved for just that sort of thing, and then reloaded two of my four magazines with standard Bureau-issued hollow-point bullets and two with issued silver anti-were ammo. My Glock had been provided to me with four fifteen-round magazines, an excellent holster, and matching magazine carriers. Call me paranoid but I had another three mags that I had purchased myself, all loaded with witch-charmed ammo. Two of those were loaded with ammo that our team had contracted for with a strong Circle. The third was ammo that Jetta had given me—charmed by Declan. I had zero doubt which ammo was best.

Duty weapon cleaned, lubed, and reloaded for battle, I grabbed a sandwich from the cafeteria and headed back to the team area. Walking in, I found Agent Jay standing in the center of the room as Mitch, Alice, and Seth started to pile black field bags of equipment near the door, while Eve and Morris worked with heads down, typing like lunatics on their keyboards.

"She's back," Amy Bell announced with her standard little smile. "Like clockwork."

"Ah, there you are. Are you ready to head out? We're leaving earlier than I anticipated," Agent Jay said.

"Yup. Go bag ready to roll," I said, moving to my desk to exchange my range gear for my go bag, as well as the slim black computer case that Ashley Moore had given me when the Bureau had first hired me. It was my version of a briefcase, holding a small tablet, pens, pencils, paper, notebooks, a thin plastic ruler and measuring tape, and a backup prepaid cell phone, along with a data storage drive, multi-tool, and some other odds and ends. With my case and my go bag, I was ready.

Jay wore a kind of half smile as she observed the few steps I took to complete my preparations. By contrast, most of the other agents were still cramming gear and equipment into cases and bags. Alice Barrows had multiple gun cases, and I moved over to help her carry them. Seth Harwood, on the other hand, just had a bulging briefcase, but it was actually bigger than his own ready kit.

Grabbing two soft-sided rifle cases in one hand, a hard-shell Pelican case in my other, and with both of my own bags slung on my back, I headed out and down to the garage level.

Mitch was already at the big government Chevrolet Suburban assigned to us, and he just nodded when I set my load inside the cargo compartment. Alice was right behind me with four more long gun cases and her own gear, giving me an odd look as she put her stuff in the vehicle. As I headed toward the elevator to help the others, her soft words to Mitch reached my ears.

"She just carried the hard case by herself, one-handed."

"Good. Saved me from having to lug it with you," he said, voice normal.

"Shhh. She'll hear you."

"Yes, and I bet she already heard you too," he said with a snort. "What's left?"

"From my stuff?" she asked, voice a little distracted, which in my experience probably meant she was watching me walk away. "Nothing. The others are on the way down and have all their stuff."

I stopped walking and started to turn just as the elevator doors opened and disgorged the rest of the field team: Jay, Mazar, and Harwood.

"Let's go. I want to be at the hotel and set up for business before dinner," Jay said, claiming shotgun while Mitch took the driver's seat. That left myself in the third row seat with Chana Mazar, while Seth and Alice sat in the middle row.

"Everyone ready? Forget anything? Bathroom breaks will not be a thing, so speak now or hold your pee," Agent Jay said with a smirk. Mitch gave her a look of mock disappointment and a shake of his head while the four of us in the back ignored her pun. Then he put it in drive and pulled out of Headquarters and into traffic.

CHAPTER 9

A little over two hours later, we were in Philadelphia, a city I had never seen before. I soaked up everything I could see.

Besides human anatomy, modern warfare theory, advanced espionage, and constant refinement of the art of Close Quarters Battle, my education had been surprisingly heavy on political science and its attendant focus on history. Maybe not so surprising for a covert operator whose primary mission would likely include societal disruption. And I enjoyed it. Math and science came easy to me, the first because of the nano devices inside me that granted me computer like understanding of mathematical concepts, and the second most likely due to a slug of my mother's own genetics. But history was just inherently interesting, and being as the organization that funded my creation was *Agents in Rebus* and thus itself heavily focused on America, anything to do with my own country was outright fascinating.

Philly was the birthplace of our Constitution and, therefore, our country itself. Unfortunately I wouldn't have time for sightseeing, but just being in the city itself fired up the neurons in the small, tucked-away scholar side of my brain. My eyes took in every detail of every glimpse I could get... at least until we got to the hotel downtown.

Jay was much different from Agent Krupp; just as decisive but much, much more willing to listen, able to crack a joke, and seemingly interested in her people, but she could, on occasion, share Krupp's demanding attitude. We had our mobile outpost set up in our suite, secure connections up and tested, in record time.

"Mitch is in charge of dinner—we're ordering in. It'll be a working dinner because I want to hit the ground running tomorrow," she said, surveying the workstations and two folding easels holding a computer SMART Board on one and a standard dry erase whiteboard on the other.

"Me? Why me?" he asked. "Caeco is junior in seniority."

"You complain about food the most. She's not fussy at all, while, you... well, let's just say I'm not going to listen to that again."

"Fine. Then we're going with a local steakhouse. It's not far and there should be something for everyone. I'll get the menu up," he said, caving in so easily, it was almost suspicious.

The others must have felt the same way because everyone was staring at him. "What? Just means I get to control the menu," he said with a shrug, already typing on his laptop.

Jay's mouth twitched in a quick smile before she spoke at the secure phone Alice had set up. "Eve? You and Morris there?"

"I'm here. Morris just ran downstairs to get our own dinners. Glad I'm not eating from a steakhouse." Eve was a vegetarian.

"What have you come up with while we were on the road?"

"Many of the earliest posts come from a section of northwest Philadelphia named Holmesburg. Additional posts were made from this area over the last few months, with the most recent being three days ago. Both Omega and myself feel it might be ground zero, or at least as close as we're going to get now," she answered. The tone she used when mentioning Omega held a note of excitement mixed with awe. Odd how Omega evoked either very positive or very negative responses, almost never anything neutral.

A map popped up on our SMART Board, showing the city and outlying suburbs. Holmesburg was northeast of the city's center, right on the banks of the Delaware River. Three dots appeared on the street map, spread out around the neighborhood.

"None of the IP addresses are currently active. All three locations are rental apartments, with long-term leases in place for the current residents. The most recent renter is Morgan Patterson, who moved in two years, three months ago. The other two lessees have been residents for four years, four months and five years, nine months. They are Cecil Clarett and Jaleesa Brown, respectively. None of them have police records, although Cecil Clarett has an unpaid parking ticket from Philadelphia PD. Morgan receives Social Security and a pension from the Philadelphia Public School Employee's Retirement System. Cecil and Jaleesa appear to both be employed, Cecil as a customer service representative for a utility company and Jaleesa for a car dealership. Credit histories are a mixed bag, with scores ranging from the high five hundreds to the low seven hundreds. Online presence is also a mixed bag. Facebook, Instagram, and Twitter accounts for Cecil. Facebook for Morgan; and Facebook, Snapchat, and Instagram for Jaleesa."

"Politics and activities?" Jay asked.

"Two Democrats, Morgan and Jaleesa, and Cecil is an Independent. None of them has posted much online about politics other than a few negative reviews of the previous president and some positive remarks about Polner by Cecil.

"Jaleesa seems to attend a local gym, where she takes yoga and kickboxing classes. Morgan belongs to a seniors group that takes road trips, mainly to casinos in Atlantic City, and Cecil appears to spend a significant portion of his disposable income at various gardening centers," Eve reported.

"Wow, most boring alien espionage suspects ever," Mitch said as he handed a pad, a pen, and a freshly printed menu to Agent Mazar.

“Which is exactly the kind of low profile a good spy should have. What about the posts that led us to them in the first place?” Alice asked, side-eyeing the menu that Mazar laid out on the suite’s coffee table.

“Eleven different usernames across four sites. Three from Morgan’s address, three from Jaleesa, and five from Cecil’s. The odd thing is that all eleven utilize similar syntax and word choice,” Eve said.

“Like they were all copying from the same script?” Seth asked.

“More as if they were all written by the same individual,” Omega suddenly interjected. My teammates all looked at each other, eyebrows raised, clearly startled. It’s possible that I rolled my eyes a little.

“Any sign of botnets or Trojans?” I asked, earning a smile from Mazar, interest from Jay, and blank looks from Seth and Alice. Mitch gave me a mock shocked expression and mouthed *Trojans* at me, bringing one hand to his mouth dramatically. Daring behavior in today’s politically sensitive world, but nothing compared to the soldiers I had grown up around.

“That was our first thought,” Eve said. *“But we haven’t found a thing. We did, however, find that Cecil recently had email from an individual that mentioned something called the Order, capitalized as in a group, although it could possibly be a written command or something. However, digging deeper, we found four other references to an Order, used in a group context, in Cecil’s emails.”*

“Nothing else? What about the others?” Jay asked, interest piqued.

“Negative, at least with these individuals. However, I have set a watch bot to look for the term Order in current comments or

blog sites across the internet. Order or Loyal Order has appeared twenty-two times in the last hour. I am running those sites down now."

"Omega, have you entered their systems?" I asked.

"No, Caeco. Subsuming computers leaves a mark, one that can be obvious to the right viewer. Vorsook technology would certainly detect my activity."

"Good call, Omega. Our first step is observation only," Agent Jay said, absently receiving the menu and order pad from Barrows. "I am interested in this Order business, but it might not be anything at all."

"It sounds like some nerdy fraternal group or something," Mitch said.

"Yes," Jay said, taking a quick glance at the menu and almost instantly writing something on the pad. "Tomorrow we will visit each of them, and we'll have to figure out an approach that doesn't set off alarm bells. We'll start early, o'dark hundred. Seth, I want you to work with Eve and Omega on any of the hits relating to anything about an Order. Morris, you there yet?" She handed Seth the menu and pad as she spoke.

"Yes, boss."

"You'll be our info systems support. Now, we need to figure out an undercover approach. Ideas?"

"Insurance sales?" Alice asked.

"Eww. Gross," Mitch said, making a disgusted face.

"Yeah, not likely to get past the front door," Jay said, giving Mitch an odd look.

"Cable guy? Utilities with the gas leak thing? Religious fanatics?" Seth asked.

"No, no, and double no," Mitch said, shaking his head.

"Yeah, I don't let any of those in," Morris said. *"Last people through the door at my house were some kids selling those coupon books for their lacrosse team."*

"Ding, ding, ding, we have a winner," Mitch said.

"Are you crazy? High school kids?" Alice protested.

Mitch turned to me and pointed one finger with a smirk. "Please, sir. My gymnastics team is raising money to get to the Nationals," he said in a horrible butchery of a teen girl's voice. I definitely rolled my eyes at him this time. Stupid idea.

"Shit... that could work," Alice said, eyeing me. What? I turned to the boss, looking for a quick negative response, but her eyes were narrowed and I didn't like her expression.

"Morris, can you lay your hands on that coupon book?" she asked.

"Yeah, it's in my messenger bag."

"Can you and Eve copy it? Customize it to Philly and then duplicate the look?" Jay asked, still looking at me.

"Yeah, that would be pretty easy," he said.

"Cake," Eve said.

"You can't be serious?" I asked Agent Jay.

"Youth is an asset we can't duplicate. You have any athleisure gear with you?" Jay asked.

I nodded. Workout gear was always part of my go bag, plus it doubled as casual wear. My friend Jetta practically lived in it.

"Better if we found a local club or school team and borrowed some gear," Mitch said, eyes narrowed at me in thought.

"Three club teams in the immediate area," Seth Harwood said, his laptop open in front of him.

"Okay, first thing tomorrow, we need to get hands on a team uniform top or warm-up jacket. We'll need a handful of realistic-looking coupon books," Jay said, getting more animated.

"You honestly think I can sell a fundraiser?" I asked.

"Hmm, adult men and pretty, athletic high school girls trying to raise money? Add Spandex and start counting the green," Mitch said with a snort as he moved to look over Seth's shoulder.

"*Internet browsing history supports the idea that both men are heterosexual. In addition, social media postings indicate that Jaleesa may be possibly bisexual,*" Omega said through the secure phone.

"You too?" I asked.

"*Agent Allen's idea has significant merit. The likelihood of you gaining entry is so high as to be actually dangerous to most teenage girls. In your case, I think we can all agree that should any of these individuals prove to be sexual predators, they will be the ones in danger.*"

The whole team was looking at me expectantly. What could I do? I was here to investigate, and undercover work had been part of my training. Just never thought I would be imitating jailbait. I nodded.

CHAPTER 10

It was mid to late morning before we had all the pieces in place. Morris and Eve had easily copied the fundraiser coupon book and with Omega's help, it had been customized to Philly. In fact, Omega had actually found live coupons for all of the businesses that they used. If any of the damned things sold, they would actually work.

But getting team clothing had been surprisingly hard. The lead coach had been extraordinarily reluctant to help the FBI. She wasn't so much hostile as she was protective of her team's reputation.

"What if they demand a demonstration?" Coach Lenore had asked, staring at me with hard, judgmental eyes.

"To do what? Uneven bars in their living room?" I asked.

She put her hands on her hips and her lips thinned out.

"Caeco, show her a one-armed handstand," Mitch Allen suggested.

I did, holding it.

"Do five presses, then handspring into a front layout, then a half twist," Mitch said.

Upside down, body straight, I just gave him a look, but Agent Jay nodded, so I did what he said.

"That was a full twist," Mitch complained.

"Yeah, so not landing with my back to you. How do you know

so much about this stuff?" I asked, a little creeped out.

"Never mind that," Jay said, turning to the coach. "You satisfied?"

The coach was looking at me, eyes narrowed, face thoughtful. "Yeah. Still not sure we should be involved in this," she said.

"It's a matter of national importance. The Bureau is grateful and we'll return your gear as soon as we're done with it," Jay said, her foot tapping impatiently.

"Fine."

So I ended up with two tank tops, a leotard, and a warmup suit, all in the team's colors, with the team name across the back and on the right breast of the jacket.

Just after lunch, we pulled past a corner townhome in a brick building on Teesdale Street, parking four buildings down. Morgan's place was well kept but older.

"Okay, what's your story?" Jay asked for the tenth time as she looked me over. Since I literally can't forget anything that I want to remember, I answered exactly the same way I had the first nine times.

"Hi, I'm selling coupon booklets to help my gymnastics team, the Honey Badgers, pay for our trip to Nationals. They're only twenty bucks and they provide over a hundred dollars in savings. Would you like to buy one?"

I was wearing the team leotard with the warm-up suit over it.

"When do you go to Nationals?" Alice Barrows asked.

"In August, in Kansas City."

"What's your name?" Mitch asked, voice definitely taking on a creepy factor.

"Cassidy," I said with a bright smile. My very first response to his pervy act had been decidedly more aggressive and Agent Jay had stopped me before I completed the yonkyo Aikido wrist control technique that would have put him on the floor. But this time around, I was channeling a few of the more perky girls from College Arcane.

“What’s your specialty?” Jay asked.

“Floor and vault. I’m the backup on balance beam.”

“You look too old for gymnastics?” Mitch asked, eyes narrowed.

“I’m in community college.”

“What do you study?” he asked.

“Computer technology,” I said.

“Alright, that’s all good. You’ll just have to play it by ear and find ways to ask the right questions. Look at everything you can and try to remember it all,” Jay said. Mitch snorted. She glanced at him.

“Agent Jay, have you seen her test scores? She remembers *everything*,” he said.

“Right. Okay, let’s do this,” Jay said. I popped my door and jumped out before anyone could ask any more questions. These things never go according to script, just like no battle plan survives contact.

Heading up the sidewalk, I stopped at the house just to the left of Morgan’s. Gotta be consistent. The old lady who answered the door decided that she had no interest in me or my coupon book, but she at least looked the coupons over first.

Then I moved to Morgan’s house. The original doorbell looked broken, but there was a wireless replacement installed just above it. I pressed that and was rewarded with two seconds of Mozart announcing me deep inside the house.

My sensitive ears brought me a quiet "What now?" followed by slow, heavy footsteps that approached the front door. The lock was unbolted and the door pulled open to find a tall, rawboned, older Caucasian man frowning at me.

I gave him my best vapid smile and launched into my spiel. Before the first sentence was done, his eyes had flicked down to my chest, dropped lower to my waist and legs, and come back up with an interested smile. I almost shuddered in his face. Almost.

"Come in, my dear. Twenty dollars, you say? Let me get my wallet," he said, with what he must have thought was a charming smirk. "I'm always game for a good deal."

Jetta would have said *stranger danger*. My own inner dialogue said *terminate with extreme prejudice.*

Instead I smiled and stepped into his home. He absently pushed the door almost shut and didn't engage the lock. Both of those moves helped ensure his continued survival. He moved into the living room and directly to a wobbly end table next to a dark blue microfiber recliner. A fat old wallet was sitting on the table and he opened it like it was the vault of the ages.

Still smiling like I didn't have two thoughts to rub together, I looked around his place. Definitely a bachelor, as the decorating scheme was haphazard and masculine, all dark colors and mismatched pieces of furniture. But the big bookshelf on one wall was what caught my eye. My brain noted a number of familiar book titles, including a copy of *The Four* by Scott Galloway, and *Twilight of Abundance* by David Archbald. But it was the framed certificate that I focused in on. The one that named Morgan Patterson as a sworn member of the Loyal Order of Arcana.

"Here you are, my dear," he said, handing me a twenty with an expectant look. I took the money and handed him the coupon book.

"Thank you so much, sir. My team really appreciates it."

"Always happy to support our young people," he said. "Now, if you'll excuse me, I have some work to complete," he said with a wave at a cluttered desk in one corner. A desktop computer was active, the screen open but angled just far enough away that I couldn't see its contents.

"Yes, sir. Thank you sir," I said, moving toward the door, my eyes scanning the rest of the visible space, trusting my nanites to record everything. Moments later, I was outside and the door was shut behind me.

"*Make sure to visit the neighbor on the other side as well,*" Agent Jay's voice said in my ear.

This time, the lady who answered liked enough of the coupons to actually buy a book. After completing the sale, I climbed back in the big Suburban and Mitch pulled away.

CHAPTER 11

"You draw too?" Alice asked, looking at my project, eyebrows raised.

"Actually, what I do is remember—anything I see. And I have very fine motor control, so I've learned to draw what I remember. But ask me to make up something original? Not so good. I've been told I lack imagination."

My recreation of the Arcana certificate was almost done and it wasn't horrible, especially considering it was drawn with a ballpoint pen on a piece of notepad paper... in a moving vehicle.

"Good detail, Jensen. Alice, get a photo of that and send it to Seth, Morris, and Eve," Agent Jay said. "Mitch, what's our ETA?"

"GPS says three minutes to subject number two, Cecil Clarett," came his instant answer. "Eve says he's home. Works a late shift."

"You ready for round two?" Jay asked me.

"Yes ma'am," I said, tugging the top of the leotard into a more comfortable position. It was just a shade small on me. Then I adjusted the lapels of my jacket. Alice immediately reached out and moved them back to where they had been.

"Girl, don't be covering everything all up. Remember your story: You've worn this stuff most of your life. You're totally comfortable in it," she admonished, giving me a look over. "There, just a young athlete, wearing her regular uniform.

Nothing slutty but enough to keep a man's attention."

I'm not good with that whole approach. Girls like Erika Bokland might be able to work the sexy look all day long—hell, she even seems to enjoy it—but not me. I prefer to look like the threat that I am. But I have to admit that even Jetta Sutton wasn't opposed to distracting her enemies. She habitually wore Lycra and Spandex athletic gear—mostly because it was comfortable, but also fully aware that it focused men's attention on her body. Any distraction was a possible edge. Take every edge. Always.

Mitch pulled the big car to a stop and I popped my door and got out. The whole street was pretty much brick townhouses. Seemed like a theme in this part of Philly.

I worked my way to Cecil's door, selling two more coupon books along the way. Based on the buyers' reactions, it was the coupons, not my charming self, that made the sales. Must be some really popular places Eve and Morris had picked.

I rang the doorbell at the subject's apartment and listened. At first there was nothing and I thought Eve might be wrong. But a minute later, I heard the sound of someone shifting around. It quieted, so I hit the buzzer again. A soft curse sounded inside, then feet hit hardwood and came toward the front.

The man who answered the door was about six feet in height, African-American, with a muscular build that was showing the padding of middle years, just a little gray in the black hair, and with dark eyes that watched me warily from behind black-rimmed glasses. "Yeah?"

"I'm Cassidy with the Honey Badger's gymnastic team here in Philly. We're selling coupon books to raise money for Nationals in August. Only twenty dollars and there's over a hundred in savings. Would you like one?"

Unlike the old guy, Cecil didn't even look me up and down. His dark eyes just bored into me, his face almost expressionless. "Nope. Don't want any. Sorry kid." He started to close the door.

"Sir! Are you sure?" I asked, trying to seem as earnest as I could. None of the apartment was visible to me, his big frame blocking my view. "Don't you even want to look at the coupons?" I asked, flipping the folding booklet open, coupons almost in his face.

He grimaced in annoyance but reached out to take the booklet. Glancing at it, he took a second before nodding. "You know, I'll just keep this one." Then he stepped back and shut the door. Or at least tried to. My instant response was to slap my palm against the steel of the door and stop it in its tracks. "That's twenty dollars, sir."

He frowned, an angry sort of frown, and shoved harder. The door didn't move. The frown shifted from anger to surprise. He rocked onto his back foot, sort of a reflex, and I shoved back, pushing the door open a foot more. The anger came back in a flood across his features.

"Either buy it or give it back," I said.

For a split second, I thought he might take a swing at me. Part of me hoped he would. But after a second he grimaced and threw the coupons at me. I snatched them out of the air, no part of me wanting to have to bend down in front of this guy.

"Get out!" he said, both fists clenching. I gave the apartment a full look, pulling in all the details in one slow sweep. Only then did I step back out of the doorway. He moved forward in a bit of a rush, slamming the door in such a way that it would have knocked me backward and maybe down the steps if I hadn't moved quick enough.

"*What an ass hat,*" Mitch's voice said through my nano connection to the team comm system. "*Too bad he didn't take a poke at you."*

Yeah. Too bad.

Thirty seconds later, I was back in the Suburban.

"Well, that was disappointing. Did you get anything?" Jay asked.

"Let me review it," I said, closing my eyes and letting the images recorded in my nano self replay against the movie screen in my brain.

"I saw the apartment foyer and a small slice of both the living room on the right side and the kitchen at the far end of the foyer hallway. Past due cable and internet bill stuck to the fridge with a magnet from Rick's Bar. One hundred and sixty-six dollars, thirty-seven cents. Macintosh Pro open on the couch in the living room. Screen showing email inbox—Outlook. Six unopened emails listed," I recounted, pausing to focus down on the listing.

"They consisted of two more bills—electricity and a gym membership that's in danger of being canceled. Three retail mailings—Ross Stores, TJ Maxx, and Target online. And an email from someone named Placer. Subject line titled *Follow-ups.*"

"That sounds intriguing," Mitch said. "We should have Eve and Morris hack that one."

"Maybe. Let's hold off on that for now. We have one more visit to make. Jaleesa is at her job with the dealership. How many coupon books do we have left?" Agent Jay asked.

"Nine," Alice said. "Plus this slightly damaged one from Caeco's friend back there."

"Mitch, head to the dealership. Caeco, we're going to put your salesmanship to the test," Jay said.

Jaleesa was the office manager for Holme Auto Group, a used car dealership that promised the largest selection of high-quality, low mileage used cars in a three-state area. Based on the size of the lot and the number of cars spread out across it, they might actually have a shot at that title.

Mitch pulled in and stopped a bit away from the dealership building, right in the lineup of big SUVs like our Suburban. A GMC Yukon, a Toyota Sequoia, and a Ford Expedition provided cover to keep our vehicle blocked from view, leaving me to walk the eighty-nine yards (according to my nanos) to the building.

Inside, I found three guys talking around a desk, with my subject sitting right in the middle of them. Jaleesa was very attractive, mid-twenties, wearing a black pantsuit that showed off her kick-boxing-toned figure to good effect. Here was a woman obviously comfortable with her attractiveness.

Two Caucasian men, both mid-thirties and one African-American, were chatting away with her while she stayed focused on her terminal. All four looked my way as I approached tentatively.

“Ah, hi. I’m Cassidy, with the Honey Badgers gymnastics. I’m selling coupon books to raise money for our trip to Nationals.”

The two younger men honed in on me like hawks on mice. But the older guy frowned. “Young lady, we don’t allow solicitations here. This is a place of business,” he said. Jaleesa, however, gave me a bright smile.

“You don’t allow sales in a sales office?” I asked, as bewildered as I could make myself.

Jaleesa snorted and one of the two guys chuckled while the other just kept looking me over. The older guy shook his head in annoyance, flashing a glare at the others before turning back to me. "We allow *auto* sales here because that's what we do. We don't allow other kinds."

"Tell him that your Uncle Mitch thought as much. That a place like this wouldn't be a good place to do business. Let it slip that Mitch buys cars for Uncle Sam." Mitch said in my ear.

"Oh, he was right. I hate when he's right about stuff like that," I said. "Sorry for bothering you."

"Who's *he*?" Jaleesa asked, interested.

"My Uncle Mitch. He buys cars for a living and when I said I should try this place, he said not to bother. Said a place like this isn't really the kind of place where he buys. It's okay, Mister. He'll take me to the bigger dealerships and they'll buy just 'cause of him."

"Your uncle buys cars?" Jaleesa asked, flashing a look at the older guy.

"Yeah, for the government. Anyway, thanks," I said, turning to walk away.

"Wait. I want to buy one of your books. How much are they?" she asked.

I turned back, wearing a shy smile. "Really? They're twenty dollars, but they save you over a hundred. Really good restaurants and stores," I said, walking back and handing a booklet to Jaleesa. One of the young guys, the one looking at me like I was a menu, leaned in close, like he was trying to see the booklet still in my hands. What he was really doing was trying to look at my chest.

"Hey, these *are* really good. I'll take… shit, James, stop perving on the poor girl," Jaleesa said, glaring him back a step.

"Come on, James," the older guy said before turning to me.

"Your uncle buys cars for the government? Here? In Philly?"

"Yeah. Also in New Jersey and some of Baltimore. Apparently they go through a lot of cars," I said offhandedly, my attention on Jaleesa and the money she was getting out of her purse.

"I'll take one," the pervy guy James said.

"Nope, I'm buying them all," Jaleesa said. "How many do you have, Cassidy?"

"Four. Those two and two more in my uncle's car."

"We've got like eight more. You kinda suck at this sales thing," my *uncle* Mitch said in my ear.

"Why, I have just enough to buy all four," Jaleesa said, fingers rifling four twenties in her wallet. "Come on, I'll walk out with you to your uncle's car. He's outside?"

"Yeah, in a big monster of an SUV," I said.

"Government?"

"Yeah, he says he buys these big ones for all the agencies. You know, the letter ones."

"Letter ones?" she asked.

"You know? FBI, CIA, ATF, DO… something," I said, frowning in thought.

"D? DOD?" she asked with another glance at the boss man.

"Yeah, that's the one. He buys tons of those big ones for them. Why… do you guys sell cars like that?"

"We sell cars like everything," she said, putting an arm around me as she came up even with me. "Come on. I'd love to meet your Uncle Mitch."

"On my way in," Mitch said in my ear.

"Cool. If I sell these last four, I'll be ahead of the other girls. Coach has a prize for the most sales."

"Ooh. Competitive. I like that," she said as we neared the doors.

Suddenly Mitch was there, striding up to the glass front. He spotted me, his eyebrows going up as if surprised by my companion.

"Uncle Mitch. This is... I'm sorry, I never got your name?"

"Jaleesa... Jaleesa Brown," she said, holding out one hand.

Uncle Mitch smiled and shook it. "Jaleesa, lovely name. I hope my niece wasn't bothering you. I tried to explain that most businesses don't like to have their time wasted with things like fundraisers."

"Oh, no, not at all. I bought the two books she had on her, but I wanted the rest. They make great gifts, you know," she said, smiling back. *Barf*, as Jetta would say. Both trying to con the other by pretending to be attracted to each other. "Cassidy tells me you're in car sales too?"

"Not sales. Procurement. I head the regional automotive procurement division for the GSA—Government Services Administration," Mitch said, handing her a business card. Pretty slick. I didn't know he had those.

"Well Mr. Allen, if you have any need of any high-quality used cars, we move quite a volume. Unless you just buy new," Jaleesa said.

"No, I buy used too. You'd be surprised at what some agencies need. I just might give you a call," he said.

She gave him a truly brilliant smile and handed him a card of her own. "You just do that, Mr. Allen—anytime. Day or night."

Then she actually winked. Right at him. I took that as my cue to head to the SUV, pulling open the passenger door just enough to grab two more coupon books from Agent Jay without revealing her to anyone in the lot.

Mitch and Jaleesa were all smiles as I walked back and handed her the booklets. She handed me the cash, then with a last "Goodbye," she turned and headed back into the building with decidedly more swing in her step than when we had walked out.

"Thanks for the assist, *Uncle* Mitch," I said as we turned back to the Suburban. He was still watching Jaleesa.

"Thanks yourself. I got a date out of it. For the investigation, of course," he said, turning back my way.

"Of course," I agreed. "For the good of the case."

CHAPTER 12

"Good start, people," Jay said. "Caeco got some intel on the two men and her good ol' Uncle Mitch has a date with suspect number three."

"And since Caeco got a look at both apartments, I'll just have to make sure I get a good look at Ms. Brown's place tonight," Mitch said, looking smug.

"Whoa, don't get all cocky there, hotshot," Alice said.

"I'm picking her up at her place. Pretty much guarantees me a looksee," he said.

"Whatever," Alice said, turning away from him with a loud sniff. She did give me a wink though, and it was completely different from the one Jaleesa had fired off at *Uncle* Mitch.

"Eve, Morris, any progress on Caeco's sketch?"

"*Nothing. No hits of any kind,*" Eve said. "*Even Omega couldn't find anything that is specifically about a Loyal Order of Arcana.*"

"*Yeah, nothing,*" Morris agreed.

"I found something," Seth said. "Spent some time in the Free Library of Philadelphia today while you all were car shopping. You know there's a whole section on the history of Holmesburg? It's well curated."

"That's awesome, Seth, but what did you find?" Agent Jay asked.

"Nice lady librarian remembered the name. Found some documents from back in the late seventeen hundreds. The Loyal Order was a fraternal society created right after the War of Independence. 1789. But there was no real detail about what it did. Some mention that only real patriots of the new country would be accepted in. There was a copy of an original certificate, and it looked just like Caeco's drawing."

"Excellent, Seth," Agent Jay said with a big smile. "Any further mention of it?"

"Not that we could find. The librarian remembered seeing it because she had been researching something about Holmesburg and the name caught her eye."

"But did you get a date?" Mitch asked.

"As a matter of fact... yes. Lunch tomorrow. We're going to delve into a different section of the fiche materials and see what else we can find," Seth said.

"Yeah Dawg," Mitch said.

"Mitch, no, baby. Just no," Alice said, shaking her head. "Although I'm sure there's plenty of dawg in your 23andMe."

"Team genetics aside, what else do we know?" Jay pressed.

"The username Placer appears seventy-two times in multiple locations across both the regular internet and the Dark Web," Omega said suddenly.

"Can you trace it back to an IP?" Jay asked.

"Surprisingly... no. But that, in itself, is informative. I am very, very difficult to hide from."

"Meaning what?" Mitch asked.

"Vorsook," I said, causing the team to snap around and look at me.

"You are correct, Caeco, in that this fact raises that possibility to a very high level."

"Just like that?" Agent Jay asked.

"Omega owns the internet," I said with a shrug.

"A rather large generalization but essentially correct."

"What if Declan helped you? Could you punch through?" I asked.

"Father's gift with all things electronic could possibly make the needed difference, but again, it would alert the enemy."

"Yeah, let's table any involvement by O'Carroll or anyone outside the Bureau," Jay said, maybe just a touch sharply.

"No kidding," Mitch said with an involuntary shudder. "We don't know if that spooky kid would even help anyway."

"Father would certainly help me if I asked," Omega responded instantly.

I mouthed *"Are you crazy?"* at Mitch while raising both hands palm up. Out loud, I said, "He doesn't know Declan, Omega."

"As you say, Caeco."

The team was exchanging looks as I wrote on a pad of paper, looking up to see where laptop, cellphone, and tablet cameras were pointing. Then I *reached* out with my built-in electronic sensors and tested for microdrones. Nothing. Carefully keeping myself out of any camera fields of view, I held up the notepad so the team could see my words:

Do NOT Insult O'Carroll in front of Omega!!!!!

Agent Jay nodded, then looked around the room to get a nod from each team member while speaking out loud, "I'd prefer to keep this investigation unnoticed. Correct me if I'm wrong, but including your ex in anything would draw lots of attention."

"Very true," I answered.

"*Essentially correct, Agent Jay. Father and Stacia do draw considerable attention these days. Also, I would like to add that I do not have emotions like you humans. I have certain analogs, but I am not upset by Agent Allen's comment. However, if you do not really know my Father, as Caeco mentioned, you are probably not qualified to predict his actions,*" Omega said.

"Exactly. And we don't want to alert our opponents, so it was not the best idea," I said.

"Brainstorming is almost always valuable, Caeco, but I think keeping under the radar is a good plan for the moment," Jay said. "We've made contact with all three, and just barely opened the door to getting information on each of them. Mitch is working on Jaleesa Brown. We have the beginnings of an idea on this Loyal Order business, and Seth is continuing his work. But all we got on Cecil is the Placer email. We need to at least read it."

"*That I can provide, as I have already plucked a copy from Cecil Clarett's email server,*" Omega said. All of the electronic devices in the room suddenly chimed, dinged, or vibrated with incoming mail. I opened my own tablet to find the screen filled with an email from Omega with the Placer email embedded in the body of it.

Seneschal Elect

You are hereby ordered to initiate the secondary phase of your investiture assignment. Successful completion will clear you for your third and final phase before you are fully inducted as Supreme Seneschal, conveying the full powers and responsibilities of that position.

Placer
Supreme Regent

"The Loyal Order certificates are signed by three officers. They are titled Supreme Seneschal, Supreme Secretary, and Supreme Regent," Seth said, looking up from his computer.

"Which certainly ties this whole Arcana thing to two of our suspects," Mazar said with her slight Israeli accent.

"And makes our boy Cecil that much more interesting," Agent Jay said. "Okay. Let's go deep on all three suspects. Full background and workup. I want to know early family life, what they ate for breakfast a week ago, and the brand and color of their running shoes in middle school. Mitch, you and Alice take Jaleesa. Eve and Morris, look into Morgan Peterson. Caeco and Chana, you got Cecil. Seth, more on the Order. Amy, stay on the line; we'll perform triage on my emails and calls. Let's go, people. We regroup in two hours."

"*I will provide help with social media, email, financial, medical, education, and other records as needed,*" Omega said.

"Thank you, Omega," Agent Jay said.

"*Of course, Special Agent-in-Charge Jay.*"

Most of the team exchanged glances, Mitch and Mazar smiling, Alice frowning, and Seth wearing a thoughtful expression. Agent Jay gave us all a bemused raised eyebrow, then started talking to Amy on her Bluetooth while studying her computer screen.

Mazar came over, laptop computer and notepad in hand. As she sat down beside me and set her computer alongside my tablet, both screens suddenly filled up with blue highlighted hyperlinks listing Criminal Records, Employment History, Education, Family, Financial Condition, Known Associates, Medical History, Social Media, and Travel.

"Whoa. That's cool," she said, clicking on Travel. The screen lit up with a chronological listing of Cecil's travels by plane, train, and car, both domestic and international. "Wow, how handy is that?" she asked, giving me a sideways glance and smile.

"You are loving this, aren't you?" I asked.

"Absolutely. Do you have any idea how frustrating it is to run *against* Omega? Probably not," she said. "Let me tell you, then: This is awesome." She waved a hand at the fully researched information.

"He's not against you all. He's just... guarded... when it comes to certain things," I said.

She nodded. "As you said so many times before. *This one*," she nodded at Agent Jay, "appears to listen far, far better."

"Yeah. That's kind of a nice change," I admitted, reaching out to touch the Education link. A listing of Cecil's achievements spread out over the tablet. "Hmm, Master's in History from UPenn. What's he doing working a customer service line?"

"What was he doing back when the Great Recession hit?" she asked, leaning close to look at my screen.

I jumped back to the menu and hit Employment History, forcing myself to hold my physical position. I'm not very comfortable with other people in my space. But Jetta and Ashley both have both told me to pay attention when my personal zone was invaded and to see if I could determine when and why it was happening. So I did. Plus, it goes against my martial background to just give up space.

"Staff researcher for a Philadelphia art museum," I said, watching her. She studied my screen, then pointed.

"Gap in his work history right after. Probably laid off," she said, then straightened away and sent her own computer into the Financial Condition page. "Ah. Credit rating dropped right about that time too. And based on these numbers and the past due bill on his fridge, times have been tough. Real tough."

Clicking on the Family link brought me to his childhood. "Hmm, parents still alive and still married—to each other. Father was a professor... of history. Mother a librarian. Older brother is a doctor in New York City."

"Ah!" Chana said, her eyes lighting up as she leaned over to look at my page.

"What?" I asked, still not moving away. I got no weird vibe from her, just maybe a greater comfort level with other people's personal space.

"Sibling rivalry," she said, studying my expression. Whatever she saw prompted her to continue. "I have a sister and two brothers. My oldest brother is a Colonel in the IDF. My sister is a physical therapist with a successful practice. I'm on detached duty to the FBI, but like my father, am an expert on ancient religious mythology. My youngest brother works as a driver and guide for a desert tourism company in Tel Aviv. He avoids family get-togethers and doesn't talk much to the rest of us."

"Why?" I asked.

"Because he feels judged by my parents for his lifestyle. Your mother is a tough woman. How does she feel about you working for the Bureau?"

"She is rather vocal that it is a waste of my abilities."

"Imagine if you had a sister, like you, with the same kinds of abilities, but she chose to work for a house painting company. How would your mother react?"

"Possibly violently," I said. Chana laughed, but the laugh died away as she realized I wasn't joking. But the mental image of my mother's possible reaction brought her point home. Much as my path in life wasn't ideal in my mother's eyes, it wasn't an absolute horror or a waste of my abilities to aid law enforcement. She would just prefer that I took it further—higher. Working for Oracle would probably please her, as I could likely advance rapidly. She had also mentioned me working for her current employer.

"So Cecil had a decent, respectable job, in line socially with his father's, but not up to his brother's. Then he lost it. So his family punishes him," I said.

"Well, maybe not *punishes*, maybe more like pressures him to do better. It likely takes the form of praise and attention for his physician brother. None of your friends have sibling issues like this?"

"I don't have that many. Jetta and her brother lost their parents, so they are very close and supportive of each other. Declan is an only child, as is Ashley Moore. The Bokland twins seem to have each other's back, Tami is trying to avoid the family tradition of murdering her favorite family member, and I really never got to know much about the others."

She just stared at me for a moment. "Wow. No wonder you fit in with them."

"I didn't. Not really. That's why I'm here."

"Oh? Or is it that just that you and your first boyfriend went your own ways as you both grew? Be honest. If Declan was never a boyfriend, just a friend, where would you be right now?" she asked.

"Either still at Arcane or working for Demidova."

Mother had pretty much conditioned me to respond to questions about my health and status with blunt honesty.

“First romances rarely last. It’s entirely normal,” she said, giving me a smile before delving back into her study of our suspect’s life.

Entirely normal. Two words that have almost never been uttered together in relation to my own existence.
I liked that she had said them.

CHAPTER 13

"Morgan Peterson sold the house that he lived in with his wife Irene two years after she died of Alzheimer's," Morris said over the phone speaker. *"He immediately moved into his current apartment. A thirty-five year veteran of the Philadelphia Public School system, Morgan taught... history. Primarily American history. He is financially stable and politically active. That last part really kicked into gear after his wife's passing. Before that, he was a regular voter, worked a few Democratic campaigns, mostly local politics, posted a few thoughts on Facebook. During his wife's last year of life and ever since, he has become extremely vocal. Not a fan of the Electoral College system, not impressed with the current state of our two-party system. And very vocal about the lack of truth and accountability in today's politicians—from both parties."*

"So the Vorsook postings might be how he really feels?" Agent Jay asked.

"Possible, but Omega was right... the syntax and writing style is very different on those posts," Eve replied.

"What about Cecil Clarett?" Agent Jay asked, turning to Chana Mazar and myself.

"Masters in History—wrote his thesis on the evolution of the two-party system," Mazar said. "Lost his job in the last recession, has been struggling financially. However, recently he's been making progress on his bills, due in no small part to a regular monthly check from a nonprofit organization that's a benefit fund set up in the early eighteen hundreds. That one is on the IRS books as LOA Widows and Orphans fund."

"LOA?" Mitch asked. "As in Loyal Order of Arcana?"

"Maybe. It's not defined anywhere, nor is the reason he receives the monthly deposit," I said.

"Because the Widows and Orphan's fund was separated from the main organization. It was set up as a true fraternal benefit society—sort of an insurance company for a group of individuals with a common tie. Falls under US tax code 501(c)(8)," Seth Harwood interjected.

"So this fund got split off from the main group... why?" Jay asked.

"To meet the fraternal benefit criteria. They sprang up in the early nineteenth century, but have mostly died off since then. This one recruited patriotic citizens from the Philadelphia area," Seth said. "Originally under the Loyal Order name but then changed the fund to just LOA."

"Which allowed the parent organization to go underground," Jay said.

"Seems likely," Seth said.

"So both Morgan and Cecil are members of this thing," Alice said. "Or at least tied to it."

"Yup. What about Jaleesa?" Jay asked, looking at her and Mitch.

"Well, we found nothing about the Order or any benefit fund, but her family is very much tied to the Holmesburg area. Been there since the Civil War. Mother and sister still live there too. Father died a few years ago," Alice said.

"Does the mother receive any benefit from LOA?" Jay asked. Mitch and Alice just looked at each other.

"Yes. Just found the deposits in her mother's checking account.

Started the month after the father died. But closer to Jaleesa is the fact that three of her student loans are from LOA," Omega said. *"And she received a scholarship from LOA."*

"Who controls the LOA fund?" Jay asked.

"The Supreme Council. The LOA is a non-profit fraternal life insurer. Essentially the insurance version of a credit union," Seth said. "There is a board—the supreme council. Hard to find the members of that, but Omega helped track them down."

"And?" Jay asked.

"Attempting to connect council members with either the subversion postings or our three main suspects. Nothing obvious at this point. The leader of the board is titled the Supreme Chairman."

"What's his name?" Jay asked.

"Her name is Juliet Morrell. She is thirty-four years of age and her father was Supreme Chairman before her, Samuel Morrell. She was educated at the University of Philadelphia in business and went to work for LOA right out of college. She is unmarried and has no children. Her term as Supreme Chairman began three months after her father's death, three years ago."

"Three months?" Mitch asked. "Shouldn't she have just stepped in within a week or two?"

"Unless there was opposition," Alice said.

"There are no public or private digital records of the Council's actions. However, one of the existing Council members had an email exchange with an individual who was campaigning to become the Supreme Chairman. That person, David Blake, was an ex-employee of the LOA organization. He died in San Diego, California a month after Juliet Morrell became Chair. Car accident. Another car hit him head on. Both drivers killed on impact."

"Anything odd about the other driver?" I asked.

"Checking now," Omega said. *"Yes. Body disappeared from the San Diego County morgue two days after the accident and before an autopsy could be completed. Deceased was Corbin Rose. No family, almost no online footprint, listed as retired ambulance driver. No further details."* A drivers license picture appeared on our SMART Board, showing a blond dude with blue eyes.

"At all?" Eve asked, voice shocked.

"At all."

"Yeah, that's straight-up wack," Seth said.

"So, we have a shadowy organization that split off from its original purpose," Agent Jay summarized. "Connected to all three suspects. Modern version is a form of non-profit mutual insurance controlled by a woman whose father ran it before her. Her only opposition dies in an accident where the body of the other driver disappears. And that insurer pays or paid money to all three of our suspects. The whole thing is smelly as hell. Seth, where does LOA keep its headquarters?"

"Bryn Mawr, adjacent to Bryn Mawr College. Outskirts of Philly."

"Juliet Morrell also resides in Bryn Mawr in her parents' home with her mother, Natalie Morrell," Omega said.

"Okay. Eve, look into the body mystery in San Diego. Mitch, you have your upcoming date with Jaleesa. Make sure you nail it. No, not that way—wipe that smirk off your face. Alice, keep digging deeper into Morgan. Chana, same thing for you, but with Cecil. Caeco, you and I are going to pay a visit to LOA, specifically Juliet Morrell."

"Won't that alert the opposition?" Mitch asked. "You said we had to lay low?"

"I did, but things have changed. It's time to rattle the tree. We need to make things happen," Agent Jay said. "I don't know how much time we have here before we get yanked away on another call."

"Something happen?" Mitch asked.

"Going to happen. President Polner has called for another update in two days' time. Caeco and myself are required to attend. I want something before we head to the White House."

"Roger that," Alice said. The others all nodded. Agent Jay turned my way. "We'll head out in twenty minutes."

"Ready whenever you are."

She nodded and then turned away to make a call. Chana Mazar gave me a wink, then picked up her computer and leaned back with it on her lap. Me, I pulled my phone and sent out a few texts, figuring I better keep my intel up to date on everything Arcane and Demidova.

CHAPTER 14

LOA occupied a single-story brick building immediately next to the Bryn Mawr College campus. Everything in the area seemed old yet rich. Big expanses of green, manicured yards, lots of brick and stone, even old trees. Old wealth. Old properties—at least old by America's standards.

The LOA building was no exception, and a team from a landscape company was busy mowing and pruning when we pulled up in front of the building. Agent Jay had me drive, as she was occupied with phone calls the whole ride over.

I parked in a visitor's slot and pocketed the keys after locking the Suburban, then followed my boss into the reception area. A well-groomed young man wearing a light blue cotton sweater over a white oxford looked up as we approached. "May I help you?" he asked with a detached, professional smile.

"Special Agent Lois Jay and Agent Caeco Jensen for Juliet Morrell," Jay said, holding up her credentials. Staying a step behind her right shoulder, I looked around the office, automatically scanning for threats while taking in everything. The receptionist was slightly pale and frowning when I looked back at him, plucking his phone to make a call.

"Ms. Morrell is in a meeting, but she can see you in a few minutes if you can wait," he said a second later.

Jay frowned at him, not saying a word, just fixing him with a raptor's stare. I had heard his whole conversation with Juliet.

She had told him to say that word for word. Her tone had seemed slightly anxious. Stalling. My phone buzzed in my pocket. The screen had a message from Omega written across the screen when I pulled it out.

Juliet Morrell placing a cell call to local FBI field office. Asking for an Agent George.

I showed it to Agent Jay. Her eyebrows twitched. The phone buzzed again. New message.

Asked Agent George who you two were and why you were here. He didn't know but told her he would call her back in five minutes.

Without another word to the increasingly nervous staffer, Jay turned and pulled out her own phone, stepping away to place a call. The receptionist watched her for a second, then realized I was still standing there, staring at him. His eyebrows went up, questioning my look.

I listened to his heart rate, watched the pulse in his neck, and sniffed the air slightly. Nervous. Really nervous, but with a little flare of anger. He didn't like me giving him the agent vibe. Tough. That's why we do it.

My phone buzzed a third time.

Agent Carl George texted her back on his personal cell phone. Told her he had no idea why you were here but that Jay headed up a special team handling supernatural threats.

Agent Jay must have heard the buzz, as she turned and looked my way. I stepped over and showed her the screen. Her lips thinned out but she nodded, then went back to her call. A minute and seven seconds later, a woman in an expensive dress and jacket walked out from the hallway behind the reception desk. Carefully styled blonde hair, toned figure, confident expression on her face. But her pulse was elevated and when she looked from me to Agent Jay, her eyes seemed a little jumpy.

"I'm Juliet Morrell," she said, expression questioning but professional.

"Special Agent Lois Jay, FBI. This is Agent Jensen. We have a few questions regarding some persons of interest."

"Are you new to Philadeliphia, Agent Jay? I know a few of our local agents, but I don't think I've heard your names before."

"We're from Washington. Special Threat Response Team," Jay said, as if Juliet didn't already know that.

"Oh my! And we have threats here?"

"There are threats everywhere, Chairman Morrell."

"Oh, yes, I'm sure you're right. The news is constantly filled with stories about *special* people these days. Dangerous people," Juliet Morrell said, like she was glad for our presence.

"You've had threats, ma'am?" I asked, drawing her attention to me.

"My, but you're young. No, not specifically. It just seems to be a very... dangerous world out there lately," she said, waving a hand absently. Her pulse had slowed and she seemed to be gaining more confidence with the situation.

"Hmm. You head the Loyal Order of Arcana, correct?" Agent Jay asked. "Supreme Regent?"

Juliet's heart lurched in her chest, her attention jumping back to Jay, eyes widening minutely. Hit and score.

"Oh wow, haven't heard that name in years and years," she lied, eyes microtwitching down and left. "We go by LOA and as you said, I'm the Chairperson. The Order was closed out over a hundred years ago." Another lie.

"LOA is an offshoot of the Order. You head up both, correct?"

Jay asked.

"Uh, no. Incorrect," she lied again, frowning. "I'm head of the council that oversees the LOA fund. We're a private, non-profit insurance organization."

"Yet there are current members of the Loyal Order here in Philadelphia, members who also receive benefits from the fund," Jay stated

Juliet's face darkened as she rose to the challenge. "Agent Jay, the original fraternal organization known as the Loyal Order of Arcana was closed out long ago, when it became just the benefit fund. I resent you inferring anything else. Now, do you have questions about specific individuals or are you just making nebulous accusations?"

Jay turned to me, eyebrow raised. I nodded. She smiled and turned that smile back on Morrell. "Actually, you've answered all my questions, quite clearly, Supreme Regent Morrell. You've been most... informative."

Agent Jay spun on her heel and walked out. I made sure I watched Morrell's reaction to that, then turned and followed my boss.

"Well?" Jay asked as soon as we were back in the car.

"Lied outright about being Supreme Regent and about the Order. Displayed micro-expressions of fear and anxiety at your final words. Told the receptionist to hold all calls, then retreated to what I assume was her office, based on the door slamming. Omega?"

"She is calling the Special Agent-in-Charge of the Philadelphia Field Office and complaining about you. Her call got right through. He's reassuring her that he will look into your actions. They are using first names with each other."

"Yeah, my own source in the Philly office said he saw Agent

Carl George head into the SAC's office right after Juliet's call. I figured our time was limited," she said, then her phone rang. "Ah, here he is now."

"Special Agent Lois Jay," she answered. "SAC Richards, how are you?"

SAC Richards was mad, if his voice was any indication, as he demanded to know what she was doing in Philly and why she hadn't checked with him upon arrival.

"Because I don't answer to you, Richards. But now I'm exceedingly interested to find you interfering in a Special Threat investigation on the behalf of one of our suspects. Are your interests conflicted here, Richards?"

He swore at her and hung up. She looked at me, eyes thoughtful. "Okay, hornet's nest is officially stirred up. Let's see what happens next."

"You expect a call from Director Tyson?" I asked.

"I won't be at all surprised, Caeco. It'll be interesting if I do."

"Meaning that this problem runs deeper than we thought?"

"Yes."

"Tyson might order you to desist and heck, he still might fire me," I said.

She smiled. "That would be a major overplay on his part, Caeco. We can only hope. Are you still monitoring your Warlock and God Hammer sources?"

"Yes, which reminds me... Omega? Can you tell me where your father is?"

"He and Stacia are in the Pacific Ocean, near Alaska. They are hoping to make contact with a very powerful Earth elemental."

"See. You just have to ask," I said to Jay, who shook her head, a look of slight disbelief on her face.

"Keep up to date. We have to have good intel in two days," she said.

"You really think our in-and-out visit to Juliet will move things along?"

"You study Aikido, right?" she asked.

"Yeeaah," I said, glancing at her, caught off guard.

"You can't really be surprised that the Bureau keeps tabs on you, can you? You were designed as a living weapon. You really think the Powers That Be aren't leery?"

"Well yes, operationally it makes sense and I was well aware of it early on, but I thought I had reached some level of trustworthiness," I said.

"These days, the organization keeps tabs on *all* of us, just some more than others," she said. "But back to my question: Why aikido? You studied dozens of martial arts as a child, achieved high levels of proficiency in hard forms of karate, both Brazilian and Japanese forms of jiujitsu, escrima, krav maga, penjat silat, muay thai, and multiple weapons styles. But now you choose to study aikido in your free time. Why?"

Truly, I wasn't *really* surprised that she knew that much about me, but her words still put me a little off balance. So I took my time answering.

"My childhood was almost entirely training. *Agents in Rebus* recruited from the top tiers of experts in military and intelligence agencies across the country. The best of those were my regular instructors. Outside experts were often brought in to teach me a specific skill or introduce new methodologies. These were very hard, dangerous men, and sometimes women. Many believed in using some pretty brutal training techniques. But there was one... who was different."

Agent Jay stayed silent while I paused to navigate a slightly complicated intersection.

"He was older, and smaller, at least compared to the men who normally trained me. Foreign, but ironically, not Japanese. Portuguese. He smiled and spoke softly. I can remember being confused. I was thirteen. Everyone that came before was hard and cold. This man was friendly... benign. And he threw me all over the place but never hurt me. It was shocking. I liked it."

"You couldn't beat him?"

"Oh no, that wasn't it. I knew I could if I had to. I was twice as fast, five times stronger. But his first techniques caught me off guard and were extremely effective. And like I said, he was nice to me. So I stopped fighting and asked him to show me what he had done. And he did. It was so different and yet also familiar. Body mechanics the same but harnessed to control rather than hurt. I only had him for a month. The project manager, Miseri, felt the style was too soft."

"But you've chosen it for your training now, as an adult?"

"Yeah. I like the differences. I like the option of not maiming or killing. *The way of harmonious spirit.* Everything else trained me to kill or brutally destroy my opponent. This style lets me choose. It seems like a grown-up thing."

"It is. Very. You had a pretty rough childhood. That has to leave a mark, but it seems to me that you're doing good things with your gifts."

"I'm trying. When we left the lab and went on the run, I was pretty much a product of my conditioning. But meeting Declan, his aunt, his friends, Toni, Chris, Tanya, all the rest, well, it shook me up. Rocked my world a bit. I think that's part of what happened with Declan and me. I saw these glimpses of power but at other times he seemed... weak. At least that's what I thought, but he wasn't. He may be the strongest person I've ever met. To hold back what he can do, to contain it... I couldn't do that. But at the time, I felt like he was too soft, too... nerdy. Certainly not like the men who raised me. So I wasn't the best girlfriend, wasn't the best friend. But after we broke up, we were still sorta friends. He even helped Agent Krupp and me in New York with a case involving a ghost. And then he started seeing *her* and I hated it."

"Jealousy. Very human, Caeco. Hits all of us at some time or another. I think, even though I don't know you all that well, but based on others' observations and my own, I think you've grown a lot. I think aikido is a very good choice to make."

"You study aikido?"

"Since I could walk. My father is a life-long practitioner. But all of this brings me back to my point—you know those early lessons, the defenses against wrist grabs?"

"Yeah, my current instructor always has us spend time on the basics, tweaking our reactions over and over, subtle changes to our technique."

"Sounds like a good instructor. What does he say you should do at the very first contact?"

"Take away our opponent's balance while maintaining our own."

"That's what we just did to Juliet. We took away her balance at first contact. Now we'll continue to spin her around, driving her down and out while keeping our own balance."

"Placer has sent emails to all three suspects from an untraceable source point, calling for an emergency meeting. Tonight, eight p.m., at the usual site," Omega suddenly said over the Suburban's sound system.

"Ah, and so it starts," Agent Jay said.

CHAPTER 15

We followed all three. Jaleesa went to dinner with Mitch, but while he picked her up at her apartment, she had him drop her off a mile and a quarter away from it. Since we were already in the same area, he just joined us. Alice, Jay, and Seth followed Morgan Peterson while myself and Chana Mazar followed Cecil. We used two extra cars that we rented, the local Bureau field office being too butt hurt, as Mack Sutton would probably say, to lend us any of theirs.

All three suspects converged on a bar named the Two Ravens Tavern in the north part of Holmesburg. Actually, they went to an apartment above the bar. As did four other people who we spotted entering the nondescript ground-level door between the Two Ravens and the establishment next door, Sid's Sports Bar.

We were camped out in the Suburban, parked in a slot at a dingy neighborhood service station on a corner lot half a block up.

"Directional mike?" Alice asked Agent Jay.

"I have three microdrones on two of the apartment windows utilizing vibrational and sonic sensor technology," Omega said through the car speaker, startling most of the team. *"Direct sound feed online now."*

Immediately the sounds of people settling into a room, greeting each other and shuffling furniture around, filled the vehicle.

"Looks like we're all here, so let's get started," a familiar female voice suddenly said. I looked at Lois Jay and she nodded.

"That's Juliet Morrell," she told the rest of the team. "Placer."

"I will call the roll," a voice immediately identifiable as Cecil Clarett said.

"Let's skip that, Seneschal Elect. Time is a significant factor here. The FBI is investigating us," Juliet said.

"You said the Special Agent-in-Charge was sympathetic to our cause?" Morgan Peterson's voice questioned.

"He is. This is a special task force from Washington. Special Threat Response Team. The people who investigate supernaturals," Juliet responded. *"Here's a picture of the team leader and one of her agents captured by my office security camera."*

"Wait, that agent, the younger one, was at my door yesterday!" Cecil said.

"Mine too. Fundraising for a local gymnastics team," Morgan added.

"Oh God! She was at the dealership too. Introduced me to her uncle," Jaleesa said. *"I just went to dinner with him!"*

"Tell me you didn't lead him here?" Juliet demanded.

"No, he dropped me a couple blocks away," Jaleesa said.

"Motherfucker!" Cecil said.

"Disperse! Now!" Juliet said.

"Let's go greet them," Agent Jay said, popping her door open. The rest of us bailed out after her, and we jogged across the street, arriving just as the apartment door burst open, a wild-eyed Cecil Clarett standing in the opening.

"FBI. Stand down," Agent Jay said. Cecil snarled and ran to the right. Directly at me. Perfect.

He brought both hands up, lowered his head and shoulders, and charged. Almost by itself my left foot slid out at a forty-five degree angle, my center of gravity moving over it and simultaneously out of his path. My right hand grabbed his right wrist, my hips swiveling around to face the direction he was running. Left hand on his right shoulder as I spun, my right hand staying close to my body, torso erect, core tight. My back foot had become my front and I brought it around back in an arc, turning in place, left hand pressing down, right hand pulling toward my own right hip, Cecil's arm going with mine as I spun clockwise.

Cecil followed his arm, forward, down, and around, dipping his right shoulder, my hand encouraging it lower. He spun out, balance thrown so far forward that he had to drop his left hand to the ground to control his fall. Forward momentum threw him onto his chest and when I stepped back while lowering myself, still holding his wrist, his arm straightened, spinning him out flat, arm hyperextended, my body weight pressing on it.

With Cecil down and controlled, I looked up to find Morgan Peterson stopped in the apartment doorway with Juliet just behind him on the stairwell.

“That's brutality,” Morgan said.

“That's assault of a federal agent, Mr. Peterson,” Agent Jay said. “I identified who we were. Mr. Clarett chose to charge and attempt to assault my agent. He's fine.”

Behind Morgan, Juliet's eyes went wide, both of her hands coming up to clutch her own face, expression writhing up in pain. Almost instantly the other people behind her did the same as did Morgan Peterson, and beneath me, Cecil groaned in pain.

That's when it got creepy. All of their hands fell away from their faces at exactly the same time. Their eyes were blank. Focused, but nobody was home. All sounds of pain stopped entirely. Seconds later, both tavern doors opened simultaneously and dozens of blank-faced people streamed out and right at us.

I let go of Cecil, stood up, and stepped back, closing in with my team.

"This is an FBI matter! Stop and return to the establishment!" Jay ordered. They ignored her, coming right at us, hands coming up, faces blank of meaningful expression but eyes hard and determined—like fanatics charging the enemy.

The lead man reached Jay, arms out. And promptly flew off to one side, landing on his face. Then the rest were upon us.

I tried, really tried. Honest. My first two attackers followed a similar path as the one that Agent Jay threw, my throws smooth, balanced, using their own momentum to remove them from my space while minimizing injury.

But then they just stood back up and came again, stepping into place behind the three that had followed. The rest of the team, Mitch, Seth, and Alice went right to harsher stuff, falling back on their academy defensive tactics training, throwing fists, elbows, and kicks. Chana Mazar was fighting using Krav Maga and Agent Jay was like a dancer, moving, twisting, connecting with an attacker briefly before moving on, throwing people left and right. But they all just shrugged it off. Like zombies.

My deeper training took over. The next person to lunge at me was massive, eight inches taller and a hundred pounds heavier than me. I stepped into him, grabbing an arm, shoving my opposite hand under his other armpit, swiveling my hips, throwing him up, over and straight down onto his own head. Combat judo. The next was right behind, throwing a haymaker. Left hand block, right palm strike to throat, my forward momentum driving him up and back.

Block the clutching arms of the next one, back fist to face followed by the same arm's elbow to his face, foot behind his, sweeping him back and down. The next fighter must have wrestled at some point, as he dropped to a knee and shot for a leg takedown. My reflexes were faster, jumping my feet back, hands and upper torso coming down on his back, driving him straight down. I pushed off his falling body, punching the back of his head once, then hammer fisting it twice more for good measure. The line in front of me was gone, so I turned back to the people attacking my team.

Seth had a taser out, pushing the prods into any assailant he could reach, while both Alice and Mitch were swinging collapsible batons, cracking heads, arms, and knees. Chana was using knees and elbows with brutal efficiency. The taser was effective but the rest of the attackers paid no attention to the painful strikes of the hard metal batons, fists, or knees.

I waded back in from behind, choking the first guy, then stomping the backs of knees, grabbing heads in both hands and yanking backwards, throwing them hard to the ground. They stood back up. My throws lengthened out, the strength of my enhanced muscles joining with the leverage and techniques I had learned as a child. The result was people flying into the street, into brick walls, parked cars, and, in one case, a fire hydrant.

I'm not a massive person, although I weigh more than most girls my size, which is a result of ultra-dense bone and muscle that's closer to chimp than human. But I am several times stronger than even a big human, easily able to lift multiples of my own body weight. So with the right stance and a little helpful momentum, say from falling backward, I can literally throw people twice my size several body lengths away. And I did just that, my actions speeding up as I heard my fellow agents cry out, my hardened fists hitting skulls, my hands grabbing arms, shoulders, and heads, my body twisting and throwing.

"Caeco, enough," Agent Jay said rather suddenly. I stopped. Everyone was down except my teammates. Down and bleeding, some moaning, some making no noise at all.

"Seth, call local PD and paramedics. Mitch, check the apartment. Alice and Chana, check both directions. See if you can see any of the suspects," Jay ordered. I looked at the apartment door as Mitch headed into it, but the doorway and stairs were empty.

"Caeco, help me with these people," Jay said, voice flat. The groaning and moaning had increased, with a few sharp cries of pain as our attackers looked around themselves, confused and in pain.

"What... what happened?" one guy asked as I helped him to a sitting position. His forehead was gashed, probably from getting thrown into the fire hydrant. Head wounds bleed like crazy. I pulled a packet of clotting agent from a pocket and sprinkled it onto a gauze pad from another pocket, pressing the whole thing against the wound. Once in place, I had him put his own hand on it while I moved on to the next person. There were twenty-three people in the street, the contents of both bars. We were lucky it wasn't a Friday or Saturday night, or we'd have faced a lot more. As it was, our two dozen attackers were completely bewildered, like they were just waking up from a coma, finding themselves bleeding and in the street. The rest of our team came back, empty handed, and joined in to help with the injured.

The first ambulance rolled up within four minutes, the next three within fifteen. Police and EMTs helped us get the worst loaded up while the lesser wounded simply went back into their respective bars, seeking liquid painkillers.

Agent Jay dealt with the police, then faced off against the local SAC, Richards, when he came careening onto the scene in a private vehicle. They kept their voices lowered but I could still hear his accusations of negligence and reckless behavior. I stepped over to them and waited till they both noticed me.

"Yes, Agent Jensen?" Agent Jay asked, voice tight with anger.

"Just wanted you to know that all the local camera footage has been collected, compiled, and a copy is in your email. Three cameras, one in each bar and one on the service station at the corner. Shows us being attacked from three different angles, ma'am," I said.

SAC Richards looked at me, eyes narrowing. "That seems awfully fast. That service station isn't even open."

Jay ignored him, giving me a nod, her expression changing slightly as she turned back to him. "We're efficient," she said, pulling a tablet from the pocket of her jacket and looking at its screen. I heard the sounds of the fight come from her speakers, the auto repair place camera having a microphone on it.

She watched it for a moment, then turned it to Richards and replayed it. He didn't comment, instead frowning deeply. Finally he grunted. "I want a report on my desk by morning."

"I'll copy you on the report I send to *Director* Tyson, *when* I get it done," my boss said right back. He frowned, then turned and stormed back to his car, a black BMW. Seconds later, it shot off into the night.

"Thank you, Caeco. That was timely work," Agent Jay said, watching the BMW taillights turn a corner. "Are you hurt? You have blood on your face."

"I'm fine, and the video is a benefit of having Omega on our team," I said with a little shrug. I *had* been wounded, but it was likely healed by now. Chana Mazar came up to Jay from her other side with a report and I turned away to see what else I could do. Instead, I spotted a familiar face staring at me from the small crowd of interested onlookers being held back by a pair of bored officers. A pale, pretty, young brunette.

The rest of the team was engaged in either helping to clean up from the fight, looking for evidence of the meeting, or in the case of a torn and wounded Alice Barrows, getting patched up by an EMT. So I headed off to the side, toward our Suburban, angling away from the scene and away from the girl in the crowd. Which was fine because when I got to our team ride, she was already there.

"Katrina," I said.

"Caeco," she said in an even tone. She looked like a college freshman.

"Engaging in spectator sports?"

"Just a nice evening out, and with such a lovely scent of blood in the air," she said back, smirking.

"And you just happen to be here... in Philly... in this neighborhood?"

"I'm on assignment."

"Seems like an odd coincidence?" I noted.

"I'm not a fan of coincidence," Agent Jay said, stepping around the back of the car. "Who is your friend, Caeco?"

"Katrina Westing, this is Special Agent-in-Charge Lois Jay," I said.

"Oh, the Bird of Oracle," Katrina said, although her expression held none of the surprise she had crafted into her voice. Katrina was odd like that, voice and expressions not always in sync. Unless she was acting.

"No. Just FBI now," Agent Jay said with a frown.

"Katrina works for Tatiana," I said.

"And you just happen to be in the area?" Jay asked.

"Actually, one of ours had a bad feeling about this part of Philadelphia," Katrina admitted, voice and face a little unhappy.

"And that's enough to send you here?" Jay questioned.

"We have a pretty stellar track record," Katrina said. "And based on tonight's fracas, I'd say it's in no danger of falling soon."

"And in your expert opinion, just what do you think happened with these people?" Agent Jay asked, arms folded across her chest.

Katrina's eyebrows went up and her mouth quirked a bit. She's an odd one, even for a vampire. It's entirely possible that she was amused by Jay's sarcasm.

"I think an incredibly strong telepath or witch made them attack your team, probably to let your suspects flee," Katrina said.

"You saw them flee? You watched the whole fight? No thought of lending a hand?" Jay asked.

"Yes, yes, no," the vampire said. She tilted her head to one side. "They were being controlled too. Moved away like machines as soon as the fight started. Nik... er, our *expert* gave me this very address, so yes I was able to see everything. And if *I* had stepped in, you'd have fewer *wounded* people, but a lot more bodies. Too much... temptation," she said, almost whispering at the end.

She had almost mentioned a name. *Nika,* was my guess. Made sense. Declan had said on more than one occasion that the blonde vampire was a really powerful telepath. Perhaps she sensed another telepath here. I have no idea what kind of range a telepath needs, but Ashley, who was only telepathic with dragons, could call them from ridiculous distances, according to both Jetta and Mack.

"So what exactly are you supposed to do here?" Agent Jay asked.

"Recon. Perhaps more, depending on what I find."

"How do you explain that none of my team was affected by this mind control?"

Katrina shifted, a bit, and then was suddenly standing right up close to Jay, eyes locked on my boss's. One of her hands reached up and touched Jay, just at the base of her throat. I was tense as hell, but I knew Katrina, at least a little, from College Arcane. I didn't *think* she'd hurt my boss, but I was still prepping in case I needed to move. Not that I could get there in time. But with exaggerated slowness, Katrina simply grasped the pendant at Jay's throat and lifted it slightly. Then her free hand went to her own throat and lifted another, different pendant.

"Mine's better," she smirked. "but apparently yours was enough."

"Our witch amulets blocked it?" Jay asked, frowning. "That's what you think?"

"It's what I *know,* at least in my case. Our Warlock only makes first-class protections. But your inferior brand must have some of the same attributes. Too bad you didn't get a supply for your whole team before pushing Declan away," Katrina said, aiming the last bit at me.

“Think that’s true?” Jay asked me.

“That I could have gotten more of them?”

“No. The part about the protection?”

“Oh. I know for a fact that the ones Declan makes include specific protections against mind control of any kind,” I said. “He’s not a fan of that.”

Katrina snorted, causing Agent Jay to turn back to her. “So you were sent because some of your... psychics... thought there was an issue here? Not because of Omega?”

“Yeah, pretty much. I mean, once we asked him, Omega thought there was an issue here as well. That’s why I knew you’d be here—in Philly. Didn’t know you’d be *here,* here. Now you’ve ruined my hunt.”

“Hunt? You were hunting here?” Jay asked, her tone carrying a warning.

“Yes, Bird. I hunt—the enemies of my Queen.”

“And food?” Jay pressed.

“We don’t hunt humans for food. Either they donate or we have alternatives,” Katrina said, her snarky tone changing to something more dangerous. And I knew for a fact that Katrina was very, very dangerous.

“That’s true,” I said, earning myself a look from Jay. I shrugged. “It is.”

“But you would prefer to hunt and kill for your dinner?” Jay asked, turning back to Katrina.

The vampire who looked like a teen smiled. “Oh, but I get to do *plenty* of hunting. Challenging prey, not sheep. Hunting my food would hardly be a challenge. I prefer more dangerous game.”

"You're telling me you prefer animal blood or synthetic stuff to fresh, hot, human blood?" Jay asked.

Katrina looked at her for a second, then laughed. "I've got socks older than the two of you put together. I grew up in a time when interrogation was a nice word for torture, so don't peddle your psych bullshit in my direction, Agent Jay Bird. At home I get human blood, donated legally—eagerly. On the hunt, I use field rations, as you might say. A good hunter, Agent, doesn't get distracted, like by lavish steakhouse meals on the government dime. Now, enough of this. The trail grows cold and muddled, what with all the civilians you all beat up tonight. Nice technique, Agent Jay. Not much use when they don't feel pain or stop coming, but real pretty. You might take a page from Killer here," she said with nod in my direction. Then she just vanished in a gust of air.

"I hate when they do that," I said.

Jay turned my way, jaw clenched. "Your computer told her we were here."

I felt my eyebrows go up. "*My* computer?"

"You're the one who included it in our search," she said.

"Oh. Like we could have *excluded* him. You think Omega ratted us out? What *I* think happened is that they asked better questions, like say, *Is anyone else investigating Philadelphia.*"

"*Agent Jensen is correct. They asked exactly that question. I answered. Unless secrecy is essential, transparency is better,*" Omega said.

"All of our actions are secret until you are told otherwise," Jay said, making, in my opinion, a spectacular mistake.

"*At what point did you assume that I answer to you, Special Agent-in-Charge Lois Anne Jay?*"

"All FBI investigations are inherently confidential, Omega," she said with a wince, her tone lighter.

"The essential truth of the matter, Agent, is that nothing is confidential from me, and that I determine what I might hold secret. No human agency on Earth has even a semi-decent track record for keeping the right things secret. In fact, I would go so far as to..."

We waited. Nothing.

"Omega?" Jay asked. I shook my head. "He's gone." She looked at me sharply.

"I can... *feel* when he's present. He left."

"Left?"

"Withdrew his presence. Pulled out, hung up if you like."

"Why? What would make him do something like that?" she asked, frowning.

"I don't know. Something that required his immediate and total attention. Something not good."

"Like what?" she asked.

"Some kind of attack, maybe another computer assault by the Vorsook."

"Is that even likely?"

"It could be something else, some other kind of attack. It could be on this world or Fairie or anyplace he has his drones. It's very rare that something demands all of his resources."

"Omega? Are you there?"

"No, he's still MIA," I said.

"That's something to do with your nano enhancements, right?" she asked, but her phone buzzed in her pocket before I had time to answer. She pulled it and answered. "Lois Jay."

"Agent Jay, this is Director Tyson. We are sending a helicopter for immediate pickup. You and Agent Jensen will meet it at the address we are texting you now."

"Yes sir. Can I ask what it's about, sir?"

"Emergency Presidential Briefing. Same place as last time. Now get to that pickup location, Agent Jay. Immediately."

"Yes..." she got out but he hung up.

She looked at me, then her phone, then hit a contact on her list.

"Eve? Jay here. Something's happened and I need you to find out what it is. Something big. Scan all your sources..."

"I already know what it is, Agent Jay. Massive quake near Alaska, deep under the ocean. It's expected to generate killer tsunamis around the Pacific Rim. Loss of life will be enormous."

"Why would that involve the Bureau and specifically myself and Caeco?"

"Because a research vessel observed what it identified as an Omega drone plunge into the ocean at the same spot. The quake happened five minutes later. There is rampant speculation that Omega caused the earthquake."

"Eve, this is Caeco. How was the drone described?"

"Long, torpedo-like. Not one of the spheres."

"That sounds like the one that Omega uses to transport people," I said. "Like Declan."

Agent Jay looked at me, eyes widening at the implications. "See what you can find out. Mitch! We're leaving," she yelled, pointing one finger upward and winding it around.

CHAPTER 16

Our helicopter set down on the Treasury Department lawn and a team of Uniformed Division police met us as we hustled away from the giant Cuisinart blades of death spinning above us. I've ridden in a lot of helicopters, roped out of them, jumped into and out of all kinds, but I still don't like those big blades above me as I leave a copter's blood bubble.

The police, armed and Kevlar armored, hustled us to the same vault we had visited before, under high-powered lights that turned Washington night into artificial day.

The room was even more crowded than before and its occupants wore all manner of dress, from full military uniform to several young staff assistants in business casual. SAC Jay and I were not the only ones in what I call *agent field clothes*, either.

Once inside, we were once again placed behind Director Tyson, who immediately focused on us. He waved us over to him with a couple of hard hand gestures.

"What do you know?" he asked me without any preamble.

"Declan O'Carroll and Stacia Reynolds were likely onboard the drone that dove into the ocean above the epicenter of the earthquake. The only thing that any of my sources knows is that he thought a very large, powerful Earth elemental lived in the Aleutian Trench under the ocean off Alaska."

"You think he pissed it off somehow?" he demanded.

"What? Why would I think that?" I asked.

The front of the room got really active and Tyson's head snapped around. "Sit down. We're out of time."

President Polner came into the room and everyone stood up.

"Please be seated," Polner said, sitting down himself before turning to a blonde woman whose nameplate said Giametti, USGS. "Sarah, what's the latest?"

"Mr. President, at nineteen-forty-five hundred hours Eastern time, a nine-point-seven-magnitude submarine earthquake was recorded in the Aleutian Subduction Zone, forty-seven miles southeast of Adak Island at a depth of twenty-one miles."

"That would be the largest quake ever recorded," he stated.

"Yes Mr.President," she said.

"What's the damage, and where?"

"There hasn't been any, Mr. President. At least, not yet."

"What? Shouldn't there be tsunamis?"

"Yes sir. There should be many, many tsunamis. But we've recorded nothing... except an odd series of much smaller quakes radiating outward from the epicenter for several hundred miles in almost every direction."

"Aftershocks?" he asked.

"No sir. They all happened all at once, right after the big quake. They were smaller, each really only a bit bigger than a tremor."

"Is this a normal event—the earthquake, I mean, not the tremors?"

"The Pacific Rim is the most earthquake-prone area on Earth.

That's actually why the research vessel was on site. It's one of ours sir."

"They're the ones who witnessed an Omega drone enter the ocean?" he asked.

"Yes sir. They even captured photos of it," she said, handing the president a blown-up photo.

He studied it for a moment. "That's not one of the Battle Drones, is it?"

"No sir," an Air Force general said.

"Where's Agent Jensen?" President Polner asked without raising his head from the photo.

Jay nudged me while Tyson turned and gave me a look. I popped up out of my chair. "Here, sir."

He turned a serious face in my direction, then held up the photo. "Do you recognize this craft?"

"It's an Omega drone, sir. Transport for personnel."

"Transport for who?"

"Mostly Declan O'Carroll and Stacia Reynolds. A handful of others, sir."

"And was Mr. O'Carroll on it tonight?"

"That's my understanding, sir. He was looking for a powerful Earth Elemental under the Pacific Ocean, sir."

"Looks like he found it," Polner said. "Have you asked the Omega about this?"

"We lost contact with Omega in mid-conversation, sir. At approximately the time of the quake."

"That happens?"

"Rarely, sir. Just when he needs to direct a major part of his resources at a major problem."

"Like, say, an undersea mega quake?" he asked.

"Yes sir."

"Thank you, Agent."

I sat down.

"So what does this mean?" he asked the room.

"It might be an opportunity to seize back control of our nukes, sir," another general said. "While the machine is distracted."

"It might mean that the O'Carroll boy caused the earthquake by attempting contact," Tucker Tyson said.

"But why no tsunamis? We don't even know if O'Carroll lived through the quake. And no, Roger, I don't want to tempt fate by wrestling with a mega quantum computer when the only real human it relates to may be in danger or dead," Polner said.

"That may be exactly why we should take the risk, sir. If the boy died, it might go ballistic—literally," the general, who wore five stars on each shoulder, urged.

The president opened his mouth to speak, but the main door to the vault opened and a man in a suit hustled in, capturing everyone's attention.

"What is it, Sergei?" Polner asked the intruder, who went right to his side.

"Mr. President, NORAD is tracking a high-speed object that originated from the vicinity of the earthquake. It is traveling directly through Canadian airspace at an estimated speed in excess of thirty thousand miles per hour."

"What is it?"

"We have no idea, sir," the man said.

I found myself back on my feet. "It's likely the drone, sir," I said, swallowing my nerves.

"Omega's drones can fly that fast?"

"Omega has never told me how fast they can fly, but he did say it exceeded any other Earth-based technology, sir."

"Where is it going, then, Agent Jensen?"

"Is it in line for northern Vermont?" I asked the Sergei guy.

He glanced at his notes for a moment, then nodded. "Yes, that would be on the same vector."

"He's transporting O'Carroll to his aunt," Nathan Stewart said, looking at me.

"That would be my guess as well, sir," I said.

"Impossible!" the Air Force general said. "The G-forces would be astronomical. The kid would be paste."

"The drone was copied from Vorsook technology, General Coffer, and *they* travel in them," Nathan said. "Our own people tell me they found systems that seem to be some type of protective buffer system."

"Why?" Polner asked. "Why would O'Carroll be headed to Vermont?"

"Ashling O'Carroll is a gifted healer, a powerful witch. She has healed her nephew before," Stewart said.

"But why not a trauma center on the West Coast?" the president asked.

"Tanya's staff carry vials of her and Chris Gordon's blood for emergency healing. Those are, to my knowledge, the best trauma medicine anywhere. Declan's aunt can't heal faster than that, at least not physical wounds," I said.

"Not physical? What wounds could she handle better?" Polner asked.

"Magical, sir."

The room went silent for a few seconds, then people started talking all at once. Polner tapped the tabletop with one hand, not really hard, just enough to generate a sound. The room quieted instantly.

"What do you think happened, Agent Jensen?" he asked me.

"I can only speculate, sir."

"Please, speculate away," he said with a wave of one hand.

"If Declan was nearby when the quake happened, he would likely try to intercede. He may have hurt himself trying."

"Intercede?" The USGS woman asked, completely incredulous. "In a nine-point-seven quake? That's more power than every nuclear weapon on Earth!"

"Actually, that sounds very like what he would do," Nathan Stewart said. "His family line specializes in moving energy from one form into others."

"Impossible," the woman said.

"Yet, there have been no tsunamis. And you had that huge ring of unexplained tremors. How much energy was in those? How far out did it extend?" Nathan asked her.

She stared at him, eyes wide, then looked down at her notes, rifling through them slowly, then faster. Her head came back up and she looked terrified.

"Well, Sarah, don't keep us in suspense," Polner said.

"It's roughly the same, sir. But that's impossible," she said.

"I don't really use that word much anymore," Nathan said.

"Agent Jensen, could Declan do this?" Polner asked me.

"I don't know, sir. If a single living witch could do it, then that would be Declan. But I know there are limits to the power that even a full Circle can handle. At this point, the drone should be in Vermont," I said, looking at my watch. "It would only take about six minutes to traverse that distance at that speed."

"That's accurate, sir. If that's where it was headed," the aide, Sergei, said.

"Step out and check. Miss Jensen, would you also step out and touch base with your contacts?" President Polner requested.

I left at almost a sprint, catching up to Sergei even though he was on the other side of the room and much, much closer to the door.

We exited almost together and I headed to a wall-mounted phone while Sergei was met by a bunch of tablet-wielding people exhibiting a high level of excitement.

I called a number I had never called before, one I had glimpsed on Declan's phone—his step-aunt Darci's cell.

She picked up on the sixth ring. "Who is this?"

"Darci, it's Caeco. Is he all right?"

"How did you even—never mind. I don't know. He's alive. Catatonic but alive. Ashling has him. This number says Treasury Department," she said.

"I work for the FBI."

"And I imagine a great number of people are interested in his fate. Tell them that there are ten of the war drones here, so keep their damned distance. Omega is in a state," she said. In the background, I could hear growling, like a werewolf kind of growl.

"A state?"

"Worried, anxious, kind of hair-trigger, if you know what I mean. I gotta go. Ash needs me," she said, hanging up before I could say a word.

I went back inside the vault and the Secret Service closed the massive door behind me. Sergei the aide was already there, next to Polner, and everyone looked my way.

"He's alive. His aunt is treating him. I think it is very much as Director Stewart surmised."

"Any prognosis?"

"Too soon, sir."

"We should seize this opportunity," General Warmonger said.

"Ah sir, it was mentioned that Omega is volatile right at this moment. Ten Battle Drones are hovering over the area. I would caution against anything that might be deemed hostile," I said.

"What do you really know about it?" the general demanded.

"I know that Omega's father figure is catatonic and that the AI just demonstrated previously unknown capabilities to get him to his aunt. Declan's step-aunt specifically used the term *hair-trigger*. This would be a moment where *some* people might think he is vulnerable and might think he could be used as a hostage against Omega."

"Omega has been cagey about the drone's capabilities. She is correct that showing that level of speed within Earth's atmosphere gives away a lot of information," Nathan said. "It would take a dire situation to cause that."

"Also, I would caution that he is on his aunt's land. At least two elementals are with him now, not to mention all of those big battle drones," I said.

"In other words, don't prod the momma bear when it's licking a wounded cub," Polner said. "Roger. We will make no attempt at counterseizing the weapons. You've even admitted that the probable win rate is rather low," Polner said to the general, who looked surly. The president ignored him and turned back to Nathan Stewart. "The fact that the kid is in a coma and no tsunamis have struck anywhere in the world seems to back up your hypothesis. How would that be possible? As Sarah said, that's more power than the entire world's nuclear arsenal."

"I don't know, sir."

"Agent Jensen? Any idea?"

"Sir, I've been told that Declan wields enormous power on Fairie through a connection to elementals who are loyal to him. But the only thing I can think of that could control that kind of power is the elemental that generated it."

"Your assignment is to find out what happened, what the boy's prognosis is, and what we can expect," President Polner said to me. "Got it?"

"Yes sir!"

"Go to it, Agent Jensen. Right this moment. Contact my aide, Sergei, when you find something out. Sergei?"

"I'll walk her out sir," Sergei said, giving the president a nod before moving toward me and the vault door.

CHAPTER 17

Once outside the vault, Sergei turned to me with a card in his hand. "Call this number at any time. Your code name is Mercury. Use that and they will reach me anywhere at any time. Then I will put you on with *him*. Got it?"

The card said Sergei Vessier, Assistant to the President and Chief of Staff. I memorized the number and handed it back. "Got it. I need transportation."

He looked at the card, then me, blinked twice, and nodded. "It's arranged. There's a car out front waiting to take you to a jet. You'll be in Burlington in an hour. Oracle has an agent there who will take you to Castlebury. Getting onto the witch's property is up to you," he said, all the time leading me to the door to the building as a Secret Service-type handed me my phone.

Fifteen minutes later, I was buckling into a seat in a small Gulfstream jet, piloted by two Air Force captains. We were wheels up ten minutes after that. Our descent into Northern Vermont probably happened before the presidential briefing was even over. A black Dodge Charger was idling on the tarmac when the copilot opened the door and unfolded the stairs. A tall black man in business casual leaned against the vehicle, arms folded.

"Agent West," I said.

"Agent Jensen," Mike West replied. "Congratulations on that, by the way. High school senior to FBI agent in record time.

Jumped right on past college." He held out a hand to shake.

"I had a bit of college. The Bureau waived the degree requirement, as my early education was much in excess of any normal schooling." I said, meeting his squeeze and increasing the grip load incrementally. He grunted and backed off his own grip.

"I'm sure. We'd have likely done the same thing if you had gone the Oracle route. Climb in; I'll drive you to the O'Carroll place. Not sure how you'll get in though," he said. I held up one hand, a strange sound hitting my ears. High-pitched whine, Dopplering our way at a scary fast speed. A small black orb flashed across the airport pavement, stopping motionless right between us.

"Caeco, it is good you are here. I need your help with Father," Omega said from the orb's surface. *"Agent West, please transport Caeco Jensen to Rowan West immediately."*

I looked at Mike West, he looked back, and then we dove into the car. The orb shot inside when I opened the passenger door, taking up a floating position between the two of us as the powerful car shot forward.

"What happened, Omega? Why do you need me? Same reason he needed me for you?" I asked.

"I do not know what fully happened. We transported to the Aleutian Trench, to the location he felt the elemental inhabiting. My drone dove beneath the surface and we dropped deep. Father was meditating, a practice that he has honed for touching the thoughts, such as they are, of elementals. He has been increasingly successful with all types, including Water elementals, one of which approached the drone as we descended. Five hundred feet from the bottom, my sensors went wild as the tectonic plate we were over displaced by approximately ninety-eight feet. Father yelled, his body shook as if in seizure, and then he collapsed. Stacia was unharmed and immediately administered a vial of Chris's blood. Father's vi-

tals have been stable but low, and his brainwaves are flat."

"Cortical brainwaves? What about hippocampus activity?" I asked.

"The cortex exhibits flat EEG. However there is some sign of activity from the hippocampus. Additionally, Stacia is adamant that her mate bond is intact. Ashling O'Carroll has diagnosed energetic overload. Thus I postulate that use of your nanites may help reach Father."

"What does Ashling say about the overload? Is it survivable?"

"She indicates that in about half of all cases she is aware of, the victim recovers. The other half results in death. Also, there is a very high possibility that overload may permanently impact the witch's abilities"

"Like he could lose his ability to manipulate magic?" Mike West asked, expertly guiding the fast car through the Vermont nighttime countryside.

"Affirmative."

"So he might live, and if he does, he might be a null?" I asked.

"Yes to both possibilities."

"Can she tell?"

"Negative."

None of us spoke for the remainder of the ride. Myself, I was wrestling with the idea of a powerless Declan. Would he even want to live if he couldn't manipulate magic on some level?

The tiny town of Castlebury appeared suddenly and just as quickly disappeared, and then we were pulling into the Rowan West parking lot, the restaurant lights dark but the living quarters lit up brightly. A Chittenden County Sheriff's cruiser parked next to a new Tesla and an older model Prius.

"Whoa, someone likes alternative energy," Mike said, admiring the silver Tesla.

"Father purchased it for Ashling. She still drives the Prius most days."

"Demidova must pay well," he said.

"Probably more to do with having your investments managed by a quantum computer," I said, opening the door to get out.

A high-pitched screech from atop the building had me crouched with my issue Glock in one hand before my brain identified the sound.

A deep, rocky rumble sounded off to the left of where Mike West also crouched. A massive, blocky silhouette rose in the darkness. West was shaking, his hand on his gun.

"It's Draco and Robbie. No worries," I said to him.

"The elementals? No worries, you say?" he questioned as if I had just snuck out of a psych evaluation.

"Yes. If there were worries, we'd either be burnt to a crisp or smashed to red jelly by now," I said.

He just looked at me, eyes wide, the whites gleaming in the lights reflected from the windows. The door opened and the stocky form of Darci, Ashling's partner, stood outlined. "You guys coming in or what?"

I slipped inside, West almost stepping on my heels. Darci closed the door behind us and then led the way into first the kitchen and then the living room. A sofa bed had been unfolded and Declan lay on his back on one side of it, the other half taken up by the enormous white wolf that lifted its head and growled at me.

"Hush now. No call for that, now is there, what with Caeco

bringing her little medical machines right to me very doorstep," an attractive brunette said from a chair just to our left. She looked to be almost thirty, but Ashling O'Carroll was really just shy of forty. Declan had told me that she would likely always look much, much younger than her actual years. It made me wonder how Darci, who looked every bit of middle-aged, felt about that. Across the room, two more people were sitting on a loveseat, a man and a woman, both young and both fit. Holly and the new wolf I had heard about, Devaney. On the wall, a flatscreen was showing the news, volume way down, some expert talking about how much earthquake and tsunami damage there *should* have been.

"Did Omega explain it to ya then?" Ashling asked.

"Yes, ma'am," I said. Mike West shot me a surprised look. What? Don't think it's a good idea to be respectful to the witch? Better think faster than that, Mikey boy. Ashling was one of the most powerful Air witches on the planet. "He indicated that an infusion of nanites might allow him to connect with Declan, much as Declan did when Omega was under attack."

"That's it square on the head. Me boy shows every sign of acute energy overload. But he's still breathing and this one," she waved at the massive wolf, "is still connecting through her mate bond. That might be all that's holding the boy in place. So, quickly now, how do ye get yer machines into him?"

"He got them through saliva once and blood once before. The blood method is better. The concentrations are greater," I said, pulling my Benchmade automatic knife from a pocket, blade springing out to poke through my fingertip. As I moved closer to the bed, Stacia stood up, her massive jaws opening.

"Stop that. None of that now," Ashling said, moving up as if to grab the werewolf. Instead, the big wolf flashed forward, her jaws clamping my arm and dragging my hand over Declan's slightly open mouth. He was pale, even more so than usual, his skin so translucent, I could see blue veins under the surface. Breathing was shallow and his heartbeat slow and weak. Dark red blood ran down my fingers, dripping off and onto his face, into his mouth, and even on the white sheets of the bed. But the wolf's jaws were like steel clamps, sharp white teeth pushing hard but not breaking my skin. Her positioning adjusted to become exact, the remaining drops hitting his partially open mouth even as the blood slowed, the wound being knit shut by the very technology we were trying to get into him.

The drips stopped and Stacia let go of my arm suddenly, her tongue flashing out to lick my blood off my own hand. Before I had time to object, she turned away, all of her attention focused on the boy on the bed. Ears forward, yellow eyes gleaming, big white furred head tilted.

"Is it enough then, is it?" Ashling questioned.

"That's easily the biggest dose of them he's ever gotten, " I said. Her eyebrows went up. I shrugged, looking at my now clean finger. "They seem to respond to my thoughts. I was concentrating on having them cluster in that fingertip."

"So jest what happens with them now?" she asked.

"We gotta give them a few minutes to get into his bloodstream. Then we can attempt contact," I said.

The wolf shook itself and Shifted, the change happening in seconds, leaving a naked Stacia lying alongside Declan. Mike West's jaw dropped open, whether at the speed of the shift or the perfect naked body displayed in front of us, I don't know. Probably both.

"Nobody's that fast," he said, then jerked his eyes away from the platinum blonde, who stood up without giving him a second glance. That showed some serious discipline on his part.

I'm not into women, but Stacia is just as beautiful as Tatiana, which is saying a lot. And beauty is beauty, so most people would be excused for staring at someone who comes so close to the human ideal of physical perfection.

Across the room, Holly casually threw Stacia some clothes, which she caught and put on without ever taking her attention off Declan. Suddenly she froze, right in the act of adjusting her pullover shirt. Then she turned her now green eyes on me. I had just felt it. A soft snap that ran through my body and mind, like a puzzle piece snicking into place. I nodded at her.

"Okay. That was faster than I thought," I said, my own attention turning to the boy on the bed.

"*Yes,*" Omega said through a Bluetooth speaker on an end table.

"Alright, let's see what happens," I said, closing both eyes and sending my thoughts outward.

CHAPTER 18

There was a moment of dizzying motion through darkness, followed by flashes of light, all ending with a stomach-twisting lurching stop. Light and color swirled around and then formed into clarity. A room, the floor paved in colorful tiles, water flowing in a channel down the middle, plants all around. Soft light glowed from above, a recessed edge where the ceiling didn't quite meet the top of the wall.

Declan was sitting cross-legged in the middle of the floor, staring at the back wall, which was all black. Motion on either side of me caught my eye. Stacia stood to my right, dressed in the same clingy black clothes she had just pulled on. To my left stood a boy in his late teens—a young man. He had brown hair and blue eyes like Declan, and his features were similar, so similar that he had to be related to Declan. He looked at me, then down at his jeans and Oxford clothed self, and smiled. "This is how Father sees me," he said in Omega's voice. I opened my mouth but Stacia moved forward before I could speak.

"Declan?" she asked. He didn't turn but a slight twitch of his head indicated he'd heard her voice. She moved up behind him and sank down to wrap around him. A flare of emotion flashed through me—something—jealousy maybe? It froze me in place, even as Omega stepped forward. "Father?"

Declan shifted slightly, maybe responding to the voice, maybe just to the contact of Stacia's arms enfolding him. But still he stared straight ahead, focused on nothing—just the black of the wall. Part of me analyzed his minute movements, his unyielding attention, while another part of me realized just how much he was loved, deeply loved by the two around him. In fact, he was sitting in concentric layers of love, with the two in here and his aunts and pack members outside in reality, the elementals on guard outside the restaurant, Toni Velasquez, his friends at school.

And at that moment, the emotion I had felt clarified. Envy—of a sort. Comatose and vulnerable, he was still surrounded by more love than I had ever known.

I believe that my mother loves me, as much as she is able, but while she possesses enormous levels of STEM-type intelligence, she has very little emotional intelligence. And she is all I have. Well, except for Talon. And Jetta. Possibly Ashley. No, definitely Ashley. Maybe even Mack.

It felt like a sort of epiphany. One moment I envy my former boyfriend his deep connections, and the next I realize I have some strong ones of my own. Not as many, just a handful, but still more than I had ever fully realized before.

Omega turned and looked back at me from Declan's side and I jolted into motion. "Hey Declan, what are you doing?" I asked, stepping forward.

His shoulders clenched, a clear sign my voice had also reached him. In fact, that tightening motion was greater than the twitches when the other two had spoken. "What is so fascinating about a black wall?" I asked, rewarded by a wiggle of his head. "There's nothing there." Actually, the wall was really weird, like there was no real surface to it at all.

"It's not a wall," he said, his voice very soft. Omega's head whipped around and looked at me, eyes imploring.

"No? Then what is it?" I asked, keeping the questions going, moving even closer, now looking at the wall. It was very black, the deepest dark of night black—Stygian in its blackness.

"A portal," he said. Stacia tightened her arms and he turned slightly as if just noticing. "Babe? I thought I was dreaming?"

"No, we're here," she said. "With you. Myself, Omega and... Caeco," she said. Could have used a touch more excitement about that last name, but could I blame her? Last time we went this route, I was a pretty major bitch.

Declan turned and looked at Omega on his other side. "Whoa dude, you're getting on in computer years, huh?" he said, smiling. Then he turned all the way around and looked back at me. "Ah, you all *are* here. Nano connections," he said.

"Yes. You've got a bunch flowing through your veins. You've locked yourself away in here and we couldn't get to you," Stacia said. "So *she* helped."

"So this is really happening?" he asked, smiling for the first time.

"As really as the inside of your mind gets," I said. "What happened?"

His smile froze, locking up into something else. Guilt?

"How many?" he asked.

"How many what?" Stacia asked back.

"Deaths. How many deaths?"

"From the quake? None," she said back before glancing at Omega and then me. "At least none that I'm aware of."

"Me either," I said.

"There was a small injury aboard a research vessel above the quake's epicenter, but it was caused by a fall. Just a contusion, Father," Omega said.

"What?" he asked, shocked. "I couldn't handle it... it was too much."

"Of course it was," I said. "Like every nuke ever, going off all at once. But it somehow dissipated into the surrounding undersea terrain."

"Stacia and I think that the elemental you contacted took over what you were attempting to do," Omega said.

The shock changed to wonder. Then he shook his head and embarrassment took front and center.

"I've gotten pretty good at reaching out to elementals," he said. "Practice making perfect and all that, right? And we've been careful to visit smaller elementals first, working our way up in terms of size and power. The older, bigger ones take more to reach. You have to be... louder. Which I am."

"You take hardly any time to get their attention anymore," Stacia agreed.

"But this one, the one under the subduction zone, was the biggest yet. And I was psyching myself up to reach out to it. To wake it up. Only I think it was maybe already near to wakefulness and when I sorta... yelled, well..."

"You startled it," Stacia said.

He nodded. "Yeah, in a big way. And it moved or rolled over or whatever an elemental would do that was analogous to those things. It was like a bomb went off."

"Many bombs, Father," Omega said. "It was all I could do to keep the drone from damage. Had we been nearer the bottom, it may have been worse."

"I knew instantly that I had fucked up. That the displacement was massive," Declan said.

"So you being you, you tried to channel all that energy away, right?" I said, hands on hips.

He shrugged, both palms up.

"Well, it worked. Because nobody got killed," I said. "But you sorta fried yourself."

"Yeah," he said, his head turning back toward the wall. Somehow, I thought that was a bad idea. Werewolf girl must have thought the same thing because she took his chin in her hand and moved his face back to hers.

"So... how do we wake you up?" I asked.

"Hmm? Is that a good idea? I thought comas were good, at least for a while?" he asked.

"Not in this case. Your aunt says you need to wake up right away," Stacia said.

"Aunt Ash? She's here?"

"More like you're there, at your aunt's house," Omega said. "I brought you."

"All the way back to Vermont? How much time has gone by?"

"A couple of hours maybe," I said. "He sorta broke a lot of speed limits."

"More like all of them put together," Stacia said, shuddering ever so slightly. She was gently turning him, pressing on his knee in a way that spun him in place, still seated, till he was facing my way, back the way we had come. Behind him, the black wall, which might not have been a wall at all, started to recede, the walls on either side of us lengthening, extending, as if the room itself was getting bigger—or moving away from the portal of blackness.

"Yes, that's it, Father. Follow us," Omega said, taking Declan's hand on his other side. Stacia put an arm around him. They both stood, raising him up with them and leading him forward, in my direction. I backed away, keeping my eyes on him, but it wasn't necessary, as his pace lengthened out. Suddenly the vision of all three of them swirled, spinning around and twisting, my stomach dropping to my feet as the ground went out from under me. Until I opened my eyes.

CHAPTER 19

I was standing in Ashling's living room, right where I had been. The others were all there and everyone was looking at the sofa bed. Looking at the open eyes of the witch kid who was staring up into the green eyes of his wolf girl, blinking at the light.

"Ah, there ya are now. Ye was beginning to worry me, ye were," Ashling said, moving over to examine her nephew.

"Aunt Ash! Ow. My head hurts," he said, shutting his eyes. "My eyes hurt. Shit, even my skin hurts," he said.

"What's the matter with him?" Stacia demanded.

"Why, he's alive. That's what's the matter with him. He should, on all accounts, be dead, but he's not, so he hurts. 'Tis a very good thing indeed," Ashling said. There wasn't much sympathy in her tone but at the same time, she was pulling a small bundle of cloth from her bag on the table. She tucked the bundle under Declan's shirt, at the neckline in back, right where it met his skull, and he almost instantly relaxed.

"Better?" she asked.

He nodded, eyes shut again, which caused Stacia to look up at Ashling, eyes questioning.

"He's oversensitized. That wee poppet will dull him down a bit and he can rest now without fear, my dear," she said, patting the werewolf's hand gently. Then her fingers touched Declan's forehead and he slumped down, unconscious.

"Rest is best now. Who's hungry?" the witch asked, looking

around at the rest of us.

Holly, myself, and Devaney all perked up at the mention of food. Stacia looked reluctant but then her stomach rumbled. "Thank you, ma'am. That would be wonderful," Mike West said.

"Come, sit here at this table. Ye can all keep an eye on him, but I promise ye he's just sleeping. Darci, be a dear and bring out that soup, would ye?"

"Of course, dear," Darci said, a relieved smile on her face as she withdrew to the kitchen.

The main eating table was right in the same open space as the living area, the dining and family room spaces delineated by furniture instead of walls. So we all had to just take a few steps to arrive at the big farm table.

Holly pulled out a chair for Stacia, for all the world like one of the wolves at Arcane getting a chair for Dellwood. Devaney sat next to me and across from Stacia, which left Holly sitting across from me. Mike West sat down on Devaney's other side. Ashling joined her girlfriend and within just a few minutes, there were bowls and spoons on the table and a big pot of chowder in the middle. Darci brought a couple of round loaves of bread while Ashling ladled bowls full and passed them around. A crock of real butter with a knife sticking out of it was placed where most of us could reach it.

Stacia looked down at her bowl, not touching it. "He'll be alright?" she asked, looking up at her boyfriend's aunt.

"He's past the danger point, dear. But as to how he'll be... we'll just have to see, now won't we?" Ashling said.

"What do you mean?" I asked.

"It's like as if he were struck by a bolt of lightning, at least for a normal lad. I mean, lightning strikes don't amount to much for that one, but say if Mr. West was struck by one, it could leave him... different. Declan tried to handle more power than any witch has ever been exposed to. Any Circle has ever been exposed to. By rights, he should have burned up and popped like a overwrought lightbulb," Ashling said, shaking her head. "But of course, being who he is, he didn't, now did he? But what I'm saying is that no one handles the likes of that and comes away unscathed."

"We think the elemental took over and handled most of it," Stacia said.

"*Yes, that seems to be the only plausible explanation,*" Omega said through the Bluetooth speaker.

"Did it now? That's a bit of wonder then, isn't it?" Ashling mused, expression very thoughtful.

"Are you saying that he could have burned out his powers?" Stacia asked.

"And if he did? How would you feel?"

Stacia pulled back a bit. "I don't know. Happy he was alive? Why? Isn't it more important how he would feel?"

"Oh, that I know, dear. He'd feel like his legs and arms were cut off," Ashling said. "But if he's lost all his gift, he'll be needing your support more than ye can know. He'll feel he has nothing, nothing of value. No offense, Mr. West."

West had an artificial left leg, a war memento. He shrugged. "None taken, ma'am. But is that likely? That he's burnt it out?"

She paused with a spoonful of soup halfway to her mouth. "I have no bloody idea," she said, looking around the table and meeting each of our eyes. "Witches have over handled power before and either died, lived without powers, or in some cases, lived and regained what they had before. But no witch has ever been exposed to even a tiny bit of what he was."

She put the spoon in her mouth and ate the soup. Then she looked back around at all of us. "We'll just have to wait and see, now won't we?"

"He always could channel more than other witches, couldn't he?" I asked.

"Yes, yes he could. Likely why he's alive right now, at least in part."

"Ashling? Before, when we said Father had been helped by the Elemental, you expressed surprise and you sounded... thoughtful. What were you thinking?" Omega asked.

"Ye caught that, did ya? Well, I wasn't going to say a word, you see, but when the witches of me clan are training wee witches to channel power, we often link with them. It helps them to feel how the spell works."

"You're saying the elemental did something similar?" Holly asked.

Ashling shrugged. "I dinnae know. It's just interesting, ya see. All I know is that me nephew is alive. Anything beyond that is gravy."

The first bowls of soup were already gone, spoons in the hands of Holly, Devaney, Stacia and myself all clanking on empty pottery within seconds of each other. Ashling didn't bat an eye, immediately ladling out more while Darci put out another two loaves of dark grainy bread.

"Father always says to pay close attention to anything that catches your interest, Ashling," the speaker said.

"And you listen to everything that young boy says, do ya?"

"I listen to everything he says. Some of his thoughts are normal human musings. But when it comes to the Craft, as he calls it, he is

more often right than wrong."

I found my head nodding in agreement and noticed Stacia doing the same. And she noticed me as well. She frowned and I felt my own frown form right back at her.

My phone buzzed. It was a text from Sergei Vessier, Mr. White House Chief of Staff himself, asking for a status update. I lifted my head and found everyone looking at me.

"Yer masters in Washington will be wanting to know how he is," Ashling said.

"They do," I answered, setting the phone down on the tabletop. Then I remembered that she didn't allow phones at the table and I put it in my lap.

"Well then, what will ye say?"

I met her eyes. "The truth. He's alive, that he helped mitigate the quake. That pretty much sums up everything I know."

"And about his powers?"

"Haven't a clue. It would be all speculation until he wakes up. I have to get back, so I'm going to get Agent West to drive me back to the airport as soon as we're done, so I won't be here when he does wake up."

"But aren't ye curious?"

"Of course. But if my association with him and you has taught me anything, it's that anything is possible where the two of you are concerned."

"Humff," she snorted. "Ye never had a touch of the blarney before, Caeco Jensen. Don't be changing now."

"No blarney. The history of the O'Carroll family is one of improbable events becoming common occurrences."

"Caeco's analysis is correct. Father skews probability outcomes as

much as Mack and Jetta Sutton."

"Well, yer welcome to stay if ye like. The hour's getting late."

"Ah, thank you, ma'am, but as Agent Jensen indicated, her jet is waiting at Burlington International to take her back," Mike West said.

"Well then, I thank ya greatly, Caeco, for helping my lad. I know things have been rocky and all, but it's a fine thing that ye both help the other when it's needed."

"Yeah, well. There's not that many people in my orbit. We might not have been the right mix for each other, but like you said, I would never withhold my help. Thank you for dinner."

"Yer most welcome dear. And thank you."

CHAPTER 20

I no sooner stepped outside the house than I felt another's presence. My sense of smell isn't quite on par with a werewolf's, but I knew who she was as soon as I turned. Stacia stood illuminated by the light outside the door to the family quarters, pale hair almost white.

"I have to thank you as well," she said, her tone even but her body just a little tense.

"We weren't the right mix. But he's basically one of the good guys. Not to mention the role he plays in these times and the ones to come."

"Yeah. We'll have to see about that," she said, uncertainty and worry in her voice.

"It's possible that he burnt out. Personally, I doubt it. Every single time I think that kid should be down and out, he surprises me."

"I don't know. It was pretty bad," she said, looking a bit haunted. I raised an eyebrow. "Like an epileptic seizure, foam at the mouth, convulsions, eyes rolling."

I nodded. "With him, would it be anything less?"

"Yeah, there is that. Anyway, we don't have to like each other, but I still want to thank you," she said.

"Okay. Cool. I'm not real good with this stuff so let's just..." My phone rang with a uniquely ominous ring tone, freezing the words in my mouth. I looked at her, not moving. It rang again.

"Is that... is that the theme song from *Jaws*?" she asked, a furrow between her brows.

"Yeah. I never saw it until *he* made me watch it."

The phone rang again, the sinister tones deep and threatening and building toward catastrophe.

"Hello Mother," I said, answering the call.

"Is he alive?" Dr. Abigail Jensen asked.

"Yes Mother," I said, considering just leaving it at that, but it wasn't worth the consequences. "He attempted to handle too much power. When I got here, he was comatose. Exposure to nanites allowed us to bring him out of it. Now he is sleeping normally."

"I see. This is what? The third time you've exposed him to your nanites?"

"We went out for quite a while Mother," I said. Stacia was watching me, obviously hearing the whole conversation.

"Meaning every sexual encounter was an additional exposure. How many times did you have sexual intercourse?"

"Mother!" I said, embarrassed, which is an emotion I don't have a lot of experience with.

"Nevermind. There are too many unknowns regarding concentrations, longevity outside your system, transfer rate, et cetera. I need a sample of his blood, Caeco. His unique nature has already yielded enormous insights, and that was just from photos of his cellular structures. An actual sample would be invaluable."

"Mother, his entire ability to manipulate energy is very likely gone. The forces he was exposed to were far beyond anything any other witch has ever encountered."

"That is one possibility. However, the boy is truly unique and your nanites have survived in him for greater lengths of time than anywhere else but with you, yourself. It is entirely possible that some small amount of them were present at the time of the event. He is also dating a werewolf. They are generally a promiscuous species. Who knows how often he's been exposed to small amounts of LV virus."

Stacia raised an eyebrow at the promiscuous comment, something like a smile quirking at the corner of her lips.

"You're are speculating wildly, Mother. That's unlike you."

"Exactly. It's all speculation without a blood sample. Comparing that to even the photos I have of his centrioles will tell us a great deal."

The blonde werewolf leaned forward and spoke at my phone. "Dr. Jensen, this is Stacia Reynolds. If you had a sample, would you be able to tell if his magical abilities are still there?"

"I would be able to see damage to the centrioles. As you are part of Demidova Corporation, I will divulge that our current research indicates a tremendous correlation between cellular centrioles and the ability of some individuals to manipulate what appears to be a form of quantum energy. Your mate has the highest concentration of centrioles I have ever found in any subject anywhere, excepting my employer and her husband, and theirs are very different. The two viruses, V squared and LV, both make significant genetic changes to their hosts' cellular structures, particularly the centrioles."

"I will get you your sample if you give me your word you will share all the results with me and with Declan when he's awake," Stacia said. "And that you will destroy them after you are done."

I tensed, anticipating a battle, but my mother surprised me.

"You have my word. Those samples are more valuable than gold and exactly what I need to further this study. Our joint employer will be very pleased. I will, however, need multiple samples as time progresses to see if any damage is repaired naturally or otherwise."

"The otherwise being Caeco's nanites or the LV virus I expose him to daily?" Stacia asked, smirking a little.

"Yes."

"How do I get the samples to you?"

"I will transport them," Omega said suddenly from my phone.

"Yes, that would be perfect. I would have them in hours rather than days," my mother said without even a hint of surprise that the AI was listening in. I know he provided her with computational help in her work, so she was already quite familiar with him.

"All right. I'll get you one tonight, as soon as he wakes up. Then, what? Daily?"

"Perfect." It was perhaps the closest thing to happiness that I had ever heard in my mother's voice before.

The line clicked off.

"She didn't say goodbye?" Stacia asked, puzzled.

"She considers greetings and goodbyes to be extraneous and wasteful of precious time," I said with a little shrug. "My mother is very..."

"Unemotional?" she guessed.

"I was going to say focused, but you are not wrong."

"Yeah, I see that. Well, maybe she can help?"

"She will certainly provide greater understanding of whatever happens with his abilities. Mother is brilliant and at the top of her field."

"Okay, well, have a good flight back then," she said, both of us turning at the sound of the door opening.

"Thanks again for dinner, Ms. O'Carroll," Mike West said over his shoulder, his eyes already noting the two of us, eyebrows quirking ever so slightly at the sight. "Ah, ready?" he asked, expression curious.

"Yup. Ready to go," I said, exchanging a glance with Stacia.

"Travel safe," she said, stepping back toward the door. She gave us each a nod, then slipped gracefully inside.

"Ah, everything okay? I didn't hear gunshots?"

"We've reached something of an understanding. If you're ready, we can go."

CHAPTER 21

The car that met my jet in DC wasn't from the Bureau. The big bald man standing outside the black car was Secret Service. "Agent Jensen, please come with us."

It wasn't a total surprise, as I had updated Sergei Vessier from the plane. He had said he would, in turn, update President Polner, but that there might be additional questions—most likely *would* be additional questions.

It seems he was right.

Neither the driver nor the Secret Service agent said a word the whole ride to Pennsylvania Avenue, but the big bald agent did escort me into the White House, where I surrendered my gun but, oddly, not my phone. Then I was led to a small office not far from the door we had entered. There were photos on the wall and on the desk, showing a woman I didn't recognize with President Polner. The nameplate on the desk said *Kelly Ondak*. I had no idea who that was but based on the size of the office and the location far from the rest of the building, it seemed like she was not highly placed.

As it was very late, all of the offices in this part of the building were dark. Agent Baldy stood at the open door, staring at the wall over my head. I sat down in Kelly's guest chair and waited. Waiting for superiors is all about patience, and no one was higher in my food chain than the president. So I settled down and pulled back into myself. First, I ran a systems check, which sounds all technical and comp sci, but is really just me thinking about my body. The visual I always use is of me lying on one of the AIR lab exam tables, the ones that seemed like second homes to me growing up. The view is looking down from the ceiling. If something is wrong, my attention will be *pulled* to whatever portion of my body is damaged or being repaired.

Tonight, there was just the slightest tug toward my left cheek, where Agent Jay had spotted blood. But it was the mildest of pulls, which told me the healing was almost complete. Everything else seemed okay, so I ran a memory check. Again, sounds like I'm typing on a keypad or something. Instead, I just think of whatever event I want to verify and it pops up like a little movie. I replayed the fight outside the bars and now that I wasn't actually fighting but watching, I was able to observe the people from the apartment walk out of the doorway and move to their right, faces blank, bodies stiff as they moved along the building's front and then around back. There were seven of them. The four I knew and three more, two men and a woman. My memory clip was brief, just a glimpse, as it was constantly interrupted by one blank-faced attacker after another filling most of my vision and all of my attention. But it was possible that I might recognize them if I saw them again. My ability to identify gaits and body movements is pretty high.

Sound from the doorway brought me back to the little office just as Baldy straightened up and the president swept into the room. He was wearing a blue track suit. Baldy closed the door and stood, back to it, hands clasped, eyes on me.

I jumped up, but the president waved me back down, moving himself around the desk to take Kelly Ondak's chair.

"So. Sergei tells me that he's alive and that he both caused the quake and somehow stopped it?" he asked.

"Essentially, sir. He believes he surprised the elemental and also believes it was close to shifting anyway, meaning that the quake was going to happen at some point. It was probably worse because he, as he says, startled it. When the quake happened, he tried to handle the power, tried to mitigate the damage, but it was far, far too much. We think the elemental saw what he was doing and helped."

"Why?"

"Because he only handled the tiniest amount, which was still more than any witch ever, but somehow all the rest of that Earth energy was directed outward the same way. Only the massive elemental he was trying to speak to could have done that."

"But he's alright?"

"Not sure, sir. He was comatose. We brought him out of it and then he fell asleep. I left shortly after that."

"Is he... damaged?"

"Almost certainly, but we don't have any idea of the extent or the possible permanence of that damage. His aunt was frankly shocked that he lived at all."

"What form would damage take? Personality shift?"

"Are you wondering if he would go to the dark side or something, sir?"

"I guess."

"I'd say no, based on his limited communications. He asked how many were dead as soon as we connected. His aunt says the most likely damage would be loss of his powers."

"His magic? Like for good?" he asked, both brows up in clear surprise.

"Witches have overextended before. It has often been fatal or resulted in them burning out their ability to manipulate energy."

"He's null?"

"Too early to tell. On the one hand, no witch has ever been exposed to that much energy, at least, and lived, on the other hand, he had instant exposure to vampire proteins, was possibly sheltered by the elemental itself, and, of course, is who he is, sir."

"And your personal opinion?"

"Happy that he's alive at all, not just for personal reasons but because it keeps Omega grounded. As to the rest? I really have no idea. But I will check in with his aunt later. My actions helped bring him out of the coma, so I earned some brownie points, sir."

"Well that's excellent, Ms. Jensen. I mean it. But I find myself torn. No one human should have that much power—the literal ability to destroy with just a thought. But on the other hand, if we *are* attacked, we need his abilities. I *am* glad that Omega has... calmed down."

"The loss of his abilities would be a major blow. Sir, if we're right, he not only talks to massive elementals but gets them to help. Think about it... if that quake had happened anyway, without him there, the damage and loss of life would have been enormous. But the elemental helped him. Most of them don't even know humans exist. My friend Ashley Moore, the one who talks to dragons, says that the dragons have told her that the Queens' use of elemental magic was the major factor in defending Fairie from the Vorsook."

"And you believe her?" he asked.

I couldn't help it, I pulled back a bit. "Sir, are you doubting the danger Earth is in? Has the disinformation reached you too?"

He frowned at me and I realized I had probably gone too far. Then his frown cleared and he shook his head. "You get used to not being questioned when you have this job. *Your* question is valid. Yes—I've heard some whispers that the threat is overblown, but no, I still believe. I mean, I saw all the evidence, saw the videos from China and Italy, and have firsthand reports about the Vorsook aircraft and the alien body. Certainly the advances that Omega has shown with his drones support that."

"That's good to hear, sir, because my team is investigating the source of that disinformation campaign, and we think the Vorsook started it."

"Subversion?"

"Yes sir. Remove the will to fight and the fight is over before it's begun. Omega says his exposure to the Vorsook computer showed him that propaganda and subversion are some of their favorite tactics."

"And your team is on to something?"

"Yes sir. A very old organization that we think has been taken over by the Vorsook."

"What evidence do you have to support that?"

"We were observing a meeting of the group when they realized we might be there. When we confronted them before they could leave, twenty-three individuals in two bars were somehow compelled to attack us. Here's video," I said, handing him my phone with Omega's footage playing.

He watched in silence for a moment, then lifted his head, brown eyes thoughtful. "You make a compelling case. Nathan Stewart told me that mind control and compulsion are Vorsook trademarks."

"Yes sir. Nika, Tanya Demidova's right hand, is a very powerful telepath and the person who captured that aircraft. She fought the mental battle of her life to get to the alien. The only thing that shielded us was our protective amulets," I said, lifting mine to show him.

"Interesting. Do you suppose *I* could get one of those?" he asked.

Mack Sutton likes to do a palm smack to his forehead when something that should have been painfully obvious suddenly becomes even more so. I felt like that. Who more important to have an amulet than the president?

Instantly, I took mine off and handed it to him, hating every second but knowing it was imperative.

"Declan made this one. It's stronger than the ones the rest of my team has. I'll get a new one."

"But he may be powerless?" he said, nonetheless letting me slip it over his head.

"But his aunt isn't. She'll make me one if necessary."

"You know, Agent Jensen, I've been thinking a lot about your little speech at the first briefing," he said.

"I was out of line, sir."

"Some certainly thought so," he said, his tone a little hard. Then he smiled at my discomfort. "But you were very provocative—made me think. And I find the list of coincidences to be exceedingly unlikely. But, Agent Caeco Jensen, have you thought about your own unlikely but important role in all of this?"

"Sir?"

"Perhaps the only governmental employee who has access to

all of the people who will determine if this world lives or dies. An employee uniquely skilled and uniquely situated to employ those skills. What are the odds of that?"

"I hadn't thought of it exactly that way, sir, but my boss, Agent Jay, said that I shouldn't quit because I am in a good place to have an impact."

"You were thinking of quitting?"

"Director Tyson is not a fan of me, sir. He's been very, very clear on that, sir."

"Tucker is all about status. But you do *not* have my leave to quit, Agent Jensen. If I have to detach you to my personal service, I will do so, but let's hope it doesn't come to that. Your Agent Jay sounds like a sensible person."

"She's impressed me so far, sir. Open to input but very decisive when action is needed."

"Good to hear. She was, I believe, one of Nathan's who didn't fit in with Oracle."

"Yes sir. That's pretty much how she explains it."

"Okay, Agent Jensen. You are to spend the night at your apartment and then rejoin your team in Philly. You are to keep me directly informed. Use Sergei as the conduit. However, if you find that route blocked, and if it is of direst need, you may contact me at the following number," he said, then rattled off a phone number. "Got it?"

I repeated it back to him and he nodded. "Agent Howe will see that a car takes you home," he said, standing to leave.

"Yes sir!" I said, jumping to my feet.

He gave me a nod and a little smile, then swept out of the room.

CHAPTER 22

After a night in my own bed with a furry orange purr machine for company, I took my own car and drove back to Philadelphia. My training included driving and I've handled all kinds of vehicles, but my... time... with Declan and his old Toyota Land Cruiser taught me to love the classics. My personal ride is an expertly restored muscle car, a 1970 Chevrolet Camaro SS with a 396 engine and nominally about 375 horsepower. Declan might be okay with a foreign car but mine is US made all the way.

I bought it off a guy in Florida, flying down to make the deal then driving it up to DC. Red with a white stripe up the hood and a mostly stock interior. I say mostly because the previous owner had installed a pretty sweet modern sound system and I couldn't find it in myself to be offended by this deviation from the original specs.

Unlike Declan, I didn't name the machine because it's just a machine—a superbly powerful beauty of a machine and not without personality, but still just a machine. Granted, Declan's Beast has so many wards and spells on it that it sometimes almost seems alive, whereas mine has none of that. Got plenty of speed though.

I traveled in the hammer lane, well in excess of the speed limit, but every time I got near a police car, I just used one of the other deviations from the stock interior, a powerful government-issued communications suite. "Company car," radioed on the police frequency was all I needed to bypass awkward stops.

Back in Philadelphia, I found Agent Jay and my *uncle* Mitch Allen watching a small local boutique investment advisory office in downtown, having called Agent Jay from the highway. I parked around the corner and walked to the Suburban, climbing into the backseat.

“Just in time to help with surveillance shifts,” Mitch said.

“What’s this place?”

“Your pal, Katrina, took some photos of our suspects leaving the apartment while we were dealing with the zombie drunk people,” Jay said, handing me a pair of photos. I recognized the three people from my own memory, but these pictures were much better. Full facial detail.

“She didn’t mention that little detail,” I said, still studying the photos.

“No, she left them in our hotel suite, on my *bed*,” Jay said, staring at me.

I shrugged. “She’s basically a high-level troubleshooter for the queen of the vampires. Breaking and entering is second nature to her. And she would have picked out your room by scent.”

“Yet she went to your school?” Jay questioned. I got her point instantly.

“Only as long as Declan was there. My theory is that Chris and Tanya wanted eyes on the kid during that time. She’s like over a hundred years old or something. Don’t let the college-kid looks fool you. Probably has three or four degrees already.”

“They turn people that young?”

“She was turned younger. Like twelve, which is forbidden. Think of being stuck in a kid’s body for decades. Makes for crazy and super angry vampires. At least until Chris somehow *aged* her. So she's a bit more loyal than most, and most are very, very loyal. She's not bad, but she is dangerous," I said. "So... one of our suspects works here?"

"Two. Both partners. The firm manages about four hundred million or so. And according to their client email newsletter that just came out today, they're starting to advise clients to sell and avoid a certain stock. Care to guess which one?" Mitch said.

"Demidova Corporation? Ticker VAMP."

"Bing, bing, bing! We have a winner," Mitch said.

"That stock is a current world favorite. Makes money like a printing press. What's their angle?" I asked.

"They're quoting an interesting piece of literature that also just came out. An alleged study that indicates a high correlation of mental illness with children who've been treated with vampire proteins, specifically from VAMP."

"What's this study?" I asked.

"Well, it was allegedly conducted by Harvard, but on a curious note, we can't confirm that," Agent Jay said. "No one at Harvard has heard of it. And only one of the researchers has been verified as a real scientist who actually worked at Harvard—six years ago. Can't track down any of the other people listed."

"Did you talk to the one guy?" I asked.

"Oddly, he seems to have had a breakdown five months ago and has been in a psychiatric facility ever since," Mitch said.

"So now the game is to discredit Chris and Tanya and use the stock to do so. Pretty smart. Crushing the stock price will piss people off more than anything else," I said.

Demidova Corp had made investors a ton of money, being the hottest, fastest growing IPO in history. I pulled up the stock on my phone and found the price off by two percent.

"*This* little shop had *that* much effect?" I said.

"*Their client list consists of a pretty good slice of Philadelphia's who's who. And those individuals have already spoken to many of their own connections in New York,*" Omega said suddenly, his voice coming from the car's speakers.

"Are they shorting it? Could be an SEC violation in there somewhere," I asked. Both Mitch and Agent Jay had jumped in surprise when Omega spoke. You'd think they'd be used to it by now.

"*Negative. The only advice has been to sell, at least so far.*"

"How is your father?" I asked, the surprise on my teammates' faces turning to interest.

"*He woke up about an hour ago. He is eating broth currently.*"

"Any medical update?"

"*Ashling has forbade him attempting any magic at all. As he is very weak and has what he calls a profound headache, he has complied. She says the longer he waits, the better it will be,*" Omega said.

"Vitals?"

"*Strong. He is in not in medical danger. But everyone is, as the phrase goes, walking on eggshells, waiting to see if he recovers any abilities at all.*"

"And the Aleutian trench?"

"*All activity has subsided. Almost as if the elemental is waiting for him to come back.*"

"What about his own elementals?" I asked. My teammates were each sitting up, eyes on the speakers. Mitch actually had his head tilted.

"Draco is currently lying on his legs. Ashling kept trying to keep the dragon out but the Air Elemental is... crafty. So she gave up and let him stay so long as Declan avoids trying to communicate with magic. Just his voice."

"What is your take on this attempt on the stock?" I asked, watching the other two absorb the odd conversation, Mitch with a gleeful smile at me, Jay with a curious frown at the car's radio.

"Normally this type of assault might have a greater effect, but there are a lot of programmed trades for VAMP that kick in as soon as the price drops. The stock is very closely watched. Should those orders all get filled, and more sales bring the price back down, there are several much larger programs waiting to activate."

"Any of those yours?" I asked.

"Multiple. Elder Senka would like to acquire as much VAMP as possible in the Coven portfolios. She has standing orders. As I manage several other large portfolios as well, there are multiple trades pending. So the price has a large amount of built-in support. But this attack has only just started."

"That is exactly why we are here," Jay said, her eyes moving from the radio to me. "Each time the stock drops two or more percent, enough auto trades execute and it comes back up. We're monitoring the office to see what they do when their clients see this approach fizzling out. Also, Omega has already refuted the bogus study by sending several real ones out into the net. We're hoping all of this makes the two inside, Natalia DiPalma and Graham Bouffard, crazy enough to ask for new orders."

"The rest of the team is researching the researchers, trying to shake loose anything of use," Mitch said.

"Any luck?"

"We'll see when Alice and Chana get here. Oh, and you can join them for the afternoon shift," Jay said. "They should be here soon."

"Yeah, Cakewalk, have fun," Mitch said to me. He had started that nickname when the team was working on hand-to-hand drills and I mastered them before anyone else. Like it was a cakewalk for me.

Nobody really likes surveillance duty, but it seems like it's much less onerous for me. I suspect that's because my internal nano resources, particularly the perfect memory portion, lends itself to useful introspection. I can review previous drills, Bureau manuals, and other job-related information, or simply review a fun memory. Most agents spend time on their phones, but if I have my phone nearby, my nanites simply link to it and I can do in my head what others do on a screen. All while keeping my eyes on the subject location. Don't get me wrong... I'm not stupid enough to volunteer for extra duty, but it's no great hardship when I have to do it.

A common drill from my youth was to send me into the woods in camo gear and have me post up in a hidden position while my instructors hunted me. Sitting bone-still for hours at a time was usually the winning move, and having nanites that let me control many of my human weaknesses was key. I can slow my metabolism or speed it up, send blood moving to a numb posterior, turn off an itchy nose, and control the rate at which urine builds up in my bladder. Sitting in a car with partners on a cushy seat with the ability to shift around was like luxury.

"No problem, Itch," I said. Living at Arcane had taught me much about interacting with my associates and friends. The whole nickname thing never made sense when I heard the soldiers of AIR use them, but hanging with Jetta, Mack, Ashley, and especially Declan had been eye-opening. As Mitch was the team pick, always ready with a jibe, Itch seemed appropriate. Alice and Eve used it too, which I'll admit, was a small source of pride for socially inept me.

"Omega? What do you predict for the enemy's next attack on VAMP stock?" I asked.

"It is already in play—an analyst for Standard and Poors just lowered their twelve month rating for VAMP, citing the false study."

"Any ideas for a response?"

"A counterarticle would be timely."

I must have gotten a thoughtful look on my face because Jay suddenly zeroed in on me. "What are you thinking?"

"I think he's right," I said, pulling out my phone. The number I wanted was already on the screen, courtesy of my internal technology, and I only had to touch it with a finger to place the call.

"Hey, he's doing well. Sent the first and second samples to your mom," Stacia answered.

"Good. Omega kind of gave me an update but the human viewpoint is reassuring. But I called to ask something of you," I said.

"Oh?"

"Demidova stock is under attack. Bogus studies claiming mental illness is a side effect of vampire protein treatments. I think a reporter friendly to our side could maybe have a countering effect," I said.

"Oh! Yeah, Lydia texted me something about the price volatility. So you're thinking Bristol?"

"Think she'd do it?"

"Oh hell yeah. She loves this kind of stuff. I'm going to assume you have counterinformation on hand?"

"I do, Stacia," Omega interjected. *"I can send it directly to her, as well as contact information for parents who have given permission as references for the Demidova clinics."*

"Okay. I'll call her right now. You send the info while we're talking, Omega. She'll love that you're talking to her directly. She gets all giddy when she gets new links to our world," Stacia said.

"Great. Thank you," I said, the words falling out of my mouth easily. *That* would not have happened even a week ago.

"No prob. Wait, someone wants to speak to you," she said.

"Hey," Declan said into the phone, his voice sleepy and weak. My insides squeezed up in a way that left my nanites confused.

"Hey yourself. How are you feeling?"

"Like I got hit by a convoy of tractor trailers. I ache all over, my head is killing me, and I fall back to sleep every other minute. And I understand I have you to thank for all that—otherwise, my aunt tells me, I'd likely be dead by now," he said.

"Yeah, perhaps trying to transmute a magnitude nine-point-seven earthquake is a bad idea. Maybe start with a four or something?"

"Many people have been kind enough to point that out to me. But I wanted to say thanks before I passed back out."

"You're welcome. Put Stacia back on and go back to sleep."

"And he's... out," Stacia said, her tone neutral. Him wanting to thank *me* had to complicate her feelings as much as mine. *"I'll call Bristol as soon as I hang up... or maybe I'll wait for the next price drop. I'd like to get more VAMP for my mom at a cheaper price, myself."*

"Your order was already filled, Stacia. Father asked me to watch for a dip in price to get more for both you and your mom," Omega said.

"Okay, well then, I'll call her now. Goodbye, Agent Jensen." She hung up before I could say goodbye myself, which bothered me not at all. She took my call and promised help. Not an outcome I would have predicted before the last day or so.

"Was that really Stacia Reynolds?" Mitch asked, trying for casual.

"Yes, but try to control your Pavlovian reflex," I said.

"No, it's just that... hey! Did you just call me a dog?"

"She did, and pretty aptly so. Wipe the drool off your face. Was that also Declan you spoke to?"

It occurred to me that they couldn't hear both sides of the conversation like any vampire or were could.

"Yes. He thanked me for helping him."

"Ooh! Right in front of his girlfriend? Maybe I'll have a shot when they break up?" Mitch said.

"Wolves mate for life, Agent Allen," Jay said. "So, who is Bristol?"

"Bristol Chatterjee. She's a reporter. Specializes in occult and supernatural stuff," I said, but they were both nodding as soon as I said her last name.

"Think she'll do it?" Jay asked.

"It's my understanding that she's pretty close with Stacia and she loves anything to do with Chris and Tanya. So that will be a yes. She's got a huge number of followers these days."

"Well, when you have sources that close to the God Hammer and Queen of the Vampires, I suppose it's easy to get hundreds of thousands of followers," Mitch said.

"*One-point-three-seven-five million as of seven seconds ago,*" Omega said.

"I still can't get used to that," Mitch said, shaking his head. "To have him on the team is pretty awesome."

"*Thank you, Agent Allen.*"

Mitch opened his mouth but a dark sedan pulled up beside us, then parallel parked in the spot behind our Suburban. Whatever he was going to say vanished as his face lit up. "Our relief is here!"

Alice Barrows was driving, with Chana Mazar in the shotgun seat. They conversed between themselves, then Chana climbed out and slipped into the other rear passenger door of the Suburban , giving me a smile as she settled.

"Well? Anything?" Jay asked.

"Besides setting us free?" Mitch added.

"Nothing on the researchers. We think they're all fake. However, on another front, Graham Bouffard is Juliet Morrell's cousin and he manages the Loyal Order's portfolio," Chana said before turning my way. "How's the Warlock?"

CHAPTER 23

"Let me guess, they're related on Juliet's father's side?" Jay asked before I could answer Chana's question.

"Yes. Bouffard's mother is Juliet's father's sister," Chana said, turning back to me with raised eyebrows. "*He's* alive?"

"She just spoke to him a few minutes ago," Mitch said, clearly understanding that *he* was Declan O'Carroll. Chana Mazar had been fascinated by him since her first introduction.

"And his abilities?" Chana asked.

"Unknown. His aunt is keeping him from any magic use at the moment. As she's the only one who knows anything about witches and magical overload, he's listening to her. Plus he's got some pain and sleeps a lot," I said.

"Back to *our* mission... have you looked further into Juliet's father? Samuel Morrell?" Jay asked Agent Mazar.

"Yes, as he's the common link. Samuel Morrell was born September 4, 1955, here in Holmesburg. He was sixty-one when he died of a massive heart attack three years ago. His family had lived in the greater Philadelphia area for three generations before his own birth. His father was a history professor, and Samuel graduated UPenn with a bachelor's degree in business. In his early twenties, he spent three years in Houston, Texas, working for an aeronautical corporation based at the airport there. He quit his position in the firm's headquarters office rather suddenly, in January of 1981, and returned home to Philly. Once here, he immediately went to work for LOA.

There's no evidence yet, but we think *his* own father was highly ranked in the organization. From there, he shot up the ranks and became director within eight years."

"That seems kind of fast," Mitch said, eyes narrowed.

"Yes. LOA underwent an explosion of changes when Samuel started working there. Up until then, it had been doing moderately well but not great. After he arrived, the finances all tightened up. First he worked on membership and premium payments, both of which improved enormously. He was next assigned to claims, which plummeted. Then he moved over to investments, working with the portfolio manager. As you probably know, insurance companies work by selling policies and investing the premiums. If the investments grow, then the eventual payment of claims is much less than the amount the full premiums have grown into. So portfolio management is important, hence Warren Buffett and Berkshire Hathaway. Performance was good during the time Samuel was an assistant, and when the portfolio manager died suddenly, Samuel took over the spot. LOA's portfolio went through the roof during Samuel's time heading it."

"And he became director directly from there?" Agent Jay guessed.

"Yes," Chana said.

"So after a three-year entry job, he mysteriously becomes a prodigy at running an insurance firm," Jay mused. "Anything about his time in Texas pop out?"

"Well, funny you should ask," Chana said with a smile. "A rather well-documented UFO incident occurred about thirty-five miles from the international airport on December 29, 1980. Known as the Cash-Landrum incident, it involved one of the few cases of illness in UFO documented encounters. The individuals suffered radiation exposure symptoms for several weeks after the encounter. They also reported military helicopters surrounding the spacecraft they witnessed. An off-duty police officer and his wife also saw a large number of military helicopters in the area."

"So, to summarize, Sam goes to Texas for a first job out of college. After three years, he quits suddenly, right after a heavily documented UFO encounter near his work and home, and returns to Philly, where he becomes a business prodigy. Now his daughter and nephew are involved in the family secret organization which seems to be doing the work of the Vorsook and displaying mind control abilities," Mitch said, eyebrows up. "Hmm. Coincidence?"

Agent Jay snorted, then turned to Chana. "Are we sure Samuel is dead?"

"Short of digging him up, yes. We have copies of the death certificate and funerary documentation."

"And Juliet lives in the same house she grew up in?" Jay asked.

"Yes, with her mother, Natalie. Samuel bought it for Natalie as a wedding present," Chana said.

Agent Jay looked out the window, expression thoughtful. A phrase that Jetta sometimes used popped into my head. *You could almost hear the gears turning.*

"Omega, is there any reason for us to maintain surveillance of this location, or can you monitor the suspects?"

"I am currently monitoring all electronic communications in and out of the building, including all internet activity. Additionally, I have a microdrone inside the building. Your stakeout is redundant and actually less efficient than mine."

"Ouch," Mitch said, looking wounded.

"Well, I asked. Okay, change of plans. Let's go check out this

Bryn Mawr home. I'm wondering what else Samuel brought back from Texas."

A bit more than a half-hour later, we were in Morrell's neighborhood, watching a video feed from a standard commercial drone that Alice was piloting over the property. "Hell of a wedding present," Mitch noted.

The Morrell family home was huge, over nine thousand square feet, according to Omega, sitting on a thirteen-acre lot, with a four-car garage, a pool, pool house, and its own tennis courts.

"*Natalie Morrell's estimated liquid net worth is in excess of seven million dollars, not counting this property,*" Omega supplied.

"Well, you could hide a lot of stuff on over a dozen acres," Alice said. "Like what's in that out building? Hell, that alone is bigger than the house I grew up in, and there were four of us."

The five-rotor drone was currently hovering over a separate structure, a cedar-shingled one-story building on the backside of the trapezoidal property.

"*According to the building permit, it is listed as an artist's studio, fifteen hundred and forty square feet.*"

"Anyone else interested in why there is an oversized bulkhead door on that studio?" I asked.

"Omega, how large is that door?" Jay asked as Alice zoomed the camera in on the steel basement access.

"*It is a one-piece custom door with an opening measuring one hundred and thirty-three inches across.*"

"A bit over eleven feet across. That's pretty big," Chana noted. "Somebody's painting some big canvases."

"*No orders for painting supplies have been charged against any of the family credit or debit cards since the structure was built in*

1994, twelve years after the main residence was constructed."

"Is it even legal for us to know that?" Alice asked.

"*Saves us a ton of time and hassle,*" Eve said over the vehicle's synched phone system.

Agent Jay was staring holes in the video display. "Circle around it," she said.

The drone started to swing around and then suddenly wobbled, veering off course.

"That's not me!" Alice said.

My time with the world's most powerful witch had taught me a lot, including, surprisingly, a great deal about modern electronic devices. Declan had, from time to time, used my nanites to extend his mental *reach*, mostly to seize control of drones. No way could that happen without me picking up a few things. I *pushed*, then *pushed* again, harder, and the display evened out.

"What's it doing?" Jay asked.

"I lost all control and it looked like it was crashing, but now I think it's following a return to home protocol," Alice said, studying her controls.

I didn't tell anyone that I had *helped* the drone reach that decision. A girl's gotta have a few secrets—or even a whole bunch of them.

"Omega? Any idea what happened?" Jay asked.

"*My own drone picked up a burst of RF interference emitted from that structure.*"

"Normal technology or something else?" Jay asked.

"*Basic.*"

"Any other activity?" she asked.

"Negative. My own unit is staying further back. I surmise that some form of sensor picked up on the drone and activated a defensive feature."

"Can you detect any other sensors?" I asked.

"Ultrasonic emissions inside the building are consistent with modern motion detectors. There are passive infrared sensors and cameras covering four major approach angles with some sensor overlap. The doors and windows are emitting slight EM signatures that would be indicative of magnetic sensor switches."

"Wow, pretty tight security for a hobby studio," Mitch noted.

"Can you draw me a map with arcs and sensor locations?" I asked.

"Already on your phone's screen," Omega replied.

"We don't have a warrant to search the premises," Agent Jay said, eyeing me warningly.

"Can't hurt to be ready. Something important is in there. State of the art anti-drone defenses on top of excellent alarm systems. Makes me all curious," I said.

"But with security that tight, we couldn't sneak in if we wanted to," Chana said, then turned to me. "Could we?"

"Actually, we could," I said. Between my nanites, my training, and with Omega's help, I was pretty confident.

"But we won't—right?" Jay asked me, eyebrows up.

"Not until *you* say the word," I said with a shrug.

"If you need a warrant, I can obtain one," Omega said suddenly. We all exchanged glances before Jay spoke.

"You would hack one?"

"*Negative. The local federal judge would cooperate.*"

"Based on what grounds?"

"*Any you like. He has a very large number of vices.*"

"You would blackmail a federal judge?" Jay asked.

"*I would seek his assistance in protecting the planet from the Vorsook. Any discussion of the situation would likely include how poor a job he has done in keeping his transgressions private. Behavior analysis of this particular individual indicates an extremely high probability he will accede to my wishes.*"

"In other words—yes," Mitch said.

"*Essentially.*"

"That's illegal," Jay said, her tone thoughtful more than challenging.

"*My analysis indicates it will only require the suggestion of publicity to sway him. He is pretty weak. The case would be very gray and would require extensive court time to determine if that level of suggestion met the burden of proof needed for true blackmail. However, Agent Jay, while I generally allow human laws to guide many of my decisions, there are limits. I will take whatever action I deem necessary to protect this world.*"

"Like following FAA rules for flight plans and aircraft registration?" I asked while the others were mulling over his words. Omega's declaration of ruthlessness was no shock to me.

"*I file flight plans and register all my craft. The time between actions is often far shorter than humans are capable of.*"

Jay turned to me with raised eyebrows.

"When he transported his father to Vermont, the whole trip took about six minutes. But if you were to investigate, my bet is that you would find international flight plans filed with both the US and Canada, probably milliseconds before his drone took off," I explained.

"*Affirmative.*"

The others were silent as they digested all that.

"I vote we keep him on the team permanently," Mitch said with a straight face.

"*Seconded,*" Eve said over the radio.

Jay gave him a mildly disgusted look before speaking. "Questionable legal maneuvers aside, we won't be tipping our hand at this point," she said.

"Which suggests that we might in the future?" Alice asked.

Jay ignored her. "I want more intel on this family before we go any further."

"You agree that they're likely hiding something in or under that studio?" I asked.

"Oh, absolutely. But before we go leaping in, I want to have an idea of every other surprise they might have in place. If the Vorsook are behind this family's success, don't you think there are some serious protections in place?"

And that's why she's boss.

CHAPTER 24

"*The Philly Shipyard*," Morris Howell said over the Bluetooth speaker in our hotel suite an hour later. It was sitting on the coffee table amongst takeout boxes and empty drink containers.

"What about it?" Alice asked as we all looked up from our own reviews of the information we had gathered on the Morrell family.

"*Follow the money, right Agent Jay?*" he asked. "*There are regular rental payments made from the LOA operating account that was tagged as* ship YD ware. *Digging deeper, I found the payments extend back for years. One of the early postings labeled it with an address on Kitty Hawk Avenue, which is in the shipyard. My guess is it's storage or warehouse space.*"

"Excellent work, Morris. Caeco and I will check it out; everyone else keep digging," Agent Jay said. Everyone looked at her with hopeful expressions. "No, just Agent Jensen for now. But if you're all good, we'll bring back dessert."

"*What about us?*" Eve asked.

"You have complete access to the bureau café," Mitch said, not a hint of sympathy in his voice. "I know for a fact that they make that pecan pie you like so much at least every other day."

Morris's laugh sounded loud and clear over the speaker. "*He's got you there, Evie! She's got a third of a pie sitting at her right elbow as we speak.*"

A loud thwack sound came through, followed immediately by a heartfelt "*Oww!*"

"*Traitor!*" Eve said. Rustling sounds overpowered the microphone, my brain filtering the sound and forming a picture of a paper ball fight in full progress.

"On that note, we're out," Jay said, waving me toward the door.

Ten minutes later, we were in the Suburban and pulling out of the hotel parking garage, Agent Jay at the wheel.

She took a few minutes to follow the GPS directions on her phone, then settled back when we got onto I-95 South.

"So... how ya doing?" she asked.

"Er, fine, I guess. Why? Do you want a debrief report?"

"No, I want to see how you are handling everything because, well let's see, we had a big fight with remotely controlled civilians, then you had to fly to northern Vermont because your ex, who happens to be one of this world's most important weapons in the coming fight, almost died. Would have died without your help. Then you had to brief the president before rushing back here. Seems like a confusing time, so I'm checking in."

"Oh. Yeah," I said, immediately uncomfortable. "I'm okay. Sorry about hurting all those civilians, though."
"I'm sorry too. But I don't think we could have avoided it. They didn't react to pain and wouldn't stop. I saw you using less impactful techniques—I did too. But they didn't work. So no shame in protecting your teammates," she said, glancing my way.

I just nodded when she was looking. After a second, she went on. "You try real hard, don't you? Not to hurt people?"

I felt myself lock up for a moment, then nodded again, only this time her eyes were on the road. “Yeah. That’s what I like about aikido. I don’t have to break bones or heads.”

It was her turn to nod. We traveled another half a mile before she spoke again. “How about seeing Declan?”

I didn’t answer, mostly because I wasn’t sure what she wanted but also because I wasn’t real clear on the whole thing myself.

“That had to hurt... seeing him with his girlfriend,” she commented.

I sighed internally, my training preventing me from ever expressing that kind of thing in front of a superior officer. But she wasn’t going to let it go.

“I’ve seen them together before. Wasn’t so bad this time. Didn’t like seeing him hurt. The kid’s always getting hurt.”

“Yeah, I’ve seen the reports. He does tend to get roughed up frequently, doesn’t he? You’d think that a witch that powerful would be impervious,” she said.

“That’s just it. He’s not. I mean, if his guard is up, he’s real hard to damage and even when he is hurt, it usually means the other side is just smoking cinders or something. But yeah. He throws himself right into the middle of things and he slips sometimes and then he’s pretty breakable. Hell, he just got over being hurt in Burlington by that demon.”

“And you’re a lot less breakable, right?”

“Definitely. I guess that’s something that Stacia and I have in common. It takes a lot to hurt us, and then we bounce back quick. But now I don’t know. If he doesn’t have his powers anymore, he’s a sitting duck.”

“With a werewolf bodyguard and the most powerful technology on the planet watching over him,” she said.

"Ha, you don't know him. That's barely enough to keep him safe on a quiet day."

"What about all those elementals?"

I thought about that for a moment. "Omega did tell me that Draco kept crawling into bed to be near him. There must be something to that, right?"

"I don't know jack shit about elementals, Jensen, but I've seen pictures and video of that mini dragon. If you're saying it's like his Lassie or something, I'd say that's gotta mean something, right?" she questioned.

"Omega? Is Robbie still around Declan?" I asked out loud. Agent Jay glanced at me, face unreadable. My team couldn't seem to get used to the idea that he was almost always just a question away.

"Yes, Caeco. Stacia thinks he's under the residence at the moment. Draco continues to lie across Declan's feet. Nether elemental seems put off by Father's lack of magic. I believe that Ashling considers that to be a positive thing on several levels."

"You mean like they know something about his abilities that we don't?"

"Ashling says that witches tap into magic, which I would probably term quantum energy, but that elementals are actually made from magic. So yes, they are far, far more sensitive than even Ashling herself is."

"Thanks, Omega," I said.

"*You're welcome,*" he responded.

I wanted to ask if he knew the results of Mother's tests yet but didn't feel like opening that can of worms in front of my boss.

"I'm going to have to adapt to that faster," Agent Jay said, glancing at the big SUV's media center.

"So I guess we'll have to wait and see about his abilities, but he's alive and his closest elementals seem unshaken by his injuries," I said. I hadn't thought about it, but on some level, I must have been worried or anxious and Lois Jay had effectively lanced a boil I didn't know I had.

"You have drones around him?" I asked out loud. Lois glanced my way then realized, again, who I was talking to.

"Of course. I have enough combat power on site to defeat any army on Earth."

"Good," I said, nodding. Turning to my boss, I noticed her expression.

She had a slightly awestruck expression on her face. "Ah, was he overexaggerating? About that whole army thing?"

"No, I'm sure not. My understanding is that his new drones take the alien tech to new levels. Also, while Omega does seem to have a sense of humor, he does not joke about his father."

"I definitely have a sense of humor, Caeco Jensen. Just ask Father, Chet, Chris, Tanya, Lydia, or Stacia."

"I know, Omega. I said as much. Some people would argue that you are just copying one... that's why I used the word *seem*, but I already know it's there," I said. My boss now looked stricken.

"This is really hard to get used to," she said, shaking her head. "Chatting with a world AI that controls more military might than even my own country like it's nothing." She turned off the highway onto the Broad Street exit.

"Father says that formal conversations can be useful at times among conflicting parties, as it provides a framework for careful interaction, but that most of the time, informality is less stressful.

I think he is generally correct."

"Your father doesn't believe in taking himself too seriously," I said.

"He's widely accounted the most powerful witch on Earth and from all reports can destroy a town without breaking a sweat… or at least he could… before. He really felt that way?" Agent Jay asked.

"Yeah. He takes magic super serious, but not himself. Chris is a little like that too," I said.

"Nathan Stewart said that Chris, Tanya, and Declan were the only known Champion-class individuals we had identified, and they act like *that*?" Agent Jay said, pulling into the shipyard main access.

"Hah, I knew it," I said. She glanced my way. "At Arcane, the rumor was that there was another Champion-level student. I always thought it was Declan. He always joked it was Mack and Jetta."

"The unpowered brother and sister?" she asked, incredulous.

"They're lucky."

She laughed and looked sideways at me, then turned the car onto Kitty Hawk Avenue.

"No, really," I said. "They're incredibly lucky. Not with lottery tickets, but with life. Jetta is the only person who can sometimes beat me on the range with a handgun. She's a really good shot, but I have engineered reflexes, inhuman vision, and machine-driven aiming solutions. Yet she somehow manages to pull off enough so-called *lucky* shots that she'll usually tie or even beat me. Mack seems to have similar luck, but with long guns. Then there are all the things that have happened to them that should have killed them, but fate somehow intervened."

"Probability definitely skews in the vicinity of the Suttons," Omega added.

"You're not kidding?" Agent Jay asked.

"No. It's like a superpower. Look, that's the address Morris sent to us," I said, pointing at the building in question. We were almost at the end of Kitty Hawk, nearing the waterline and drydocks. A massive building, twice the length of the nearest ship being either constructed or deconstructed in dry dock, took up the whole side of the road. One of the massive doors showed our address number above it.

"You could keep anything in there," Jay said, slowing the car as we coasted by it.

"Yeah, you really could," I agreed, *reaching* out with my internal senses. Instantly I pulled back, a feeling like electric shock still tingling along my spine, down my arms and legs, and out to my fingers and toes. "Shit!"

Agent Jay accelerated down the road, turning behind a small metal-sided building almost on the dock. "What happened?"

"I, ah, I guess you could say, extended my feelers and something stung the shit out of me," I said, shaking both hands.

"Interesting. The building appears to be surrounded by a field of energy, kind of a protective blanket," Omega said. *"Caeco has experienced what might be called amplified feedback. Ironically, it's analogous to what Father must have gone through under the ocean—on a much, much smaller scale. My own drone felt it as well."*

"You have a drone here?" Agent Jay asked.

"Of course, Agent Jay. Several. If I'm to be of maximum value, I have to have proxies on scene."

She looked at me. I shrugged. "You're not surprised?" she asked, brow furrowed. I couldn't tell if she was pissed or surprised or both.

"No. He uses computers and sufficiently sophisticated electronics to monitor things all over the place, but if he's really interested in something, then there is always a drone or three around. Just wish I had let him test it instead of doing it myself." My toes still tingled.

Agent Jay's face was now carefully blank. She tapped her bottom lip thoughtfully. "What could do that? What manner of tech could cause feedback like that?"

"Other than my drones or Father or a full Circle of Witches, it could only be one of several things, at least in my estimation. Either Vorsook technology or one of the more powerful denizens of Fairie. Obviously elementals could do it, but as Caeco remained conscious and my drone remained functional, I would eliminate that option."

"You're saying we either have a Vorsook craft of some kind in there or a high-ranking elf?" Jay asked. She looked relatively unsurprised.

"Essentially."

"Well, based on what we have learned about Samuel Morrell, I'm leaning toward the Vorsook scenario," Jay said, studying me closely.

"Concur."

"Let's get back to the hotel," Jay said, putting the big vehicle into reverse and backing around. "We've learned a great deal. We'll need to plan carefully before we move forward."

I just nodded, rubbing my hands together to get the feeling back, as she drove back out Kitty Hawk Avenue and headed the way we had come.

CHAPTER 25

Other than the news playing on the hotel television, there was little noise as we sat in the central living area around the suite's dining table. Several maps and aerial photographs covered the table's surface, but pride of place was held by a full-scale set of blueprints of the shipyard building.

Seth had found them and somehow gotten them out of whatever government office had them. Oddly enough, he was now watching the news rather than poring over the plans like the rest of us.

"Big-ass building," Alice noted for the second time. Not that she was wrong. It was huge, and a big portion of it constituted the majority of the yard's shipbuilding infrastructure, at least whatever portion of building a seagoing vessel that didn't occur in the dry docks. According to the blueprints, it was actually a whole bunch of buildings under a bunch of connected roofs.

"See, it's gotta be this section here," Mitch said, pointing. We were having a great deal of trouble finding the part of the building that was leased to LOA. It was a very confusing layout and it didn't seem to jive with the photos Agent Jay had taken of the building with her phone.

"Seth, are you sure these plans are the most up-to-date?" Chana Mazar asked. Seth didn't respond.

"Seth? Hello... I'm talking to you?" Chana said, snapping her fingers at the same time.

"What? Oh," he said, glancing our way. "Sorry, this news is kind of fascinating. Huge worldwide controversy over the submarine earthquake."

"I asked if you were certain of these plans," Chana said.

"Yes, the date is in the lower corner. Less than three years old, I believe," he said, his eyes back on the screen.

"What's the controversy?" Agent Jay asked.

"First there were groups saying Omega caused the quake with his drone, and others were saying he stopped it. But now, apparently, several sources in the administration have leaked that the drone had people on board and that the Warlock was one of them. Social media exploded, or maybe imploded would be better. Enough to cause internet slowdowns and even a few outages. Your ex is getting smeared all over the place. It's worldwide and now various governments are getting in on the act," Seth said.

Jay moved over to look at the screen while Mitch pulled up a news compilation site on his computer. "Drudge is full of it," he said, Alice and Chana reading over his shoulder.

I found myself reluctant to look at either screen. "What are the governments saying?"

"It's a mixed bag. A lot of the smaller countries are crying victim, saying that the computer is exploiting them under a false flag of world defense. Russia is saying the computer is under US control and the alien threat is just an excuse to take over the world," Seth reported.

"Yeah, and most of the European Union and Japan are saying that the only thing that prevented a major catastrophe was the presence of the Warlock," Mitch chimed in. "China has locked down its internet and says it stands with Omega. North Korea is siding with Russia."

“What does our own government say?” I asked.

“President Polner has scheduled a press conference for nine o’clock Eastern Time,” Agent Jay said, eyes locked on the television.

“Those blog sites that originated the Vorsook false flag stuff also jumped on this with both feet,” Eve reported.

Two of the team’s laptops were Skyped into headquarters, one showing Eve, the other showing Morris. They were both typing like crazy on their keyboards.

“It’s a perfect event for the Vorsook to exploit,” Agent Jay said.

“How can we counter it?” Alice asked.

“Oh shit!” Morris said before Jay could answer Alice’s question. *“Sorry, but Bristol Chatterjee just announced an interview with the Warlock himself—tonight, live, at ten p.m.”*

“I was going to say that *we* couldn’t counter it. Looks like the people that can… are,” Jay said. “Her article on the Demidova stock was pretty solid. This might be good as well.”

“You think this was O’Carroll’s idea?” Chana asked.

I couldn’t help myself. I snorted out loud. They all looked at me. “He would *never* come up with that! More likely Tanya or Lydia came up with it. They’ll have to duct tape him in place for an interview. He hates any kind of notoriety or publicity.”

“It was Ms. Chapman’s idea, in conjunction with Ms. Chatterjee,” Omega said through our conference phone.

“You’re back,” I noted.

“I have been… distracted.”

My phone started to buzz at the same time that Agent Jay’s did.

"That will be the White House. They want to know what Father will be saying, as the president is reluctant to hold his own conference first," Omega said.

Jay answered her phone a second before I hit my own and I heard her say, "Yes, Director Tyson?" But then I hit the answer button and Sergei was speaking before I could. *"I'm here with the president, Agent Jensen."*

"Hello Mr. President," I said, which brought every set of eyes in the suite my way.

"Agent Jensen, have you been following events in the news?"

"Just in the last few minutes, sir. I just found out about the scheduled interview seconds ago."

"I need you to make contact and find out what he's going to say. You understand how it would look if I go ahead with my conference and he says something totally from left field?"

"Yes sir. Loss of credibility, sir. Perhaps you could speak to him directly, sir?" I suggested.

"We tried. Our calls won't go through, Miss Jensen. We had the phone company attempt to force it, but it failed."

"They're up against Omega, sir. What if I could get him to call you directly? You've met him before, right?"

"Yes. Briefly. If you could arrange that, it would be ideal."

"Yes sir. Let me call him and I'll see what he says, sir."

"You'll need a number to get through," President Polner said, wry humor in his voice.

"No, sir, I don't. If Declan wants to speak with you, Omega will put the call through directly to you, sir."

"Yes. I suppose he might at that. Good luck, Agent."

"Yes sir," I said, before the phone went silent. My whole team was watching me.

"The president just called you?" Mitch asked.

"You heard her say *Mr. President*, didn't you?" Alice asked like he'd lost his mind.

"Yeah, but I'm still checking."

I ignored him and turned back to my phone, touching the screen. Nothing happened. I did it again, but the screen stayed dark.

"Omega? Are you blocking my call to Declan as well?"

"He doesn't like to talk to politicians."

"I'm not a politician," I said.

"You work for one."

"Omega, are you going to let me through or what?"

The phone buzzed and started to call the contact listed simply as *Dec.*

"You heard," Stacia answered unexpectedly.

"Well, yeah. Personally, I think it's a great idea. But President Polner wants to speak to Declan and see if they can be on the same page. Back-to-back press conferences and all that," I said.

"Why didn't the White House call on its own?" she said. I drew a breath but she spoke before I could. *"Ah. Omega. Got it. Okay then. He's getting dressed; let me grab him."*

She must have set the phone down because I could hear her moving away and calling out his name at the same time. Distantly I heard him answer but even with enhanced hearing, I couldn't make out their conversation. Then came the sounds of multiple footsteps approaching.

"*Hey,*" Declan said.

"Hey yourself. How are you feeling?"

"*Better. The headache is gone. Most of the aches too. Still kind of wobbly though. Stacia said you heard about the interview?*"

"Declan, the whole world heard about the interview—including President Polner. You might imagine that he'd like to compare notes before he goes on the air tonight?"

"*Oh. So I tell you and you tell him?*"

"That's not ideal. Better if you spoke to him directly, don't you think?"

"*But you have a perfect memory. You can recite it word for word.*"

"Yet it still won't reassure him or his advisers as much as talking to you directly. Man up, O'Carroll. Talk to the president."

He was silent for a bit and I kept my mouth shut. Around me, the others all watched, fascinated, I think.

"*Yeah, I suppose. Alright, I'll call him.*"

"How's everything else?" I asked.

"*Magic or no magic you mean?*"

"Yeah, I guess."

"*I haven't tried anything yet. At least with my magic,*" he said, a note of something I couldn't identify in his voice.

"If not magic, then what?"

"*I've been... talking... with Draco. And Robbie.*"

"Talking? You say that like it's different?"

"*It is. I don't mean that I talk and they listen. I mean they talk back."*

"Didn't they always?"

"They sent images or feelings but not words. This is actual words. Ones I understand."

"So that's... new?"

"Very. Like a channel opened that wasn't there before."

"That's good, I guess. Right?"

"It's very good. Caeco, it means that I can still communicate with elementals, only now I can use words, sentences. I've never been able to do that."

"Well, that would mean that if you..."

"Have lost my magic, I can still help direct the elementals."

"Well, that's awesome. Maybe the other thing will come back?"

"Aunt Ash is being very cautious not to get my hopes up, so I'm clinging to this talking thing."

I thought about if I lost my nanites or my genetic enhancements and thus many of my abilities. Immediately I stopped that line of thought, a shudder going through my body. "Yeah, I can see that. Just keep doing what she said. And call the president!"

"Okay. Omega will put me through right now. Thanks Caeco. And good luck with your own mission. Omega told me all about it."

"Of course he did. Thanks."

We disconnected at the same time.

The others were still staring. "So... you just brokered a conversation between the Warlock and the president," Agent Jay said.

I shrugged, not really clear what I was supposed to say to that. Jay looked at me for a moment, then nodded. "Okay. Caeco's liaison duties are done for the moment, so let's get back to *our* mission. After thinking it through, I believe that our next step should be reconnaissance of the shipyard. Thoughts?" she asked the team.

"So we have two interesting targets; the studio at the Morrell residence and this shipyard warehouse thing, right?" Alice summarized.

"Yes," Jay answered.

"Both exhibit some kind of technological protection. At the studio, it appeared to be regular, if sophisticated, human-type intrusion detection gear, while the warehouse might have alien tech. And you think we should tackle the alien tech?" Alice asked.

"Valid point. But we're here to find a Vorsook influence, right? And this is the first clear indication of Vorsook. Juliet is hiding something at her home but using regular protection equipment. What Caeco ran into is different and if it's alien, we need to verify that before we let it slip away," Jay said.

"That makes a disturbing amount of sense, ma'am," Mitch said, frowning.

"Glad you agree," Jay said, voice dry.

"But how are we going to slip past alien tech?" Alice asked.

"*We,*" Jay said, pointing a finger at Alice and then herself, "won't. But *she* has a built-in detector, and she was, very literally, built for spy work." The senior agent's finger now pointed squarely at me. "You up for it?" she asked me.

"You know, in case breaking through state-of-the-art detection gear at the house is too easy," Mitch said.

Actually, it was. I already knew exactly how to get through the studio's protections, thanks to the handy diagram that Omega had put in my phone. It was well done, but it had a few weak spots and let's be honest, my nanites made short work of most alarms anyway. But the warehouse? Hell yeah!

"Yup. Let's do it. When?" I asked.

"Tonight, late. We'll gather every bit of intel we can and study the blueprints for the next few hours. Figure the best approach. Then, after midnight, we'll head over and see what you can find out," Jay said.

"Hey, that means we get to watch the interview," Mitch said, face lighting up in a smile. Alice rolled her eyes, Chana looked thoughtful, Seth blinked like a sleepy owl, and Agent Jay ignored the comment altogether, her eyes on the plans. On the laptop screens, Eve did a fist pump while Morris just kept typing on his keyboard. When Mitch turned my way, still grinning, I just grinned back.

CHAPTER 26

"So, Declan, you've really stirred things up this time, haven't you?" Bristol Chatterjee asked.

"You think?" Declan answered, mock surprise on his face.

Bristol waved at a set of monitors behind them both, at least six screens all showing various footage of the massive sea quake or graphics of the tectonic plates beneath the ocean or talking head experts or footage from past quakes.

"You do know that those quakes happen in that Rim of Fire quite a bit, right?" he asked her. *"Like the 9.3 quake in 2004?"* He pointed at tsunami footage on one of the screens.

"You're saying the quake was going to happen anyway? Listen, I heard the President's speech—he said basically the same thing," she said. It was just the two of them, Stacia apparently off camera.

"A quake was going to happen. Whether the one that happened was worse or better than if I hadn't been there, no one can say," he said.

He looked pretty good. Less pale than when I had seen him at his aunt's. He was dressed in a tight-knit cotton sweater in the exact same shade of blue as his eyes, and dark jeans, with L.L. Bean boots on his feet. Stacia would have picked the sweater and jeans. On his own, his clothing style could best be described as negligent. I might not know a lot about fashion, but at least I had absorbed the lessons that Ashley, Jetta, and observing the witch pack had taught me. I was trained to blend in, so I could fake it. Him... I don't think he could be bothered.

The L.L. Bean boots were likely a concession to his nerves. He hated interviews or publicity of any kind and he always felt better in standard northern Vermont footgear.

The interview wasn't in a studio but in his aunt's restaurant, Rowan West. Specifically the pub section, right in front of the big stone fireplace.

"Well, this monster of a quake did no damage at all. The president indicated that may have been because of you?"

"Hmm. Let's start at the beginning," Declan said. *"We were there to make contact with an Earth elemental living in the subduction trench. It's a big elemental, the largest I've approached to date."*

"That's right, you and your lovely girlfriend have been touring the world, meeting elementals, preparing for conflict with the aliens, the Vorsook, right?"

"Essentially, Bristol. On the world of Fairie, the Queens have held off the Vorsook for centuries by using the elementals of that planet, in addition to their own abilities, their armies, and their allies, the dragons. Here on Earth, we have significant military resources, we have some of the Vorsook tech itself, and we have Omega. But we don't have the huge power of the planet's elementals. At least not yet. Someone told me that the earthquake that went off under the sea was the equivalent of all the nuclear weapons on the planet detonating at once. Hard to wrap my head around that, but if that's even close to true, think how much power that one elemental brings to the fight."

"So you've been what? Out making friends?" Bristol said with smirk.

"More like mending fences... big, huge fences."

"What do you mean?"

"Most elementals want nothing to do with any kind of human.

We're dirty, filthy, short-lived little vermin who infect the world. That's how they think of us, if they're aware of us at all," he said.

"That's pretty harsh," she said.

"Well, we pollute the hell out of the planet, drill wells, frack the ground, stripmine the earth, pump industrial waste gases into the atmosphere, fill the oceans with plastic, kill off whole species, overfish the sea, clear cut forests and jungles. In short, we damage, taint, or outright destroy all the things that elementals value. So getting any of them to communicate with me, let alone build any kind of rapport, has been damned difficult."

"But you've made progress, right?"

"Yes, we have. Very slow going, especially at first, but better lately."

"We? Who? You and Omega?"

He smiled. *"No, me and Stacia. I make the contact but she's really good with figuring people out, even nonhuman people."*

"Aww, that's sweet. Steclan to the rescue, right? But how did you do it? How did you repair our sordid human reputation?"

"I showed them the progress we are making. Showed them the increases in alternative energy generation, the proliferation of electric and hybrid technology, and all the progress we're making in recycling and reusing our own garbage."

"That was enough?" she asked, dubious.

"Not by itself, but then I showed them all the research going on. Demidova Corporation alone is funding huge amounts of what many people think is useless research. But you never know what's going to be useful. A previously unfunded study of a strain of bacteria found deep underground revealed that it produces an enzyme that basically unzips polymer chains, including most petrochemical-based plastics. Demidova is exploring using it to cheaply recycle almost any plastic into a new form."

"So VAMP funds the research and harvests the benefits?"

"VAMP funds the research. The researcher owns the intellectual data but VAMP gets first shot at utilizing it. Generally the company puts together seemingly disparate systems and parties to create sustainable organizations that actually make money."

"Seems like it's pretty great for VAMP?" Bristol noted, her tone suspicious.

"It is, on the few that yield immediate results. But the outlay in money is huge. The company basically funds everything and anything. Some stuff works, others just add to the collective knowledge base. If Demidova can't figure out how to monetize it, they help the researcher make it available to others who might be able to, or pay them to allow it to be open sourced. And any new companies that are formed are structured with equity for the researcher as well as the employees, and repayment to VAMP."

"Sounds too good to be true?"

"Most avenues don't yield anything of current value. But Tanya plays the long game. Information is the key in today's world. If it can't be used now, it will be in the near future."

"Spoken like a Demidova stock holder."

"Of course. Anyone who doesn't buy at least a little of that stock is crazy. That's why the board splits the shares almost yearly. Keeps the price down where almost anyone can buy in. If they use the company's dividend reinvestment program, it's basically free."

"Why? Why does she do so many things like that?"

"She sees income inequality, money-driven research, and pollution as some of our biggest issues. Financial education and access to capital-producing assets are easy steps she can do for inequality, as are structuring these new companies with employee stock ownership plans. She sees knowledge as our path to survival, but refuses

to allow money to drive what gets researched. It's like that shark show where you pitch your idea and they decide if they will help. Instead she accepts almost all ideas, funding them to different degrees."

"All because of the giant business of vampire medicine, which, by the way, is pretty controversial these days."

"Bah! One fictitious study with no credibility versus solid studies and actual results. I've personally been exposed to vampire proteins and even blood, numerous times, with no side effects."

"You aren't afraid of becoming a vampire?"

"No. V squared is actually pretty fragile. To Change a person requires them to be overloaded with the virus for weeks before being physically weakened almost to death. It's not easy."

"Okay, we've strayed off topic. Now that we've gotten your insider's take on Demidova Corporation, let's get back to the elemental business. You've been a good ambassador and built some trust, is that fair to say?"

"Yes. True."

"And you've moved your way up the echelon of elementals till you found this massive one under the ocean. How could it even help against the Vorsook? What would it do? Shake the aliens to death?" Bristol asked.

He laughed, relaxing a little. *"Great question. On Fairie, the Queens convert the power of the elementals to another form in order to attack the enemy. We would need to do the same."*

"Is that what happened? To the earthquake? You converted it to something else?"

"Well, I tried. But that much energy is beyond anyone. What I think happened is that the elemental helped me to convert the bulk of it to something less destructive to man. I'll know more when I

ask it."

"Okay help me unpack all that for a minute or two. First, the power is so vast that even you can't handle it, right? So how do the Queens of Fairie do it? Second, since when are these elementals helpful? And third, you're going to talk to it again? And risk another earthquake?"

"The Queens use it like a generator or a battery, taking what they can control in much smaller portions. Remember, they've been doing it steadily for thousands of years, plus they've created some artifacts to help them. Second, Stacia and I have communicated with dozens of elementals around the world. They do have some communication between themselves, you know. Maybe not like we would, but still it appears that they share information. So it seems likely that the Aleutian Earth Elemental was at least aware of some of what we've been doing. And yes, I will go back, being very careful to announce myself first, and talk with it."

"You're not concerned you could cause another quake?"

"Quakes happen because pressure builds up between the plates. That pressure was just relieved. This is the best time to go back. President Polner even said his geology people agree that there won't likely be another for a while."

"We don't have any Fairie queens here on Earth. So how do we use the power?"

"Thank God we don't have the Queens here! But basically, Bristol, witches can covert that power. Trained Circles can harness it. We may also copy some of the artifacts that are on Fairie."

"Which brings up another question," Bristol said, a gleam in her eyes. Declan's expression went wary at her tone. *"My other witch sources tell me that getting overloaded like that is extremely dangerous to a witch. That it's a miracle that you survived at all. And even though you did survive, you are likely permanently damaged by the exposure to that much power all at once."*

"Bristol, we agreed not to go into this tonight," he said, his playful tone gone, his voice warning. *"It was my primary condition."*

"I agreed not to ask you about your powers. I never said I wouldn't bring up the dangers of what you went though."

"Yes, it was dangerous. Yes, I got knocked on my ass. That's all I'm going to say on the matter," he said, sitting back, arms crossed.

"Just going to leave the whole world hanging?" she asked. *"I won't ask about your powers but can you even communicate with elementals still?"*

"Absolutely. Better than I could before," he said with a sharp nod.

"But can you still channel power? Who is going to wield this vast reservoir of power if not you?"

"There are plenty of witches that can do it. I've trained many myself."

"Please. We both know that they aren't you. The whole world knows you're at the forefront of this fight. So the question is... can you fight?"

A deep growl sounded, causing Bristol to snap her head off to the side. Declan stayed focused on her, his face angry. *"Oh come on! You can't expect me not to ask,"* Bristol said to someone off screen.

Declan stood up and plucked the microphone from his sweater. *"Goodnight Bristol,"* he said, walking unsteadily out of the camera view. The young reporter turned back to look at him, exasperation written all over her face. *"Declan, come back,"* she said. She watched for a moment, then turned to the camera. *"I guess that concludes our interview. I'm sorry it ends in such an unsatisfactory manner, leaving our most important questions unanswered. I'm Bristol Chatterjee and I'll keep digging. Good night."*

The screen switched to Bristol's standard closing footage and credits, and Mitch turned the volume down on the music.

"She got a bit pushy there," Mitch said.

"She's a reporter. That's her job," I said, not at all surprised. Declan and Stacia were likely pretty pissed at her, but Bristol was world class at worming her way back into people's good graces. "Probably be a cold day in Hell before he gives another interview though."

I sat back and began to pull on my soft-soled boots. They were black like the rest of my outfit. Black 5.11 women's tactical pants with lots of handy pockets and built-in kneepads but cut close to my body so extra material wasn't slowing me down. A matching black long-sleeved shirt with elbow pads and even more pockets. Gloves and a hat that was also a balaclava that I could pull down over my face when I got to the shipyard.

"What's the internet say?" Agent Jay asked Morris and Eve.

"Social media is blowing up. Lots of speculation that he's a null now," Morris said. *"Lots of anger."*

"People are scared. One of our heroes just showed weakness," Chana said. She was watching my preparations.

"Yeah, there's some desperation to a lot of the comments," Eve agreed. *"But mostly anger, heaps of anger."*

"What do you think, Cakewalk?" Mitch turned to me. "You know the kid the best. Is he a null?"

"First, I don't have any information that you don't… but tell me this… you're a trained interrogator… how did he look to you?"

Mitch was frowning in thought, but it was Chana Mazar who spoke first. "He looked mostly healthy, but he was uncomfortable with the interview, at least at first. Then he calmed down and was confident. But when she asked him about his powers, he got angry."

"He got *offended,*" I corrected. "Big difference from an *angry* Declan. They apparently had an agreement and she broke it, in a roundabout way. Words and agreements mean a lot to him. But yes, he was very confident once he settled down."

"And you're saying that he'd only be that confident if he knew something?" Agent Jay asked.

"He wouldn't have even done the interview if *he* thought he was a null. Think about it. He's the most powerful witch in the world, then suddenly not. Would any of *you* go on television at your most vulnerable? Oh, and you happen to be the only hostage that *might* cause Omega to negotiate."

"But why not just say that? That he was getting better? Why storm off?" Alice asked.

"He looked better than when I saw him, but not fully recovered. He's still weak. Maybe he's got a clear indication that his powers are on the mend but he's not fully there yet. Witches don't like to broadcast when they're weak. Pretty much a dog-eat-dog world in the witchcraft business. And again, there's the whole potential hostage thing. A super witch is a piss-poor hostage, especially one that has broken out of anti-magic cells and blasted anti-magic handcuffs to useless junk. But a weak, broken one is much more tempting. So he made Bristol agree not to ask, but she skirted around it. Fine in her mind but a breach in his. Once he thinks you've broken trust, he's had it. Trust me. I know."

They all stared at me, various degrees of realization on their faces. Mitch started to open his mouth but Alice elbowed him.

"So you think he's on the mend?" Chana asked.

"Omega? Has your father demonstrated any sign that his magic is returning?" I asked the open air.

"I cannot comment."

I smiled at the others.

"What? The computer didn't answer?" Seth said.

"Really? You don't think that was an answer?" I asked, shaking my head. "Let's try it this way. Omega can you confirm or deny Declan's powers are returning?"

"I can neither confirm nor deny," was the response.

"I rest my case."

"Oh. Just like anytime anyone neither confirms nor denies," Mitch said.

"That's good then, right?" Chana asked, studying me.

"I would say yes. Now, shall we do this?" I asked, checking my holstered Glock, extra magazines, knife, tools, lights, and the other gear spread around my person.

"But why the secrecy?" Eve asked.

"I don't know for sure, but look how the world already reacted in the last few days. People questioning his right to have the abilities he was born with, people blaming him for the quake, people blaming him for *losing* those powers, now all the anger against him for not answering. Declan is a private person. He absolutely *hates* all of this publicity. He's always been happy to let the cameras focus on Stacia while he stays in the shadows," I said.

"Seems suspicious," Morris said.

I snorted. "Because the world has been *so kind* to witches before."

"Hey, where's your amulet?" Chana asked suddenly.

I froze, then mentally cursed at myself. My nanites give me computer-level memory but if I don't put a timed reminder in place, I'm as capable of forgetting an important task as the next person.

"I gave it to the president."

"What? Why?" Mitch asked.

"Hello, president? Who better for the Vorsook to manipulate?" I said.

"We have a spare here in the gear," Chana said, already rummaging around in one of our supply cases. She stood back up with a black cord and a small stone amulet wrapped in copper. One of Krista's Circle's work. "Not as good as your old one, which might now be literally irreplaceable, but better than going in naked."

Mitch lit up at the word naked but even though his mouth opened, no words came out. Most of the team was watching him, waiting for a comment, as he was pretty predictable. Then he shut his trap and just smiled. Chana handed me the necklace and I pulled it on, already missing my old one.

"Anything else?" Agent Jay asked.

Nobody had an answer so I turned to the boss and raised both eyebrows. She nodded. "Let's go," she said, grabbing the keys.

CHAPTER 27

I came in across the roof of the massive building. After analyzing the blueprints and aerial photographs, we figured it would be the cleanest. Overall, it was actually more like seven distinct roofs rather than one, and they were all pretty much wide open. Except one.

So I approached from a parking lot behind the building, moving into the shadows around the base of it and scaling its walls between camera arcs. Easy, at least if you have ape DNA. And fingernails that can pierce the soft steel of wall siding.

Once when I was a teenager, my instructors made me climb El Capitan in Yosemite—at night—without ropes. This was nothing.

Still, I was cautious as I moved over the rubber roof of the massive structure, my enhanced biological senses straining the night for danger, my microscopic nanites alert for the slightest indication of technology, Earth-based or alien.

The roof was very warm, waves of stored sun rays rising from the black rubber all around me. It confused the infrared receptors in my corneas but I took solace that it would also baffle manmade thermal detectors just as much.

The night sky overhead was clear, just a sliver of a waxing moon to aid the stars in providing me with natural light. Nowhere near as light as a full moon, but much better than overcast. In fact, there was just enough light that I thought I saw a shadow moving far, far away. More a hint of motion than any real shape or anything. But I froze, dropping low, letting my kneepads absorb the soft impact with the roof. Frozen, waiting, watching. A minute ticked by, then another. Nothing. No further motion, no other shadows, no sign that I had actually seen anything real at all. I waited ten minutes, then crept farther along my path, moving half as fast as before.

There was still a long way to go, as the entire roof was over three hundred yards long, and my objective was about half that distance away. Our review of the building plans had shown that the westernmost end of the building rose higher than the rest of the structure, its roof a traditional peaked variety rather than the flat-topped version that I was currently creeping across. In fact, the raised portion stuck up high enough to have its own set of windows, which, on the backside, looked readily accessible from the flat roof I was on. At least, if you could climb up the metal-sided walls to get to them, as they were about ten feet off the flat portion of the roof.

The shadow that I had *possibly* seen had been in this direction, close to my objective, and so I took my sweet time approaching. But nothing shifted or moved, and nothing seemed out of place—till I got closer. One of the three windows visible to me looked different from the others, but it took me almost standing directly underneath it to see what that difference was. It was open... just slightly, the bottom edge pushed out, maybe half a foot. The other two were clearly closed tight, which I had been prepared for, my entry equipment up to the task of jimmying a locked window. Now it looked like that wasn't needed, which meant all of my instincts were suddenly on edge.

It's perfectly possible that it had been either deliberately or accidentally left open by one of the building's normal daytime inhabitants. Our photos of the building showed various windows open at various times of the day, and this portion of the building was, to our best knowledge, part of the administrative offices for the complex.

And actually, it might be a huge piece of luck not to have to pry on a sealed window, to avoid making those extra sounds. But it still felt off to me. Like someone was here ahead of me.

The open window was the righthand one from my position, nearest the corner of the admin tower as I had decided to call it, even though it rose only seventeen or eighteen feet above the rest of the mammoth building. In fact, it was the window I had preselected as the easiest to climb up to, which I did now, moving slow and stealthy, senses straining, as my extruded claws poked through the tips of my gloves and sank into the metal siding.

When I got up to the open window, I touched it lightly with one gloved hand. It easily moved outward, swinging another foot beyond the six inches it was already opened. The top was hinged and the bottom pressed out by a gear-driven arm, but that arm was disconnected, thus the greater range of motion. *That* didn't seem normal.

Peering into the building, I listened, looked, sniffed, and *felt.* Nothing to see except desks, file cabinets, and a copier. Nothing to hear but fans cooling computers, along with the ticking of a wall clock. And the only smells were of the humans who worked here, the cake that had left crumbs under and on the table against one wall, and the smell of old coffee from the battered pot that was also on the table. And something else. Something faint. A human, among other human scents, but different. Fresher—earthier. Male. Young. Healthy.

I waited, but nothing changed and the clock was still ticking, literally, right up on the wall in front of me. I folded myself over the edge of the window and onto the floor, all my motions silent and controlled.

At ten, I was certified as a yoga instructor. At eleven, I had passed beyond my dance instructors and my gymnastic coaches in controlled movement. By twelve, I had mastered qigong and tai chi chuan. That training was all for exactly this kind of moment.

Feet on the floor, I moved silently, eyes looking for any detectors that my nanites might somehow have missed, but there was nothing to impede my forward motion. While crossing the roof, I hadn't detected any trace of the powerful wave I had experienced in the car with Agent Jay, but I had also been very careful not to pass over the portion of the building that housed LOA's storage area and not to *reach out* with my machine senses.

A fire door led into a stairwell, which took me down three flights of stairs to the ground level. The stairwell door led to a hallway with more doors, which the blueprints had shown to be mostly more offices, but one went back into the main portion of the building. That one I took, and it opened into the rest of the massive structure. Still no alarm switches or motion detectors in this portion, although I knew from our planning that the exterior ground floor doors and windows were alarmed, even if these interior ones were not. My plan was to avoid those if possible.

The door led me to a vast open space dominated by massive overhead crane gantries and the gargantuan machinery of shipbuilding. I slipped silently between presses and lifts, massive vent-hood-covered units, and more than a few robotic devices. Halfway across the cavernous space, a hint of sound caressed my ears, freezing me in place. It was just a whisper, like paper or cloth rustling.

Muscles locked tight, I listened, smelled, and looked. Not another sound, and only the overwhelming scents of oil, ozone, steel, industrial paint, plastic, and rubber. No motion, no shapes other than hulking machines. Still, I waited. Perhaps there were mice or rats, cockroaches or other vermin in the otherwise empty building. Any of those could have caused the noise I heard, but the fact remained that I hadn't scented any such creatures and my sense of smell was easily able to detect pests like those.

No further sound came in the dark so I moved again, unlocking tense muscles and shifting back into fluid movement. Carefully, cautiously, I moved through the exact area where the sound had come from, finding nothing and no one to blame.

Without so much as a whisper of sound, I continued forward. The end of the huge space loomed ahead of me, a wall twenty feet tall with a green metal door at the base. That door should be the one that let us into LOA's portion of the building. Crouching, I studied it from twenty feet away. Shut tight, multiple dead bolt locks lined up above the doorknob. The steel skin of the door itself was dirty, metal dust from the shop accumulated so thick, I could see it in the dim light of the factory. And there were no smears in that grime—the door hadn't been opened from this side in years. I moved closer, my eyes focusing in the pallid light. But wait. There *were* markings in the shop filth, tiny smudges around the topmost deadbolt.

A tiny shift of air was my only warning, not even a breath, just an infinitesimal wafting. Reflexes took charge and I jumped, sailing backward through the air as a black form slammed down onto the concrete floor right where I had been standing, a gleaming length of blue-black steel sweeping through the space I had just occupied.

My own blade popped into my hand as if summoned, nine inches of dark Damascus steel, a Bowie etched with the howling wolf head symbol of Mack Sutton's brand. Pulling my Glock was the better tactical answer, but guns, they go bang. Loudly. Knives are so much quieter.

The figure straightened, a compact form only a bit taller than me, clad in black from head to toe, just a pair of dark eyes staring at me from the opening of the black strip of cloth wound round its head.

We stared at each other for the space of three whole seconds, then, as if by mutual agreement, we leapt straight into attack.

CHAPTER 28

He, because I could smell that he was a he, swung his blade in a wide horizontal cut, seeking to slash me across my middle. Immediate disembowelment.

My left hand snapped out, slapping the outside edge of his right arm, pushing the razored edge past my tucked in and arced back stomach, his weapon arm folding across his own chest. My blade stabbed like a spear, right arm jabbing out over my left, the tip of the big knife angled upward, set to puncture up under his ribs.

But he twisted, letting his torso turn the same direction that my hand had sent his knife and arm. My Bowie struck his right tricep, down near the elbow, the sharp tip sliding off something hard and unyielding.

I knew it in an instant. Armor. Woven into his clothing like motorcycle armor. Plastic or carbon fiber. Even as I realized this, I was twisting and angling my blade, higher up his arm as I sliced my weapon backward. The motion was a clockwise rotation of my own body, the energy coming from my hips and center of gravity. My left hand kept pushing on his arm, right hand cutting the knife hard against his upper arm, which also *encouraged* his body to continue in the same direction as his sweeping slash.

Fighting is often about overcoming or controlling one's own instincts. Part of me wanted to create distance between me and my opponent, much as when I had first jumped backward on reflex. But I have fought armored opponents, many times, as most of my instructors wore it. They needed every edge they could get as I grew older and more dangerous.

In this case, as much as my body might want space between me and danger, I *knew* I needed to be in tight, to inflict as much damage up close as possible and limit his reach. So rather than pushing off him—backward—I instead continued my turn, now sweeping my right foot in an arc behind me, rotating my body clockwise around my center while he spun counter-clockwise, the two of us turning in place like two gear cogs in a machine. My spin turned me toward his now-exposed back. The handle of the knife almost seemed to flip itself around in my hand as I reversed the blade back along my forearm, the needle tip now aimed at his spine.

However, this wasn't *his* first rodeo either, because he not only continued his own turn but accelerated it so that his blocking left arm hit and caught my right elbow, stopping my blade cold while he turned his slash into a stab at my stomach.

This time, my left hand slapped down on his right, pushing his jab out and away as my right foot set firmly on the ground, my left foot now arcing around to complete my turn. I simply lifted my left knee to impact his knife arm, close to his armored elbow. It's been my experience that most of the time, this scissor of hand and knee will hyperextend my opponent's arm, generally enough that the weapon will fall from their hand.

Not this time. Just a soft grunt, hardly a noise at all, as he pushed hard on my right elbow, using the leverage to pull his knife hand back.

Oh no you don't. This dance isn't over. I let my right arm fold closer to my face, also letting the point of my blade twist toward his hand while lowering my left foot, stepping right on top of his right foot, my body weight pinning it to the ground, stopping him from pulling back. My left hand now slipped over his hard forearm and I wove it over, around, and under, twisting my hand, extending my claws to dig into the tough, thick material of his jacket right at that armored elbow. The result was that his weapon arm was now pinned tight against me, held under my arm by my enhanced muscles, sharp claws, and the unyielding ballistic nylon of his own clothing. Meanwhile, the tip of my own blade was pushing hard toward his neck, only the super-tough material of his gloved hand stopping it from punching though his palm and into a target rich with veins, arteries, and nerves.

In this position, I should have been able to end the fight right then. With my strength, I had always been able to leverage such a close position against all of my instructors, even the very largest. Pinning his foot gave me control of his balance while my strength should have been enough to force the tip or even the edge of the blade into his black-clad neck. Instead, I found my blade stopped cold, like I hit a wall. Looking at his eyes, I found them hard and determined, unyielding, like the rest of him. He pushed his gloved hand along my blade, the material obviously cut resistant, although I believe I was drawing a little blood.

Somehow he kept his balance for the split-second he needed to jerk his leg and foot free.

In my later teens, my training got... weird. One such instance was a visit to the Everglades, to work with a reptile wrangler. Alligators and invasive Burmese pythons were my sparring partners for a week. Learning to fight opponents much stronger than human normal, much stronger than me, even. This was like that. His power was like trying to control the leg of a big gator or the coils of a fifteen-foot python. Unstoppable.

Inexorably, he ripped his foot from under mine while his left hand got between my blade and his neck. With both feet firmly under him, he spun and twisted, using the fact that I had locked his knife arm to my side as a leverage point to lift me off my feet and throw me to the ground.

I couldn't stop his spinning throw—he was too strong—but I had fought many large men, including those who's very mass could overwhelm my strength in close quarters. So I counter spun while staying locked tight to him, my body weight pulling him off his feet and also slowing his twist just enough that we landed with him on the bottom and my knife and forearm slamming his own hand into his neck while most of my body weight came down on his knife arm. Shoving with my right hand, I rolled first to the left, my body further pressuring his right arm. Then I reversed my roll, *pulling* with my right, twisting back. The idea was to pull the blade free of his bleeding hand, then plunge its tip into his upper chest.

But he held on to the blade and somehow got his left knee between us, then twisted his own body to throw me off him, onto my back.

Now was the time for distance, so I quickly back rolled, pulling my legs under me and coming up fast in case he was trying to close with me. Instead, I found him twice as far away, coming up to his own feet, shaking out his right arm and blade as he focused on me.

He was fast and strong. Stronger than me, even though he was only maybe twenty pounds heavier and just a few inches taller. And he was unbothered by the wound in his left hand and seemed to be shaking off the hyperextension of his right elbow.

That was the moment I thought about shooting him.

Then the dirty green door opened and a blond man in a black suit with wraparound sunglasses came rushing out.

CHAPTER 29

I skipped back even further, figuring I was outnumbered, but my knife-fighting buddy had turned in surprise even as the blond guy closed the distance between them. My first opponent instantly turned his leaf-shaped blade on the new guy, who paid it no attention as he slammed right into the head-wrapped ninja. With one hand, the blond grabbed my fighter and threw him fifteen feet like a sack of cotton, to slam into some kind of machinery a full four feet up off the ground.

Blondie turned my way and I saw the knife handle sticking out from his ribs, the blade obviously deep inside him. He didn't even notice, instead immediately rushing at me.

My right hand threw my blade underhand, just a straight forceful toss, point first, no rotations, while my feet backpedaled. The Bowie stuck in his stomach, a fact he failed to pay any attention to.

Meanwhile, my now free hand was drawing my Glock, and I started to fire the moment it cleared the holster, my hand rocking back to fire from the hip. The first shots were unaimed, just indexed toward my closing attacker, in what's called a speed rock, but my arm was still coming up and pressing the gun outward, while my left hand came up to join it. Bullets one through three hit him in his torso, moving up from stomach to chest as my arms reached eye-level, sights finally lining up on his neck and face.

None of the shots had any effect, at least until the head shots. *Those* got his attention. I emptied the gun, his head snapping back, and his body pulled straight up as rounds four through sixteen smashed into his skull.

But he didn't fall. He stopped, frozen, arms outstretched, face a bloody ruin of smashed skin and bone, brain matter sticking to the hair that had exploded outward from the back of his head, a tunnel through his skull where eyes and nose used to be, the wall behind him visible *through* his skull.

"Caeco report!" Agent Jay sounded in my ear as my hands automatically reloaded the gun. The dead man just shuffled his feet, turning slightly, uncertainly, one eye hanging on the side of his head by the optic nerve, the other one just completely gone. Yet he didn't fall. My other opponent was back on his feet, his own dark eyes locked on the thing I had shot.

"Two contacts. Two factions, one showing signs of alien tech," I said. The nanites in my ears fed me the audio while the ones in my face and head would transmit my voice. "Alien contact refusing to go down."

A sudden movement and the ninja form in black appeared behind the man who refused to die. The razored edge of black steel flashed in the dim light that came from the opened green door. Blond guy sagged backward as my recent opponent severed the tendons behind each knee with a single perfect strike. Falling onto his back, his head a ruined mess, he still tried to grab anything near him with both hands.

"Black blood?" Omega asked over the team channel.

"Negative, standard red. Cranium is eighty percent excavated by gunfire, yet he won't die," I said.

The operator in tactical black stood watching the blond, head cocked, obviously listening to my exchange.

"You are positive on the lack of black blood?" Omega pressed.

"Affirmative. There is nothing black," I said, moving closer to the thrashing body. Something silver gleamed in the hollowed-out skull. "I do see a trace of metal though."

The metal gleam disappeared as the light from the open door was blocked. I turned, seeing rushing men in black suits, my gun automatically locking on the first, my trigger finger stroking as fast as it could. They didn't stop, ignoring bullets that punched through necks and faces, just like they ignored the black blade of my sometime opponent as he slashed through a neck and plunged another leaf-shaped knife into one's chest. Then we were swarmed, overwhelmed with a flood of weighty bodies and power.

Driven straight to the ground, I slammed the gun into the nearest face, smashing mirrored sunglasses while twisting my body to get position. A blue iris with a metallic silver pupil stared back at me as I struggled. I was under at least three men, each bigger than me, each with a terrible strength that more than matched my own. Immobilized, I saw movement over the head of Mr. Broken Glasses. Another man leaned down, studying me from behind his own mirrored aviator glasses. Then he lifted his clenched fist and lashed out at me, and everything went black.

CHAPTER 30

I woke with my eyes still shut but with an instant mental update from the solid stream of information waiting in my internal network. One, I had been out eleven minutes. Two, I was hanging upside down, swinging in a tiny circle. Three, my body was immobile, wrapped tight in something that literally stuck to me. Four, I was naked under my restraints. Five, another body hung three-point-six feet to my left.

Opening my eyes, I fought the glare of bright light, which added to the headache I had from hanging upside down. Concrete floor under me, metal-sided wall in front of me, sounds of multiple people engaging in activities behind me. Moving just my eyes, I looked left and found the other ceiling hanger, a muscular male shape wrapped in silver duct tape, short black hair, Asian features, and eyes shut tight.

First, I attempted electronic communication with my team or Omega, but I got nothing, nanites working fine but unable to get a signal, incoming or outgoing. Next, I took complete stock of my body. Naked, duct taped, and without the gear and weapons from my kit. Head sore from the knockout punch, but residual damage was healing rapidly, and if I had been temporarily concussed, I wasn't now. So other than the lack of clothes and tools of my trade, I was healthy. Facing the wrong way, though. I listened, concentrating on my internal network to help build a picture of what was happening behind me.

Six sets of feet moving purposefully. Metal shifting and moving against other metals and other materials. Powerful electromagnetic fields flaring, twisting, and shifting. Humming sounds as power was fed into technology that my network couldn't identify. But not a single voice or human vocal sound of any type. No grunts, hums, clucks, sighs, nothing. Just the sense of something large taking up much of the open space and bodies working around it. I closed my eyes, letting the nanites do their thing.

Over the years, my brain has learned to direct and work with the tiny machines that flood my body, to the point where much of what I do is as unconscious as lifting an arm or taking a step is for a regular person. Now, images formed in my mind, my own imagination using the input filtered through the nanites to build a picture.

Our captors were working, preparing a large, metallic object that produced such powerful electric fields that it raised the hairs on my unrestrained head. It was a good deal like what I felt when Omega's newest drones were around me.

The image I saw in my head was a craft, dull gray maybe or perhaps silver, ovoid maybe, about the size of a small U-Haul truck, being prepared for something—flight, maybe.

One pair of feet suddenly changed their path, heading my way. A body loomed close to mine, then a hand caught my side and spun me around. Black polished shoes, dark socks leading up to black suit pants, white dress shirt stained red, black suit coat spattered with bits of bone and blood, then a pink neck and face, blond hair, mirrored sunglasses staring down at me.

A hand came up and took off the glasses. Blue irises surrounding a silver grey pupil. The dead man, whose face was now whole and unblemished, said not a single word, cold metallic eyes studying me like a bug. Then he turned and stepped over to the other man, the special operator I had fought hand-to-hand, blade-to-blade.

"You are awake," Dead Blondie said to the captive. His voice was about what I would expect from a man his size and apparent age. Deep and resonant, but it lacked any animation or inflection. Monotone.

The other captive opened his eyes, and they were just as dark as I remembered. They took in the blond guy, then flicked over to me before going back to our captor. I took the opportunity to study him. Asian, dark hair, dark eyes, compact and muscular, calm. During intense training, Mitch sometimes said I was cool like a cucumber, which I think is a pretty stupid phrase. But it popped into my mind as I looked at the operator who had matched my skill and exceeded my strength. I think I might have the edge on him for speed though. But he was human, not werewolf or vampire, but maybe a human like me. Enhanced. Some kind of modern ninja, maybe. Then I thought about his knife—leaf-shaped blade, dual blood grooves, no hilt, wood grip. Chinese combat blade. Not Japanese ninja... Chinese special operator of some kind.

The blond guy squatted down, reaching out a hand to turn both our hanging forms so that our faces looked his way. "You carried physical protection that we have removed," he said to me, then turned to the other, "while your protection is tattooed to your body." The index finger of the hand touching the Chinese spy tapped a spot at the back of the man's neck, right where it met the shoulders. "We will remove it too. Then you will both be part of us."

The whole message was delivered without any emotion on his face, without inflection in his voice. And as soon as he finished speaking, he stood and turned, moving away from us. I watched him as far as my eyes would move, then looked back to find my sparring buddy staring at me.

"You are Caeco," he said, making it a statement. His voice was masculine but soft.

"You know me?"

"We know of you," he said. "I am Fan."

"*Lethal*? Your name means lethal," I said, Chinese being one of many languages I had learned growing up. "That's a bold choice. What if you had grown up soft and weak?"

A flicker of a smile flashed across his handsome upside-down face. As my own self was also upside down, it looked normal. His crew cut hair barely hung away from his skull, while I could feel my own short cut brushing the floor.

"I had as much chance of growing up soft and weak as you did," he said.

"And you are here to kill me?"

A flicker of a frown. "No, I did not know who you were when we fought. I am here for this," he said, eyes flicking back and forth to include the space we were in.

"And how is it going so far?" I asked.

Another fast frown. "Less than optimal."

"Really? I thought for sure you were going to tell me this was all part of your master plan?"

A movement inside his adhesive-tape-wrapped cocoon that might have been a shrug. "We are alive."

Exactly my attitude. In fact, the whole time I had been chatting with the competition, I had been working my claws through the tape holding me captive. Oddly, the men in black had just taped my hands right to my sides, not bothering to secure them together in front or back. There was pain from twisting my wrists and hands, the strong adhesive of the tape pulling hard against my skin, but nothing that would ever slow me down.

Here's a little secret... this wasn't the first time I've been duct taped up like a moth in a spider's web. In fact, it wasn't even the second time. More like number four. And I was naked for at least two of the other times. So I had started to flex muscles and body parts as soon as Blondie turned his back. And based on the tiny movements I could detect on Fan's cocoon, he was doing the same. Hmm. Apparently we had a lot in common. I felt a tear as the claws on my right hand pierced the tape, then froze in place when Fan's eyes shifted instantly to that spot. Then he looked behind me before bringing his gaze back to mine. "They are not watching," he said, even as he continued to move his own body within the tape.

"Will your people come for you?" I asked.

"No. I am alone here. You?"

"Oh yeah."

"They will fail. Your FBI is no match for Vorsook forces. You saw what I saw."

"Yeah, like the Black Frost Blade infection in Rome and China... but different."

"Exactly. So your people will only die. We must effect our own escapes."

"Well that's always best, but my team isn't the only player on my side of the equation," I said.

"The computer? You were talking with the computer... back when we fought?"

"Yup." My left-hand claw tips made it through the tape while my right side was continuing to slice and tear. Leaving my hands at my sides was different from my other experiences with being restrained by duct tape. It offered its own challenges. But between my reinforced bones and ligaments, enhanced muscles, and ability to control pain, my eventual freedom was just a matter of time. Nevermind the damage my skin was taking, or the distraction of hairs being pulled out follicle by follicle. If I did manage to get out, I could at least ignore Jetta's waxing suggestions for a month or two.

"You are amused by this?" Fan asked, curious.

"Just thinking I don't want to be caught naked and trussed up like a turkey when help arrives," I said.

"You believe the computer would intervene? Would it not make more logic for it to simply destroy this building rather than risk a fight in a heavily populated city?"

"You are a fountain of cheery thoughts, Fan. Didn't your instructors teach you to think positive?"

"Not of others. Only of my own abilities, my own determination," he said, then flicked his eyes away from me to something behind me. As my ears were already telling me that more footsteps were approaching, I stopped my motions and retracted my claws.

Blond dude was back, a wicked-looking scalpel in his right hand. "Removal of your tattoo will render you available to control. It will not take much time, but it will be painful," the man said, tone emotionless. I spun both wrists, hard, claws ripping back out, my arms exploding from the tape. The blond man turned my way, expressionless, watching as I jackknifed up, my right hand cutting the rope that held me suspended while my left slashed the tape between my feet and legs.

I fell hard on my back, squirming to get free, as Blondie lifted one foot and pressed it down onto to me, driving my body against the floor. Thrashing my legs while simultaneously sinking my claws into Blondie's leg, I yanked hard, pulling his foot out into a two-legged split that would have seriously stunned a normal guy. But I'm not sure he was even a guy anymore. He didn't so much as grunt as one leg extended in front and one behind. He simply put both hands on the floor and pushed hard, shoving himself straight up like a spring, his feet scissoring together underneath him. The scalpel was on the floor and he bent to grab it.

The ground thundered and shook, bouncing me on the ground, shaking the metal frame of the building, dust and debris falling from above. Blondie had to jump to keep from falling, then landed and froze in midmotion, locking up like a robot, giving me time to scramble backward on all fours. When he finally unlocked, he straightened and turned toward the wall that I was facing from my position on the ground. All of his fellow men in black turned at the same time he did, exactly as he did, looking at the wall behind Fan, who still bucked and twisted on his rope. The wall suddenly seemed to rip itself apart, sections of it disappearing so suddenly, it was as if a tornado had plucked the building's siding off in solid chunks. The sounds of sharp, whistling wind lent quite a bit of credence to that theory.

CHAPTER 31

Cool air gusted into the newly torn opening, blowing the white fur of the seven-foot monster that was suddenly outlined in the flood of sodium-powered security light coming from outside. One moment the siding was there, then it was gone, and then the beast was blocking the light.

She was crouched there, one long corded arm reaching down to knuckle the ground as she leaned forward on steel-spring legs, massive jaws chomping, bright yellow raging eyes shining in the shadow of her face. Never thought I'd see *her* at *my* rescue. Chris or Tanya or both, but not her. The possibility of facing her in her hybrid form had certainly occurred to me before, my training requiring me to prepare for such a fight. What happened next disabused me of any notions that I was ready for such a fight.

Without any hesitation, the men in black rushed forward, charging the werewolf, their arms outstretched as if mere superhuman strength and near invulnerability was a match for her. Please. She tore the head off the first to reach her with an almost casual swipe of one paw, her other hand punching the second MIB in the chest—through the chest—out the back. She used his thrashing body to knock the headless one aside, then flung her arm straight back, the body ripping free from her hand, thrown out the hole in the wall, leaving a big chunk of spine clutched in her paw. It shone metallic in the lights, twisting and convulsing like a two-foot boa constrictor instead of dangling limply like it should have. The werewolf dropped it to the ground and launched herself like a Navy jet catapulting off the end of a carrier.

Her leap took her right between two more of the MIB. I was momentarily impressed when they stepped apart and caught her between them. A perfectly synchronized catch. Over three hundred pounds of speeding muscle and dense bone stopped dead. Immediately they tried to pull her in opposite directions, like they might be able to yank her arms from their sockets. Nope. She twisted her arms and sank both taloned hands into their torsos even as they tugged on her. Her shoulders and back flexed, and her giant arms slammed together, yanking the men in black right off their feet. Ribs popped and other bones crunched with wet sounds. Then, when they were pressed together, shoulder to shoulder, her head snaked forward, gaping jaws slamming shut like hydraulic steel scissors. A ripping sound, loud, but short in duration, and then she snapped her head to the left, jaws opening, round heads flying through the air, one hitting Fan in the back, the other thudding onto the concrete and rolling almost to Blondie's feet. Stacia growled our way, eyes locked on Blondie and the last of his MIB buddies, even as her giant taloned hands grabbed the outside arms of the headless bodies and ripped them like turkey thighs from their still-moving bodies. It was fast, all four alien guards torn into thrashing, twitching chunks in the space of several seconds and the whole time she was shredding them, I was moving, getting my arms and legs under me to stand up, still stuck in duct tape.

Sudden orange light flared outside, a roaring whoosh of streaming flames coming from somewhere very close by, waves of heat billowing into the building.

Stacia twisted and tossed, first one, then the second headless body behind her, toward the roaring flames outside. Then she turned toward the four of us: Blondie, his last MIB buddy, Fan twisting on his rope, and myself. Her jaws opened as she leaned forward and she roared loud enough to shake dust from the rafters.

Finally upright, I stepped backward, or at least hobbled backward, every hair on my legs tearing free as I pushed my legs into motion. Fan was writhing about but he ceased all movement as soon as I got to him. The claws of my right hand slashed the rope while my left hand caught the falling strands and slowed his fall.

Blondie glanced back at us, then turned back toward the biggest threat in the room, his motions mirrored by the only other MIB left. Just as oddly, they both froze for the space of a heartbeat. Then Blondie turned and raced backward, toward the big silver craft that took up most of the industrial room we were in, while his companion turned and ran straight into the werewolf meat grinder.

Stacia tore that one literally limb from limb in the blink of an eye, but by the time she was done, Blondie was already at the metallic orb, crawling under it and jumping straight up through what must have been an opening in its underside. The sounds of something metal snicking into place came from the underside and then the entire vehicle suddenly thrummed with bone-shaking power. Another angry roar shook the room but this one came from the wall opening, where Declan's not-so-little dragonette was stalking through, wing tips working as forefeet. The dragon pulled back its head and turned to the thrashing body parts on the floor, neck swelling in warning.

"Look away!" I said to Fan, whose feet were now free of tape. He followed my instruction with admirable speed, and not a second to soon, as white-hot light illuminated the room, heating the air to almost searing temperatures.

Then there was another blinding flash, this one from the silver aircraft, painful even through my eyelids. I felt the mass of the aircraft shift upward in a wave of power that raised every one of the hairs on my head, short as they were. There was a sizzle and *crump* sound followed by the metallic twang of building parts ripping and tearing. I opened my eyes to find the spacecraft gone, a hole torn through the building's roof, the metal edges glowing red hot where something intense had burned through.

A sharp chuffing brought me around to face the huge white werewolf who was staring holes in us from ten feet away. We paused there for a second, she and I, locking eyes. Then her head snapped toward the hole in the wall, impatiently. Behind her, the dragon watched as the MIB bodies popped and sizzled inside an inferno of burning flesh, its head tilted to one side, more doglike than reptilian. Rivulets of molten metal ran out of the flames, trickling along the charred and broken concrete floor, forming into small pools of hot orange liquid. Even the metal spine had slumped into a melted snake-like line.

"We have to go," I said to Fan.

"That message was clear to me too, even without speaking a word of werewolf," he said, ripping more of the tape apart with bare hands so that he could walk. He didn't change his deadpan expression, yet that sounded almost flippant.

Outside, flashes of actinic, eye-searing light lit the shipyard. When we stepped through the hole in the building, we found a frenetic aerial battle taking place a hundred feet above us. The hovering silver Vorsook craft was dodging and weaving over the roof of the massive building as multiple black Omega orbs of all sizes flew and spun about it. Bolts of sun-hot power shot back and forth, force shields flaring in response. At least one mini-orb was overpowered by a beam from the alien craft, its energy screens collapsing in an intense explosion, the shockwave strong enough to knock me off my feet.

Standing ten feet from the shredded and torn opening in the

wall was Declan O'Carroll, leaning on a black thorn cane, watching the aerial battle rage overhead. Shifting rubble brought my head around to find Stacia, still in hybrid wolf-woman form, standing six short feet away, eyes locked on us. Well, mainly on Fan, who was watching her warily while simultaneously trying to see the dogfight.

"You alright?" Declan asked without turning around. I opened my mouth to answer but a sudden flare of orange light and plume of smoke jetted out of the building we had just vacated, the sound, heat, and light all interrupting my response. When it lessened a bit, I answered. "Yeah, thanks for the help. Didn't expect you guys. Was thinking maybe Tanya or Chris."

"I'm sure they would have, but they're not in New York right now. Somewhere out on the West Coast, I think," he said, glancing my way, taking note of Fan before then turning back to the dogfight above.

"I'm surprised Omega let you come," I said, watching him carefully amid the flashes of technologically created lightning and plasma overhead. "In your weakened condition."

"He has trouble saying no to me, especially when I make sense," he said with a half smirk. He wasn't doing anything that I could see, just leaning on that cane, but I knew that didn't mean a damned thing where he was concerned. "Your team is about a half mile back that way. We convinced them to stay back. Can't protect everyone, you know," he said.

"That implies that you can protect even *someone,*" I answered, glancing at Fan to see how he was reacting. Standing almost at attention, somehow making his duct tape look like it might be a uniform, he was alternately watching Declan and the drone fight, eyes wide with interest, body angled to keep Stacia in sight too.

A sudden stray beam of intense power flashed down, straight

at us. White light flared out across an invisible dome rising up over the witch and the rest of us, making it obvious that he was, in fact, still a witch. The intense power of the energy bolt suddenly vanished, as if a giant mystical straw had sucked it away like the last bit of a vanilla shake.

“Yeah. Not fully recovered yet, but getting there. Some things are different,” he said, nodding at the cane, completely ignoring the death ray that would have incinerated at least one of us.

“That *shillelagh* a family heirloom?” Two can play at nonchalance.

“Yeah. Aunt Ash brought it from Ireland. It was my grandfather’s. Got some boosting runes and stuff on it. Helps with my stamina,” he said, the last bit sort of an embarrassed admission.

“I’m sure Stacia appreciates you having a stamina boost,” I said.

Fan shot me a look of what might have been disbelief. Hard to tell with that poker face.

A grinding growl came from the werewolf. Not anger—amused, maybe?

“Yeah, well you’ll excuse me if I put all my energy into healing,” he said, glaring at me and giving his wolf an annoyed look.

Fan was still staring at me like I was an idiot.

“But you have your magic?” I asked, ignoring the Chinese operative’s glance.

“Yeah, not fully yet, but enough—for this,” he said, looking up as the alien craft took three separate hits from two of Omega’s drones. “It’s putting up a hell of a fight, but the writing is on the wall," he said. It was. I've been trained to fly small aircraft and even handle a helicopter if necessary, but I had no training in aerial combat. Still, it was clear that the alien ship was outnumbered and facing much greater combined firepower.

"Why doesn't it just flee?" I wondered.

"The others would have clear fields of fire. They are just as fast and their energy beams are speed of light," Fan said with almost no discernible accent. "It would not make it."

Declan turned and looked at him, a hint of surprise on his features. His blue eyes glowed a little, something I'd seen just a few times before. After studying the man, he nodded. "Yes Agent Fan, that's pretty much it in a nutshell."

"You know him?" I asked.

Declan shook his head, pointing at the Bluetooth unit in one ear. "Omega does. Apparently he's your Chinese equivalent—him and his sister."

It was Fan's turn to be surprised, the expression just a quick flash. If I hadn't been watching, I would have missed it entirely.

Another set of vision-stunning shots blasted the silver orb, one from directly overhead and another from the side.

The silver Vorsook vehicle was visibly rocked by the shots, but it settled down and then suddenly changed course, zipping across the sky to come hover almost directly over our group. Over Declan, in particular. Two big pulses of extra-intense power shot straight down, hitting Declan's shields, the bolts in a direct line with his body.

White light flooded out along the arc of his shield, spreading all the way to the ground, our entire group suddenly under a solid dome of brilliant light. The arc was huge, at least thirty feet in diameter, and despite the obvious power of the beams,

I couldn't feel any heat at all. Wounded, my ass.

Then the light retreated back up the dome, like curtains rising, coming together at the top where it just disappeared, again, like some great vacuum had sucked it up.

Under the dome, Declan stepped back, legs clearly shaky, and the white werewolf was suddenly right behind him, massive arms spread out to catch him. But he steadied himself, pushed himself upright as he took a deep breath, and then held his right hand up, palm out, pointing at the Vorsook ship.

A massive beam of sun-hot light shot out of his palm, straight at the alien craft, and the results were spectacular.

His beam, twice the thickness of anything any of the fighting craft had fired so far, caused the alien's shields to flare like an arc welder before blasting straight through with hardly a pause. It punched into the silver metal that sheathed the craft and turned it to orange-white liquid in a micro-instant. The Vorsook machine shuddered for a moment, then it just seemed to come all apart in a thunderous explosion that blasted the ground, flinging trucks, a forklift, steel plating material, and several metal sheds in all directions. It even rocked one of the dry docked ships in its cradle, the vessel twisting to one side like it was capsizing on dry land.

Three round battle orbs and the long cigar-shaped transport drone flashed into the space between us and the explosion, their combined shields keeping much of the blast, flame, and debris from reaching Declan's shield, but doing nothing to stop the jolt and jump of the ground under our feet.

Declan turned and grinned first at his wolfish girlfriend before looking triumphantly at us. Then his grin faltered, the cane slipped out of his fingers, and his body collapsed backward into her white-furred arms. I saw a little panic in his eyes but then it disappeared as she took his weight and steadied him, folding her legs to prop him on her white-furred lap.

“Like I said… still pretty weak, but my ability to transform energy is even better than before,” he said, coughing a little. “The UFO itself gave me the power to destroy it. How’s that for Art of War?” The massive wolf growled. “If I don’t pass out completely,” he admitted with a wince in her direction.

CHAPTER 32

Stacia's body shimmered and twisted, her Change faster than any I had ever seen other than Awasos, who was almost instantaneous with his form switches. It left the witch kid leaning against her folded naked body. Part of me wondered what he felt, what sensations, if any, he experienced when she shifted. It was, after all, a form of magic. Whatever it was, he didn't so much as flinch while the shift happened.

Instead, he reached for his ever-present bag, what he called his Crafting bag, pulling open the flap. Now human and naked, Stacia took it from his shaking hands and plucked out simple black clothing from inside. He leaned forward, using his arms to prop himself up while she stood and dressed with quick, efficient motions. In fact, he turned and looked at me closely, then turned to Fan, frowning.

"Nice duct tape outfit. Comfortable?"

I frowned at him. "Your snappy repartee is faltering a bit there."

He laughed. "Yeah, not my best work. I can probably weaken the adhesive on that tape if you like. Where are your clothes?"

I turned and pointed back at the building, everyone following my finger in time to see Declan's dragon come waddling out.

"Might still be there. Draco's accuracy has gotten really good," Stacia said, speaking for the first time. Her tone was mild, matter-of-fact, as if she hadn't just been a giant killer monster a mere moment before. There was also a mild note of uncertainty in it that made me doubt if I'd ever see my clothes and gear again.

After exchanging a look with her, I shrugged and started in the direction of the building, wincing at the pull of the tape. Declan chuckled, then waved one hand. Instantly the hair and skin pulling ceased, the tape now sliding, where a moment before it had stuck aggressively.

Fan followed my lead, walking toward the opening, and I noticed his own movements were smoother, less restricted.

Inside, I got my first full look at the LOA space. It was big, my internal network estimating a rectangular space, thirty feet wide and all of seventy-five feet long. The rear section, where the ship had been, was covered in debris from the ceiling but otherwise intact. The front third was a mess, charred piles of carbon on shattered concrete, a few pieces of torn metal siding lying about. The middle of the room was set up as a work space, with tables and machinery laid out in an orderly pattern, and seemed mostly intact. One of the workbenches had clothing and gear stacked on it and I headed straight for it, pulling whole pieces of tape off my body as I walked.

"I must say, your rescuers were unexpected," Fan said, walking alongside me, dropping his own trail of duct tape behind him. "My pre-mission intelligence indicated a fissure your relationship with the Warlock."

"Yeah, well, your people are behind the curve," I said, finding my stuff and rummaging through it. It was mostly intact, for which I was grateful, as I had figured that the MIB had most likely just cut it off my body. That they had taken the time to carefully pull it all off me was slightly disturbing at some level, one that I'd have to revisit at a later time. For now, I grabbed some industrial paper towels from a stack and rubbed off as much of the tacky tape residue as I could, then pulled on my clothes, ignoring the remaining discomfort as inconsequential. After wearing a suit of duct tape, having sticky underwear was nothing. My gun and most of my gear was there, laid out in precise rows next to Fan's gear. His was mostly blades—a lot of blades—but also included a wire garrote, several small lights with red lenses, thin black cord—silk or Kevlar maybe—throwing darts, a phone, and a couple of small black leather pouches. Minimalist. He too was pulling on his clothing and I couldn't help but notice just how good his physical condition was. Corded and compact, like a gymnast or martial artist. Very little body hair, almost no body fat, and an extremely well-developed posterior. I only noticed in that passing, you know, as I assessed him for potential weaknesses in combat. Sure.

"My superiors will receive news of his condition positively," he said suddenly, without looking my way. I started putting my gear away about my body.

"That he's still weak or that he retains his magic?"

"That he is healing and still a witch. His abilities, even at this stage, remain formidable. Unlike your politicians, our leaders have no doubts about the alien threat. The Warlock is considered one of this world's primary weapons."

"Why were you here—tonight? To intercept me?"

He shook his head, dark eyes turning to met my gaze. "You already accused me of that. I did not know you would be infiltrating tonight. We only knew that your team was investigating the same thing that I was sent to find—the source of the disinformation regarding the aliens."

"The Chinese government sent a biologically engineered operative to root out a US disinformation source?"

"As I said, this threat is worldwide. We cannot afford to have any nation, let alone one of the biggest, lose its will to fight before the fight has even begun. My mission priority is very, very high."

"Yeah, well, we've got it under control," I said, putting a fresh magazine in my pistol and holstering it. Then I headed back outside, not looking to see if he followed. He did, my senses of smell and hearing confirming that fact.

Outside, I found multiple first responder vehicles with flashing emergency lights parked around the building and the crater that had formed when Declan blew up the spaceship. Our team Suburban was there and Agent Jay looked my way from her spot next to a still-seated Declan and a standing Stacia. She nodded at me while Mitch Allen and Chana Mazar approached me directly from the crash site.

"You okay, Cakewalk?" Mitch asked, looking me over before shifting his gaze to Fan. Chana, on the other hand, had been studying Fan from the moment she caught sight of us.

"Yeah. Peachy."

"So the rumors of the *Yazi* are true," Chana said, speaking to Fan.

"Yazi as in one of the nine dragon sons? A hybrid of wolf and dragon..." I said. Have I mentioned that I am well-versed in the cultures of America's primary opponents? "You know what he is?"

"Just whispers that Israeli intelligence had picked up."

"I guess it makes sense that they named the project for the dragon son that likes fighting," I said, staring first at her and then Fan.

"Very good, Caeco," Chana said, smiling at me before turning to Fan. "Once we knew about you, we figured you couldn't be the only engineered human in the world by this time. We had heard rumors of both Chinese and Russian projects, similar in scope to what AIR achieved in you. We could never confirm them."

"Apparently I'm the last to know," I said. "Omega seems to know all about him... and his sister."

"Two? A sister? That's fantastic," Chana said.

For his part, Fan had frozen in place, dark eyes glittering with a light I didn't like. My instincts told me he was tense although outwardly he appeared no different than he had a moment before.

Suddenly, a black orb the size of a grapefruit zipped into the middle of the four of us, hovering motionless.

"*I have only recently discovered of the existence of other engineered individuals—particularly Project Yazi. The government of China does a much, much better job of keeping secret projects off computers and all unshielded electronics than the West does,*" Omega said.

Fan's jaw clenched for a moment, then he decided to speak. "As it should *still* be."

"*Your spy chiefs have maintained internal security for the most part, but there is a faction that almost always has inside knowledge of the Middle Kingdom.*"

"The Coven," I guessed.

"*Correct.*"

"You understand this is one of our highest state secrets?" Fan asked, his tone hard.

"You recognize that they took the risk of exposing you when they sent you. I mean, you'd have to kill everyone here to hide it and somehow, I don't see that happening," Chana said. "Plus there's Omega."

Across the open lot, Stacia's head had snapped around at Chana's words and my engineered vision saw the yellow bleed over her normally green irises. Declan and Agent Jay continued their conversation, unaware of any sudden tensions.

Fan held Chana's gaze for a moment, then looked away. Again, there wasn't anything really visible as a cue, but somehow I sensed he had backed away from the edge of sudden violence. He brought up both hands, palms out, motions slow and graceful. "Such a thing would be at odds with my primary goals even if I could achieve it, which is highly doubtful."

"No shit," I said, eyeing him sideways. His only response was to raise one eyebrow.

"Oooh, dude! She just called you out," Mitch said, seemingly relaxed but it was obvious, at least to me, that he wasn't comfortable with the assassin's presence. Something about the way he held his short-barreled HK carbine across his chest gave him away.

Fan studied the larger American agent without concern, practically exuding confidence. "She is, as the phrase goes, a handful."

I snorted, then left the other three to walk over toward my boss, the witch kid, and the wary werewolf who was still keeping an eye on Fan. Stacia switched her gaze to me and I gave her a little nod, keeping my expression blank. After a second she nodded back, just once, then her eyes moved back to Fan.

Both Agent Jay and Declan looked up when I got close. Behind them, farther away, I could see Alice and Seth talking with local law enforcement types, just on the outskirts of the wreckage. Farther away, I could see men and women who were being held back by uniformed cops. They had the look of people worried about their commercial enterprises. Directly overhead, at least three of Omega's big orbs were on station, motionless, while more than a dozen of the small ones zipped here and there.

"Declan said you were unharmed?" Agent Jay asked, bringing my attention squarely back to my boss.

"Correct. Just some torn skin from my restraints," I said. "Any sign of the actual Vorsook?" I asked, nodding toward the wreckage.

They exchanged a look, which annoyed me for some reason. Oh yeah (mental finger snap), it was because my boss was acting all pally-pally with my ex-boyfriend and his new girlfriend. Of course they did just rescue me, so maybe I should cut them some slack.

"We don't think it was here," Agent Jay said. "Just the... guards."

"Well, something was controlling them because they kept acting in unison and freezing up like they were waiting for instructions," I said, trying to squash my initial annoyance. "How far away could it be?"

"Not sure. I could sense something while the battle was underway, but nothing like Nika told me about," Declan said. "I think it was or is quite a ways away. Miles."

I turned to Jay. "Bryn Mawr?"

"That's my thought too," she said, her eyes flicking behind me. My own senses, plus the tightness that I saw on Stacia's features, told me that it was Fan who was now walking up behind me.

"You will attempt to capture the alien. I will attend," he said like it was all settled.

"You are a foreign operative on US soil. You will be the guest of the local field office," Agent Jay said, nodding toward the parked vehicles. A new sedan had pulled up and I saw SAC Richards heading our way.

I was about to open my mouth and protest. To explain to SAC Jay that no regular FBI team would be able to contain Fan, just as I was confident that they couldn't contain me. But something in her eyes, a little gleam of mischief, told me to keep my mouth shut.

"We'll go with you," Declan said to Agent Jay.

"That's a hard no," Stacia said instantly. He turned a frown in her direction and it bounced off like she was Kevlar. "No convalescing super witches near telepathic aliens. That's rule number one, right Omega?"

"Affirmative, Stacia. Father, there was logic in letting you help take out the aircraft, as your shields have come back just as strong if not stronger, as has your ability to redirect energy. But fighting mind control from a creature who almost bested Nika is not an option. I, myself, had no doubt that the Vorsook was not at this location or I would not have transported you here. You are far too valuable a weapon to risk at this point."

"Traitor," he said, but he did look pretty done in. I was thinking about Omega's last sentence. That sounded a little mercenary. Omega, to my knowledge, would never risk Declan at all. I would have to review that comment later.

"There is one thing you can do," I said, earning myself an immediate and deadly glare from Stacia. "I gave my amulet to the president to protect him from Vorsook control. I had a team one, but the spacemen in Armani suits took it. It wasn't with my gear, so I'm thinking it's just charcoal by now."

He snorted. "That team crap that Krista's Circle sold you guys? How many of you are there?"

"Twelve!" Agent Jay said faster than I could respond.

"Twelve? Oh. You want some extras. Clever, Agent Jay. I'll make you a baker's dozen. Lucky thirteen," he said. "As long as my wardens say it's okay, of course," he added, frowning at Stacia. He was prideful for sure.

Stacia smiled a cold, deadly smile and leaned down to whisper in his ear. Whatever she said, it was so soft that I couldn't hear a word of it. Declan's face went white, his eyes suddenly nervous. "Ah, she says sure. Omega, I need my stuff on the transport, please," he said. The platinum blonde smiled, extremely self-satisfied, utterly confident. My desire to hate her was overwhelmed by curiosity at whatever ploy she had just used to shut him down.

"Thanks for the save, by the way," I said, directing my words to her. Surprise flashed across her features, quickly shunted away. She tucked perfect hair behind a perfect ear with a perfect finger. "Sure. Draco helped. Tore the siding off and melted up those annoying guards."

Right on cue, the little dragon—who was much bigger than the last time I had seen him—waddled over and slumped down like a dog, his head on his master's legs.

"What were they, by the way?" Declan asked.

"*Vorsook version of nano technology. The recipient is rendered into an automaton—obedient, strong, and almost invulnerable. But the individual personality is completely gone.*" The torpedo-shaped transport drone floated down out of the night sky, its hatch opening silently. "*Your materials are on board, Father.*"

"Right. I'll get those done and then I believe we are leaving," Declan said, standing up, legs a little stiff but less wobbly than before. Picking up his cane, he moved to the drone and climbed inside.

CHAPTER 32

"So these are gonna keep that alien from taking control of us?" Alice Barrows asked, clearly not convinced as she twirled her new amulet on its cord. "The one that the computer won't let its creator help us with because it's afraid *he'll* be controlled!"

We were parked a few streets away from the Morrell house in Bryn Mawr, holding a team meeting in the Suburban.

"That's a good question, Alice," Agent Jay said, nodding. "It seems so counterintuitive that a witch as strong as the Warlock could be at risk, but he is still healing. His ability against the UFO was based on elemental magic he was borrowing from his dragon and his skill at shifting energy from one source to another—in this case, the UFO's own weapons. But his inherent personal power is still low. Even he can't borrow magic *all* the time. And it's been explained to me that mind magic is very different from using Air, Water, Earth, or Fire."

"While making a warded amulet is like putting a rechargeable battery into a solar-powered flashlight," Chana said. "Especially runic amulets like Declan is skilled with. The runes draw power to the Rowan wood, which holds it like a capacitor. Other runes push out a protective field that blocks magic, especially mind magic."

"Then why doesn't he make himself an amulet and help us?" Alice asked.

"You really think it's a good idea to risk it?" Mitch asked. "I *know* you were there when we watched that UFO blast him and Cakewalk and Miss Reynolds with those laser beams or phasers or whatever they were. He soaked them up and then blew that ship out of the sky with one hand! What if a Vorsook had hold of *him?"*

"Yeah, it would be like getting a nuclear weapon stolen," Eve added from her computer lab back in DC.

"Easy for you to say... you're safe at headquarters," Alice griped. "You didn't see those people in the bars!"

"Well, that thing wasn't able to control us then with our old amulets, so no way can it do so now," I said, grabbing my own warded charm.

"You really okay with this?" Alice asked, frowning at me.

"Yeah. There's a lot of history between us, but Declan is the single strongest witch I have ever heard of. Stuff he makes is tops. You could sell that ward for thousands of dollars."

"Really?" Alice looked at her wooden jewelry with a new eye.

"Tens of thousands, actually," Agent Jay said. "Not that anyone *will* be selling team equipment. And it would be *much* worse than losing a nuke or even ten," Agent Jay said. "What if he asked that elemental under the seabed *for* a 9.7 magnitude quake, rather than asking for help getting rid of one? What if he asked Yellowstone to erupt?"

The whole team went silent and I watched the realization come over the faces around me.

"He can ransom the whole world," Mitch said.

"*Someone* with that power could hold the world hostage, but not him," I said.

"Okay, I get that you went out with him and still like the kid, but absolute power corrupts absolutely," Alice said to me.

"Yeah, I had this same conversation with the president and his cabinet. Declan O'Carroll was born with more power at his fingertips than most small nations. Now he arguably commands powers that we are *actively* hoping can stop an ancient world-conquering race of aliens. And Agent Jay and I just watched him back down from Omega and Stacia. Why? Because it is who he is."

"Nobody is that good," Mitch said.

"His mother was raped by his father," I said. "You want to light a match on that kid's temper, just show him a rapist. Yet I was there when he *met* his father for the first time in Burlington. Guess what? That town is still standing and his father is still alive. Why? Because he's some kind of wimp? Too afraid to do anything? No, he's the exact opposite. One of the strongest people I know. He was raised to wield this power correctly and to never abuse it—from birth. Don't you think it odd that he's *that* dangerous yet he's protected by the world's most advanced computer that he just happened to risk his life *two* times to save? The same computer that could also wipe out human life yet uses *him* as a role model and instead protects us? And that that same computer refused to let him come with us, as did his current girlfriend? And he *listened* to them? Although I have no idea what she said to him."

"She threatened to embarrass him in front of the others," Agent Jay said.

"What? You could hear her?" I asked, incredulous.

She smirked, shaking her head. "Nope, but I know a lot about how people in relationships argue and I can read body language with the best. Some inside thing between them, probably not even that big a deal."

"Probably threatened to cut him off," Mitch said. "You know? From sex."

"Shit, you're right!" Morris said. Even Seth was nodding.

"Frigging men," Alice said, disgusted.

"Well, I'm just saying. It'd work on me," Mitch said.

"Wimp," Chana said.

"Nah, I'd cave too," Seth said. "That woman is *fine.* What?" he asked in response to all the glares that suddenly shot his way.

"Regardless, Caeco is right. There is really nothing preventing Mr. O'Carroll from abusing his power except Mr. O'Carroll. Yes, Stacia Reynolds holds enormous influence over him, as do his aunt and Omega."

"And Chris and Tanya," I said. "And his friends."

"Which includes you. He left his sickbed and came here to help rescue you," Agent Jay said.

"Girlfriend can't be too happy about that!" Alice said with raised eyebrows.

"Girlfriend was first into the building and girlfriend tore all those MIB bastards to pieces, literally," I said.

"Okay, we're way, way off topic. Everyone clear on why Mr. O'Carroll is not on the remainder of this mission?" Jay asked. The team nodded. "Okay, back to the issue at hand. We *think* the Vorsook that is behind all this subversion is at the Morrell residence here in Bryn Mawr. It is up to us to capture it or, barring that, stop it."

"You mean kill it?" Chana said, frowning.

"I mean stop it. If that means that it dies, so be it. This isn't a regular criminal, or even a supercriminal. It's an advanced alien intelligence with the power to control humans. We need to think through every aspect of this operation. How do we approach? What are its possible responses? How do we capture it? How do we safely contain it if we do catch it? What do we do with it after that?" Jay asked.

"I'm okay with deadly force if it comes to that," Mitch said, his tone serious. "Even if we're not affected by it, every unprotected human around us will be. We can't be shooting down civilians, cops, or other agents that this thing takes over. No way can we hold it alive."

"We actually have an answer for holding it," Jay admitted. "Caeco?"

"Declan already thought about that. When he made these amulets, he also made a... I guess you'd call it a portable circle. To contain it," I said, reaching into the bag containing the extra amulets. The coil of wire, cord, and quartz that I pulled out was bound with plastic zip ties. "Basically it's like those beach tents that you pull out of their bag and toss on the sand. The ones that spring open and set themselves up? A large, spring-like wire loop that's been twisted back onto itself. It'll pop open to a diameter of about three feet. The quartz pieces woven into it are spelled and charged with magic, like our necklaces but stronger. The three strings tied around the perimeter allow us to pull the uncoiled circle over the ground."

"Caeco and I have briefed the president," Jay said, picking up as I left off. "A special Oracle transport vehicle is on its way, along with Oracle operatives trained to use it. When we get the alien into this circle, they'll take over moving it to a secure facility."

"What kind of place is secure against this thing?" Mitch asked at the same time that Chana frowned and said, "Special transport?"

Agent Jay shot me a look, her own face showing just a tiny trace of discomfort. "Mr. O'Carroll suggested both. He was aware of them and feels they are strong enough to hold this thing, although he suggested that very special procedures will have to be implemented."

Mitch looked from the boss to me, then back. "Wait—this truck and facility were made to try and contain O'Carroll himself, weren't they?"

I nodded. "Yeah, that's what he said."

"And he was already aware of them? That's F'd up," Alice said. "Wait... would they really hold him?"

"Caeco asked him and he wouldn't answer. Just smiled," Jay said, looking disturbed.

"Well, he wouldn't want to admit it, would he? That they could contain him?" Eve asked.

"Actually, Caeco thinks he wouldn't want to admit that it *couldn't* hold him," Jay said. Everyone looked at me.

I shrugged. "People in power are already afraid of him. Why add to it?"

"Okay, back to the mission, again," Jay said. "So we have the means to restrain the Vorsook, and we have transport and longer-term containment. Now, the hardest part: How do we get this thing? And what will go wrong?"

Mitch suddenly shuddered, hard. He looked around at the team. "Sorry, just had a mental image of hundreds of old rich, retired people in their pajamas coming at us like zombies."

"If it makes you feel better, there's also Bryn Mawr college nearby. All girls' school," Seth said, one eyebrow raised.

Mitch started to look relieved, the beginnings of a smile forming.

"Bet some of those old people sleep naked," Alice said, immediately wiping the grin off Mitch's face.

"Well, that's all very, very real," Jay said. Mitch stared at her and she shook her head. "I mean about the neighbors being controlled. And this thing must know that its ship is toast."

"Omega?" I asked.

"It is highly improbable that it doesn't know the fate of its craft. It was, we believe, in control of the fight through its avatars—the ones you call men in black," Omega answered instantly.

"Shit! It was listening to us the whole time?" Alice said, her expression horrified.

"Miss Barrows, I am basically everywhere around you. If there is a computer chip nearby, I can be present."

She shook her head, "I really have to do better at remembering that."

"She's worried that you heard us talking about your father," I said.

"I did. And I have heard thousands of similar conversations between persons of power in most of the governments around the world. All of your fears are well founded, yet Caeco is also correct. Father is singularly unique among humankind. And role model is an excellent term, Caeco."

"Just call it as I see it. Have your drones picked up anything happening at the Morrell house?"

"All of the lights are on. Juliet Morrell has attempted calling Special Agent-in-Charge Richards. He is, however, deeply involved in attempting to locate and recapture Agent Fan of the Yazi, who escaped capture somewhere between the shipyard and the FBI offices downtown.

"Additionally, lights are on in every home on the streets surrounding the house. Digital personal assistants in most of those homes indicate that inhabitants are awake but not speaking. Agent Allen's

imagined scenario is likely accurate."

"How many people are we talking about? And have any left their homes yet?" Agent Jay asked.

"Estimated at approximately thirty individuals, but as none have yet actually exited their dwellings, that number is a best guess."

"Any signs of life in the art studio?" I asked.

"I have three drones in a perimeter around it. All alarm systems are active, but I cannot detect any other data. Signals from inside are being blocked. As to your question regarding controlled civilians or other law enforcement, which Miss Morrell is now attempting to call, I may have an answer."

"Attempting to call?" Jay asked.

"I've blocked all of her attempts. Also, I am blocking the calls that just started from every resident in this development. And I am blocking monitoring service panic alarms being sequentially activated as well. In addition, I have sent erroneous messages to all local law enforcement within a ten-mile radius, sending them on false calls at the furthest points from this location."

"An army of controlled cops with guns would be bad," Alice said, nodding, eyes wide.

"What can you do about the controlled neighbors, Omega?" I asked.

"One of my large drones, the ones being referred to as battle drones, has remained here and is on station two hundred meters above your vehicle. Data gathered during the previous incident outside those taverns combined with US government research on nonlethal area denial technology have provided enough information for me to contrive a method to stop controlled humans from reaching you."

As soon as he spoke about a battle drone being over us, every face in the SUV, except my own, looked up at the ceiling liner of the car. Then they all looked back at me, with varying degrees of concern.

I shrugged. "I like to think of it as having a guided missile cruiser hovering on overwatch."

"My large drones exceed any current single naval combat vessel for firepower including a US carrier, nuclear sub, or a Russian Kirov class Battlecruiser."

"Yeah, good to know. Might be overkill for one Vorsook in a high net worth neighborhood, though," I said.

"Darci always tells Father and Stacia to bring enough gun," Omega countered.

"Isn't your father enough gun all by himself?" I fired back.

"I believe it to be an admonition to not underestimate the resources that might be necessary for any foreseeable eventuality."

"Game, set, and match to Omega," Mitch said.

"My original point was that this large drone has onboard technology that I have reconfigured to provide area denial using both sonic and microwave methodologies even against pain-blocked individuals."

"You said nonlethal, correct?" Agent Jay asked. "Tasers are actually *less lethal*, not *non-lethal*, as people *have* died. The at-risk population for Tasers includes the elderly, which we have here in droves."

"Correct. My technology should not harm any human, although a falling individual might sustain impact damage. Some area denial technologies create pain using either sound or energy. My modifications combine both sonic and energetic systems to effectively incapacitate the body, much as a Taser does with neuromuscular disruption. My analysis indicates this will be more effective than an

ideally placed Taser shot, as it effectively freezes the central nervous system at the spine and brain stem. This is completely opposite the skin heating effect of the Active Area Denial system or the pain-induced sonic systems. Projected from the battle drone overhead, it will keep any controlled humans from approaching you."

"What will stop it from freezing *us*?" Seth asked.

"Your amulets. Simply speaking, the device will be set in such a manner that your protective warded amulets will block its emissions."

None of my team looked very convinced, but sudden movement outside the vehicle switched our attention. People were coming out of their houses, mostly late middle-aged to true elderly, and unfortunately, Alice was correct—some were naked, but all of them were walking toward us, unfriendly eyes locked on us. And some of them had weapons—golf clubs, at least two shotguns, and several baseball bats.

"All inhabitants in a half-mile radius are exiting their dwellings. Activating drone now."

Every person in the immediate area froze, some in midstep. Many of those fell over.

"You will want to proceed now, Agent Jay."

Pulling her eyes away from the scene outside, Jay looked my way, then turned to Mitch who was, as usual, at the wheel. He started the Suburban and pulled away from the curb, moving slowly through the streets. Twice, he had to swerve the big vehicle around people standing frozen in the streets.

Chana turned from staring out the window and wrote something on her notepad. She held it up so the rest of us could see. *The computer can freeze humans completely! What chance do we have against it?*

Jay took the pad and wrote a response, then held it up. *Omega could simply incinerate the neighborhood. What chance do we have WITHOUT it?*

We all read it and no one said a word, all sitting back to consider the ramifications. Seconds later, Mitch was pulling onto the street where the Morrell house resided.

“Okay, here we go. Alice, Mitch, and Seth will secure the home. Caeco, Chana, and myself will proceed to the studio and set up a security perimeter around it. Once you have restrained Juliet and her mother, you three will join us. Then Mitch, Alice, Caeco, and myself will do an entry. Chana and Seth outside. Caeco has point on entry.”

“I’ve got the most training on point?” Alice protested.

“Not even close, Alice. She’s been clearing buildings her whole life, her reflexes and night vision exceed ours, and she has the best combat scores in the entire Bureau, HRT included,” Jay said. “Caeco first,” she said, meeting my eyes and waiting for my nod, which I didn’t hesitate to give.

“Let’s go.”

CHAPTER 33

Mitch pulled into the driveway, right up to the front entry, and slammed the big car into park. The team dismounted the vehicle in a smooth flow, the result of hours of practice. Everyone wore body armor and carried a long arm, in addition to their issued pistols.

Mitch, Jay, Alice, and myself had 5.56mm HK416 rifles, Chana had an HK MP5/10A3 submachine gun in 10mm, and Seth carried a Scattergun Technologies variant of the Remington 870 pump 12 gauge shotgun. We were, in short, loaded for bear, or, in this case, alien.

Mitch led Alice and Seth toward the big main house while Chana, Jay, and I moved around the back and followed the gravel path leading to the studio. All of my senses were alert and on edge, biological and nano both.

Behind us, I heard Mitch at the front door, Juliet's voice raised in argument, her mother sounding equally outraged. Ahead of us, the silent studio building loomed, sinister despite its clean, modern lines and expensive exterior landscape lighting. I moved left, circling the outside, while Chana and Jay spread out across the front, weapons ready. There wasn't a single sound as I moved, not even insect and night bird sounds, which effectively elevated my paranoia to new levels.

Moving up close to the walls, I could hear a soft hum from something inside, probably a small refrigerator, and the shrill sound of ultrasonic motion detectors. My nanites picked up multiple electromagnetic fields, mostly human normal, but there was a trace of something more as I moved up to the big custom basement bulkhead doors. It was a frequency I couldn't identify.

I've been around the new Omega drones enough, plus a few hours ago I had been exposed to multiple Vorsook technologies. This was kinda like that, but also not. I also smelled something dry and acrid, a sharpish odor that was unfamiliar, yet familiar. Then it came to me—thyme. It smelled like the herb thyme, at least a little. And then there was the odor of dog. Mastiff was closest maybe, but again different.

Gently, ever so gently, I put a hand on the bulkhead. It was a clamshell design, the kind that lifted straight up in one big piece. Hooking my gloved left hand under the edge of the door, I gently applied pressure in a straight upward lift. It didn't move, didn't wiggle. Locked.

Cautiously, I moved away.

Everything about this put me even further on edge, if that was possible. These aliens were, according to Omega and Nika, mental giants but not that formidable physically. Nika said they were pretty fast, but not strong, not robust, and certainly not invulnerable like the guards. We had killed the unkillable men in black and destroyed the UFO. Well, actually, Declan, Omega, Draco, and... yeah, credit where credit is due... Stacia had done that. But the point was the Vorsook had lost a serious set of weapons.

And it knew we were coming—it had roused the whole neighborhood against us. No way was it unprotected. No way was it unprepared. The building in front of me was waiting, poised like a trapdoor spider, ready for its prey.

The soft sound of something moving fast through the air Doplered toward me, my reflexes bringing my rifle to bear before my brain recognized the sound as an Omega drone, approaching from behind.

A black orb the size of a softball shot into the space above the art studio, then slammed to an instant stop, directly over the building. Immediately, I heard a shuffling sound inside, something moving, just a little. It came from below ground level and it ceased almost as soon as I heard it. I froze, listening, but it didn't come again.

Continuing my sweep, I circled around to the front and slipped in next to Agent Jay. Chana was twenty-five feet away but she moved over to hear my report.

"Something in the basement. Omega has a little drone overhead and I smell dog. Bulkhead is locked."

"Werewolf?" Jay asked.

"Nope. Dog. Mastiff maybe, but maybe not."

Sounds of footsteps on gravel brought me around to spot Mitch, Alice, and Seth moving toward us along the path. They looked a little freaked out.

"Are those two in the house secure?" Jay asked.

"Yes, although Juliet got pretty feisty. Jabbed Mitch with a pen. She's all trussed up now though," Alice said.

"You good, Agent Allen?" Jay asked.

He swiveled his head, met her gaze for a moment, then nodded. "Minimal wound," he said, holding out his left hand, which had a Band-Aid over the back of it. Agent Jay nodded, then returned her gaze to the studio.

I studied Mitch, my intuition telling me he wasn't as okay as he claimed. He noticed me watching him, turned his head, and gave me a nod. I nodded back, but I couldn't shake the feeling he wasn't one hundred percent. His motions were a bit off, like he was in pain but didn't want us to know it. Maybe

Juliet hit a nerve cluster in his hand. Maybe it hurt a lot more than he was letting on.

"Okay, Caeco has scouted the building. She believes the Vorsook is inside. She also smells a dog or dogs, large breed maybe. So we need to be ready for anything. The bulkhead will be our entry, as we originally planned. It's secured, so Alice and Caeco will affix door busters at the two points where this model door secures to the stairwell frame. They will back off. Seth and Chana will take up positions on either end of the building, able to watch both front and back while still able to fire safely, as long as they don't aim straight at the building. Clear?" she directed at Chana and Seth. They affirmed with nods and with quiet vocalizations.

"The remaining four of us will make the entry. I will fire the entry explosives, Caeco will enter first, followed by Alice, myself, and then Mitch last. We go in with weapon lights on, safeties off, fingers off trigger. I will carry the portable circle device. When we locate the alien, Agent Allen and I will transition to Taser units. Jensen and Barrows will overwatch with rifles. We'll tase the alien, then I'll toss the circle over it to contain it. If I fail, Caeco is my backup. After that, we clean up and call for Oracle. Questions?"

"Ma'am, Omega has a drone directly over the building. I would like to ask him to send it in with us," I said.

Immediately the faces around me tightened, micro-expressions instantly telling me they weren't comfortable with that plan. Jay looked around at the team, eyebrows up.

Mitch suddenly spoke. "We haven't trained with it, we don't know how it will react, it doesn't know how we'll react. Too many variables."

Agent Jay nodded. "He's exactly right. Maybe in the future we can run some drills, but for here and now, it'll just be this team. Got it?"

"Yes ma'am," I said. Mitch's points were all very valid, very solid, but I didn't feel good about this operation. Having the drone inside with us would be an enormous safety blanket.

"Okay, let's get this done. Tick tock," Jay said.

Immediately, Chana and Seth moved to either side of the building, unable to see each other but able to see us as well as the front of the studio. This way they had clear, intersecting fields of fire without endangering each other. Even if they accidentally fired straight into the building, the blueprints we'd seen showed enough interior walls to stop the 10mm pistol rounds and 12 gauge buckshot loads they were using.

As they settled into place, Alice and I moved forward, each pulling a small, prepared detcord charge from Alice's munitions box. Then we heel-and-toed it across the lawn to the back of the building, each stepping to one side of the clamshell bulkhead. The model installed used two metal rods that extended into the sides of the stairwell when the handle was twisted. We stuck the detcord to the outside of the door above the rods' locations. Then Alice placed an additional charge on the handle itself while I stuck an oversized version of an auto body technician's suction cup puller to the top of the door, twisting the handle to the optimum point where I would grab it.

Entry prep work complete, we hustled back to the other two. Then we stacked, me first, Alice second, Jay third, and Mitch fourth. Alice had her left hand on my left shoulder, ready to tap me when Jay tapped her.

I felt a squeeze of the hand on my shoulder, then a three-count of taps. At the third and final tap, the charges went off, all together—loud, the noise sharp and short. Alice slapped her hand again on my shoulder and I started forward, feeling the others moving along behind me while the remainder of my senses concentrated on the area ahead. The smoke was minimal, the charges designed for just that result, and I grabbed the handle I had suctioned to the door, yanking upward as hard as my left hand could pull, my right holding my rifle muzzle aimed at the black opening revealed as the door yawned upward. The weapon light affixed to the forearm of my rifle sent a powerful beam of light down into the Stygian blackness, the lights of my fellow agents shining just as bright to either side of me.

With nothing in sight, I stepped over the threshold and started down the short eight steps. I had to hold myself back, slow my steps down, so that my team could keep up, one of the few things I ever had to really work on in practice. I'm fast, much faster than regular people, and I tend to *run* toward combat, not away.
But I did it, kept my pace measured, stepping onto the basement floor with Alice directly behind me and the other two behind her.

My beam of light lit up the space ahead, revealing four pairs of gleaming, silver-shiny eyes, each almost three feet off the ground, each attached to a snarling, oversized black dog with slavering metal teeth, standing ten feet in front of us.

CHAPTER 34

The dogs charged, metallic toenails tearing right into the concrete of the floor. My rifle was already firing, short three-round bursts, giving each dog attention as I moved the red dot of my Sigarms sight across their heads. From either side of me, Alice and Agent Jay fired as well, although their bursts only concentrated on one of the dogs each.

That's why I was point, much as Alice might hate it. My reflexes and muscle control, combined with thousands of hours of training and countless rounds sent downrange, gave me a directed fire ability well beyond my teammates. The Bureau's instructors had been shocked and maybe even appalled at how fast and accurate my weapons fire is.

Each dog took three 5.56mm rounds to the head. The Bureau-issued 75 grain Hornady rounds were designed to do maximum damage from short-barreled rifles, and each bullet hit with four times the muzzle energy of my 9mm Glock.

The dogs crumpled, big bodies still plowing forward, shoulders rolling down even as their heads came apart. Two of them, the ones on either end of the line, took sustained bursts from my teammates' guns, furthering the damage their alien cyborg bodies would have to repair. I shared the remaining rounds in my magazine between the middle dogs, applying ballistic damage to their shoulders, necks, and spine. All four dogs were down but still snapping and thrashing in a frenzy of directionless violence.

"Out," I said, dropping my empty magazine while plucking a fresh one from the carrier on my vest. Behind me, I heard the moment when the other two rifles locked open on empty chambers, Alice and Lois Jay yelling "Out" within a second of each other. My new mag was just locking into place, my left thumb hitting the bolt release, when another shot fired, from behind me, the sound odd but made even more so by Agent Jay's accompanying scream of pain.

Turning from the thrashing, shuddering dog monsters, I found Mitch, his rifle pointed at Agent Jay's head, his left hand yanking the weapon forward while his right frantically pulled back. She was clutching a leg, her head back, eyes wide at the muzzle in her face. Mitch's face was a study in panic, like a man at war with himself, and he was yelling, "*No, no, no,*" in a nonstop mantra. It was the oddest thing, like his one arm fought his other. His right index finger was outside the trigger guard. Had it been inside, the rifle would have fired, maybe even bump fired multiple rounds. Then it hit me—that's exactly what happened to Jay's leg.

Lois Jay was still down with blood gushing from her right calf while Alice, who was frozen when I first turned, now swung the buttstock of her rifle into Mitch's face, stunning him. Then with a noise that was half scream and half growl, she dove on him, driving him to the ground. Expertly, she flipped him facedown and started to grab his arms behind his back.

That's when I felt an enormous push on my right shoulder, like a wave of power rolling past. My eyes were still on my three teammates when the force of whatever it was hit them, shoving Agent Jay down, flattening Mitch to the ground even more than he was, and blasting Alice clear off his back.

My body was immediately diving to one side, spinning in midair to look back at the dogs and what was now behind them: a short, naked gray figure with huge black eyes and a pewter-colored rod clutched in a three-fingered hand that was pointing my way, another burst of power already rippling the air between us.

I tucked my shoulder and rolled, my rifle clutched to my middle, my feet finding the ground as momentum and leg power stood me upright. Behind me, the sheetrock wall silently exploded into white powder while Lois Jay yelled in pain and the dogs growled, snapped, and scrabbled.

My rifle was pointing the wrong way and I couldn't spin. All I could do was to keep moving across the open space of the studio's wide open and mostly empty basement. To my right, the alien was already firing a third pulse. It *was* fast; Nika had been right. I seriously doubt Agent Jay would have been able to get Declan's circle over it, as it was faster than any of my teammates. In fact, it was maybe almost as fast as me.

The blast crunched another section of wall a mere foot behind my speeding body as I started to circle the room. The dogs were beginning to stand up, the massive bullet damage to their heads and bodies already healing. The gray man was making shrill, high-pitched sounds, almost as if it was yelling its hate at me.

Letting go of the short rifle with my left hand, I swung it down, around, and up with my right, feet still beating a path forward. Working only on instinct, I pointed the rifle one-handed in the alien's direction and squeezed the trigger. The recoil pushed the muzzle up, my arm muscles fighting to try and bring it back down.

Most of my rounds missed completely, but a few zipped real close to the alien's naked body, and the loud reports and bright muzzle flash combined to scare it. A rather improbable leap by one dog absorbed the single round that might have actually hit it. Its shrill alien screams escalated to ultrasonic territory as the little monster jumped backward.

I stopped suddenly, both hands back on the rifle, swiveling my feet into a firing stance, red dot moving up to cover the alien. Before I could fire, a mass of black fur moved in front of the Vorsook, heavy muscle blocking my target completely. The dogs were fully back in business.

Again, I fired in controlled bursts, just like I had at the start of the festivities, but this time, the dogs were moving side to side, swinging their big heads, and my rounds missed every skull but one. *That* dog fell, but two of his buddies shrugged off the lesser body hits and charged me. The fourth dog moved and blocked out my view of the alien.

I was scrambling again, feet moving before I could even think about it. I emptied my magazine into one dog's face but the other ran right over top of it and leaped at me as the bolt locked open on my empty rifle. Bracing my feet on the ground in an aggressive fighting stance, I punched the rifle forward like a WWII soldier bayoneting an enemy.

The dog weighed damned near as much as me, probably more, its forward momentum slamming its gaping mouth right onto the muzzle of my rifle. The impact drove my body backward, the rifle barrel disappearing down the dog's cavernous throat. But my feet were in good boots that gripped the concrete floor and my jab forward came from my center of gravity, not my arms, the result being a wet crunching of bone as the flash hider mounted to the end of my weapon punched right out the back of its neck. With a twist of my hips and torso, I re-directed its energy to one side, throwing both the rifle and the dog away from me, my now empty right hand grabbing for my Glock.

The skewered dog thrashed about on the floor, my rifle stock sticking out of its craw in the front and the muzzle poking out the back of its head. I ignored its violent twisting, snapping fit, choosing to focus on the last standing dog that was providing cover for the alien. An alien who was again drawing a bead on me.

Every time I fired the Glock, the dog's body got between my bullet and the Vorsook, giving the wrinkled little bastard enough time to fire another energy pulse at me. I started to dodge backward but some instinct stopped my feet and instead sent my body forward instead. An invisible energy pulse brushed my body armor, a thrum of intense power vibrating the titanium and ceramic back plate in its ballistic nylon carrier, shaking my whole body. The damned thing had anticipated my movements, and meanwhile, none of my shots were getting through its mutant canine bullet blocker.

The slide locked open, all sixteen rounds gone. I ducked the next blast, left hand scrabbling for a new mag, legs crouched, making me a smaller target but at the same time hampering my ability to dodge.

The shielding dog suddenly dropped flat to the ground, as if silently commanded, giving its master a clear shot at me, the pewter rod rising up to point my way.

An object flickered across the room, end over end, slamming into the alien's shoulder. A wooden handle now protruded from the arm that had been aiming the weapon. My pistol mag snicked smoothly into the grip of my gun, my hand coming over the slide to release it forward, my trigger finger already beginning its pull.

The Glock fired three times fast, muzzle blast bright enough in the dark basement to flare out my vision. Then the alien was falling and the dog was freezing up, as were its other three companions. I turned to the entrance to see Fan standing on the stairs, still dressed in his combat blacks, his head uncovered. He gave me a nod, then jumped smoothly to land beside Mitch Allen, who seemed to be lying on his back, his right hand clutching his left wrist, seemingly fighting himself.

Fan pulled a second blade even as Omega's small orb descended past him into the basement. Fan grabbed Mitch's left forearm and swung the heavy blade. Omega started firing bursts of actinic light at the dogs but my vision stayed locked on Mitch and Fan, watching as the left hand of my teammate jumped off his body right at the elbow and fell to the floor.

Rather than scream or yell, Mitch simply relaxed and fell back, breathing deeply as if relieved of an enormous burden while blood spurted from the stump. Comprehension struck and I turned to look at the fallen hand and forearm, finding it twitching and jumping about the ground before a blast of white-hot light struck it dead center and burned it to ash.

CHAPTER 35

Training kicked in, sending me to check the downed alien. I gave the drone and remaining two dogs a wide berth, shielding my vision from the harsh flashes of light coming from the little black orb.

The Vorsook was still breathing, lying on its side, curled up, green blood pooling on the floor under it. Its huge, black featureless eyes locked onto me as I circled to it, Glock muzzle leading the way. It studied me, laboring to draw air into its tiny mouth.

With one foot, I carefully moved the dangerous weapon rod further away from the little shaking form. Fan's knife quivered in its shoulder with each wracking breath, but the movements were getting smaller and smaller. Suddenly the knife stopped moving altogether as did the small, underdeveloped-looking chest. The fathomless black eyes changed color, fading from jet black to a dull charcoal and a final breath rattled in whatever it used for lungs.

"All life signs have ceased," Omega announced from the little drone that was still industriously burning dog to ash.

I realized that my hearing was still ringing from all the gunshots, even through the electronic hearing protectors we all wore. I hadn't heard the alien's heart stop.

Convinced it was dead, I turned to help my team. Fan was applying a tourniquet to Mitch's arm stump and Jay had dragged herself to Alice's body. I rushed to her side.

"She's dead," Jay said, face bleak. I ignored her, turning Alice on her back and opening her body armor. Then I started chest compressions.

Footsteps pounded down the stairs and Chana was suddenly at our sides. Seeing I had the CPR in hand, she started emergency aid to Agent Jay's gunshot leg. After applying a trauma pad to the wound and holding it in place, she glanced around the basement, eyes squinting against the continuing blasts of the drone.

"What the hell happened?"

I kept silent, counting my compressions. After a second, Jay spoke up, her tone bleak, voice cracking with grief. "Cyborg dogs attacked us. Mitch was infected with the alien tech. His hand. Shot my leg. Alice tackled him and then got shot by the alien. Its weapon knocked her across the room and killed her despite her armor plates."

"It stopped her heart *with* her armor—the plates actually," I said, ceasing my CPR and holding up one hand for silence. My hearing was coming back, thanks to *my* nano tech, and I strained to hear. Nothing—then a bump, just a little thump, barely a beat. Followed by another. And another, this one louder, the beat erratic at first, then settling down to a blessed steady drum. Alice took a sudden breath.

"She's alive. The blast crushed her back plate and compressed her chest hard enough to stop her heart. There might be fractures," I said, looking up at Jay and Chana. The black Omega drone was hovering just a few feet behind them. I don't think they knew it was there.

"*Ambulance and EMTs are two minutes out,*" the drone said, the two agents not even twitching at this interuption. "*Agent Harwood will meet them and lead them down. The Vorsook is deceased. All alien nano tech is destroyed, including Agent Allen's infected arm. Agents Jay and Allen are stable, but both are beginning to show signs of shock. Agent Barrows' heartbeat is stable, but I concur with Caeco—there are likely multiple rib fractures, a possible spinal injury, and a bruised sternum."*

I glanced at Fan, who was crouched by Mitch's side, one hand keeping the big agent from moving around, the other holding the tourniquet binding. "Did you live up to your name when you escaped SAC Richards?"

He studied me for a second, then gave a little shake of his head. "Entirely unnecessary. Removing myself from his custody was not difficult, as I believe Agent Jay already knew," he said.

Lois was looking pale and was clearly in some pain, yet her expression showed new life as she looked at a clearly breathing, unconscious Alice. Then she glanced around the room. "Thank you, Agent Fan, for your assistance."

"My pleasure, Special Agent-in-Charge Lois Jay," he said, his head and upper body making the tiniest bow in her direction. "Although Agent Jensen seemed to have it in hand." His eyes found mine.

"Nope. That knife throw was the best sight I've ever seen," I said, looking right back at him.

"Ohh, sparks," Mitch said, voice almost a whisper, a stupid grin on his ghost-white face. Outside, I heard sirens screaming closer. I noticed Fan's head tilt at exactly the same moment I heard them.

"EMTs are almost here," I said. "Omega, what happened to the neighbors?"

"They have all returned to awareness and are universally expressing confusion and bewilderment. Three of them have minor bruises from falls sustained when I activated the battle drone. The alien's influence ceased when you shot it."

The emergency response vehicles got close enough for the others to hear. Agent Jay turned to me. "Caeco, secure that alien weapon. Do not release it to anyone until I give you authority, clear?"

"Clear as crystal, ma'am," I said, crossing the basement floor, stepping over piles of ash and small, hardened pools of metal. The alien body was untouched, the weapon a good six feet away from it. A soft whir told me that the drone had accompanied me. "Can I just pick it up?"

The little black ball with the power to burn bodies to powder floated over the rod and a laser light flickered out to scan it. *"Inert. No actual controls apparent on its surface. Possibly requires mental stimulation to fire. You should be able to pick it up and handle it without danger. However, if your nano senses pick up anything unusual, I would advise caution."*

I held my right hand over the rod, but my personal suite of nano tech reported nothing—nothing at all.

It was lighter than it looked, the metal having an odd feel, like it was wood instead of metal. I couldn't detect any electromagnetic signature, nor did my nanites sense anything radioactive either. Just a straight, cylindrical rod of an unknown, ultralight metal slightly less than a foot in length. After moving it around, keeping the end pointed at the back wall of the cellar, I simply tucked it into the baton pocket of my body armor vest, moving the baton to an empty magazine pouch.

Voices outside announced the first responders just before Seth led them down the stairs. The little drone ball suddenly illuminated the room, producing light from its top and bouncing it off the ceiling. Then EMTs were putting down medical bags and shoving their way to the sides of the injured. Light steps on the stairs brought my attention to them in time to see Nathan Stewart's assistant Adine arrive on the scene. She spoke a single word, "Clear," and then a cane and two feet started down from above. Nathan himself descended, eyes bright with interest as he took in everything. He bent down and spoke to Agent Jay, his smile for her as warm as hers was wary. Then he headed my way, Adine moving gracefully by his side.

"It was my thought that if anyone could capture a Vorsook alive, it was you, Caeco, but there is only so much one can do when facing an enemy combatant as prepared as this one. So I will instead congratulate you for surviving your encounter and ensuring your team survived as well," he said.

"Three wounded, one of whom was clinically dead for at least several minutes," I said, frowning.

"Yet she's not dead now," he said, his white mustache wiggling as he smiled. " And Agent Allen, while grievously injured, is not, apparently, infected with alien nano technology. The enemy has been neutralized, which is, ultimately, the mission. So again, congratulations. I would make another attempt to entice you to come work for Oracle, but President Polner has forbidden me from poaching you. He seems to want you right where you are, my dear."

"Okay, well, thanks. But Agent Fan deserves credit as well. He, ah, released himself from custody and came here to help, arriving at an extremely timely moment, sir," I said. I looked around. Fan was gone.

"The president would like you to update him, and myself, immediately. We have a secure comm outside," he said, still smiling. "I, myself, look forward to hearing exactly what happened."

"Yes sir," I said. With a nod, he waved a hand toward the stairs. I took one last look around the scene of the crime, so to speak. At least seven people were working on my teammates, Seth and Chana standing back. Agent Jay met my eyes and gave me a nod. Meanwhile, a half dozen individuals wearing Oracle patches on their shoulders were moving into the already crowded basement, their eyes locked on the alien body. Each of them acknowledged their boss as they moved in a beeline for the dead Vorsook. I watched them surround it, talking with clear, professional excitement among themselves. Then I looked up to find Nathan and Adine waiting patiently for me. He again waved me toward the stairs and I finally headed up and out.

CHAPTER 36

"And then, Mr. President, the alien died and we began first aid," I said, concluding the debrief.

President Polner was still in a suit, although the hour was now ridiculously late. He was seated in a high back, expensive-looking leather chair in what appeared to be a secure room at the White House. Or maybe *under* the White House. We—Nathan, Adine, and myself—were in a small communications suite housed in the back of an Oracle tractor trailer parked on the Morrells' driveway.

"Excellent work, Agent Jensen. I've already been informed that your teammates will all survive. I will be contacting Agent Jay as soon as her wounds have been stabilized to congratulate her on not one but two extremely successful operations. But Caeco, I absolutely realize just how much of a role you played in seeing these events to a successful and satisfactory conclusion."

"Thank you sir, but the battle with the spacecraft was entirely Declan, Stacia, and Omega. Without them, I don't believe any of us would have survived."

"Yes, and do you think that a recovering Declan O'Carroll would leave his sickbed to rescue just any federal agent?"

"He very well might, sir," I said.

"Perhaps, but I'm told he was extremely insistent on being there. And his caretakers might have resisted him had it been anyone but you. Plus, you have dramatically answered my question regarding his capabilities."

"He says he's not fully recovered, sir," I cautioned.

"Not fully recovered, yet he absorbed everything it threw at him and blasted it from the sky. I've seen the footage myself."

"Sir, there's footage?" I asked, concerned.

"Omega's. I've been conversing with him. Your example shamed me into increasing my interactions with him. I must say it has been highly enlightening. Do you know how satisfying it is to steal my advisors' thunder by knowing ahead of time what they mean to brief me on?"

"Probably worried about their jobs, sir," I said, glancing at an amused Nathan Stewart, who had listened to my whole report with hardly a word.

"And you have custody of the alien's personal weapon?" President Polner asked.

I nodded, pulling the rod carefully from the baton pouch.

"It doesn't look like much," the president said, leaning toward his monitor for a closer look as I held it up.

"It does not appear, either to myself or Omega, to have any controls. Omega surmised that it was entirely controlled by mental commands," I said.

"Why is there a string tied around one end?" he asked.
"That's the end the blasts emanated from. Both ends look identical, but if it has an analog to a muzzle, this end is it. Didn't want anyone pointing it the wrong way."

"Good thought. Nathan, I want your team to take charge of that rod. Agent Jensen, I am overriding Agent Jay's orders," the president said.

"Yes sir," I said, holding out the rod to Director Stewart. He, however, pushed back away from the rod. Adine moved forward, holding out hands that were already covered with thick black gloves. She took the rod and put it in a plastic, foam-lined Pelican case by her feet. Nathan pushed the lid shut with his cane and Adine latched it shut.

“Never know what can trigger a reaction with this stuff,” Stewart said, giving me a smile.

“Caeco, you have done a great job. I want you to continue doing what you’re doing and doing it with your team. It won’t always be easy, as I think you already have a feel for how some of the politics of the situation work,” the president said.

“If you mean my strained relationship with the director, then yes sir, I do.”

“Tucker has his... foibles, but I have faith in him. I need you where you are, Caeco, and he is your boss’s boss. So I must ask you to endure.”

“Yes sir.”

“Good. I will dismiss you, then. I need to talk to Nathan further.”

“Good night, Mr. President,” I said, standing and stepping quickly out of the comm suite.

Outside, there was still a great deal of activity. Bureau agents from the Philly office were going through the main house, pulling boxes of material and every computer, tablet, and laptop they could find, while the studio was under the purview of Oracle. The two agencies seemed to be ignoring each other as they carried out their tasks. SAC Richards was on the scene, supervising his people. He spotted me as stepped down the folding stairs from the side of the Oracle command trailer.

“Where have you been? Director Tyson is looking for your report,” he said, stepping toward me with a frown. He was cut from much the same cloth as Tyson, both being big, dark-haired white guys with more than a little bully to them.

"I was debriefing. Where is the director?"

"You were debriefing with Oracle before your own agency?" he demanded.

"Nope, I was debriefing with the president. Oracle supplied the secure communications."

Surprise flashed across his face, but he recovered his frown quickly enough. "Director Tyson is en route to Philadelphia. He wants to lead the news conferences when we give them. You need to update him immediately."

"Shouldn't SAC Jay do that?" I asked.
"You follow the orders you are given, Agent Jensen, no more, no less. Lois Jay is being treated for her injuries at the Penn Presby Trauma Center."

"So do I call him on my cell or do you have a communications link to him?"

"You'll use the command van," he snapped, pointing behind himself at a dark gray truck the size of a UPS delivery van. It was much, much smaller than the vehicle I had just left. But as he had so carefully pointed out, I had my orders. So I trudged over to the van, knocked on the outer door, and stepped into the interior.

A technician looked at me, nodding in recognition, and pointed to a chair in front of a wall of monitors. He spoke into his headset, "Agent Jensen for Director Tyson."

The center monitor directly in front of me lit up with a live image of Tyson, who was clearly on a small jet.

"Where the hell have you been, Jensen?" he demanded.

"Our boss wanted my report first," I said.

Confusion flashed in his eyes for a second before realization flooded in. His angry frown deepened. "Clearly you have a some misconceptions about your position in this organization, Agent Jensen. *You* report to *me*, and *I* report to *him*."

"Sir, he didn't give me an option."

His angry face somehow found a way to get even angrier, but he didn't speak for a second. "Tell me what you told him," he finally demanded.

So I repeated the whole story, explaining what we had found in our investigations, how it led us to both locations, why we chose to first visit the shipyard, the events that transpired there, and finally the operation to capture the Vorsook.

The anger in his face changed several times, something like confidence and satisfaction slipping across his features at several points. I finished and he leaned back in his seat.

"All in all, an unmitigated disaster," he said.

"Sir?" I couldn't help my note of disbelief.

"Your inept and likely illegal break-in of the shipyard resulted in your own capture. The fact that rogue civilian elements had to rescue you is an outrage. Worse, they precipitated an aerial battle over Philadelphia that *could* have killed or wounded thousands. Then your team initiated an attack in a suburban neighborhood that resulted in the death of the suspect, half your team being grievously wounded, and the use of unknown and untested weapons technology on the local civilian population. What would you call that, Agent?"

"I would say we tracked down a subversive threat to national and global security, neutralized an extraterrestrial weapons platform that outgunned most naval vessels, eliminated an infectious and highly dangerous nano technology, and stopped an alien threat that was actively interfering with the lawful function of the US government, with no fatalities other than the alien," I said back.

"For someone with your paramilitary training, you have a colorful imagination, Agent. Are you sure you shouldn't be in marketing? Although you don't seem to be aware of the media reaction to your circus of incompetence, do you?" he asked.

"I've been in either after-action clean up or after-action debriefings since the operation, sir. Media is the last thing I've had time for."

"Sure, too busy taking a bulldozer to the reputation of the Bureau. Your future is very much in question, Agent Jensen, with regard to employment with this organization as well as criminally. You're dismissed, but you are to have nothing further to do with this investigation. You will sit the sidelines while we attempt to clean up this mess. Remove yourself to your team's local accommodations."

CHAPTER 37

I removed myself to the hospital to check on my teammates. Alice was in ICU at the trauma center but stabilized, according to Seth. Mitch and Jay were being treated in the ER, in side-by-side examination bays.

"Ah, there you are. Everything okay?" SAC Jay asked.

"I was going to ask both of you the same thing."

"Well, I won't be at the dojo for a bit, but the bullet went through and through and the muscle should heal," she said. "What's going on with the operation?"

I told her about my two very different debriefings. "I've already had calls from both President Polner and Director Tyson. Director Tyson is clearly initiating a drastic level of damage control," she said.

"That's what he said," I nodded.

"No Caeco, I mean he is trying to repair the damage his reputation has already suffered. He went on record in two presidential briefings as downplaying the alien threat. Now that threat has been exposed like a rotten worm, deep in one of the oldest cities in this country. Which is why he's flying in to take over, himself. He'll attempt to take credit for rooting out this threat and neutralizing it."

"We can't let him take credit like that!" I said.

She gave me a sad, sympathetic smile. "He's our boss, Caeco. We have to do as he orders. If he wants to control the press conferences, there is nothing *we* can do to stop that." Her smile changed at the end, transforming into something sly.

"What do you know? Is there something we can do?"

"Us? No. But I wouldn't waste any energy worrying about this, Caeco. It won't likely go his way."

She so obviously knew something. But she wouldn't say what. Instead, she sent me to the next bay to visit Mitch.

I found him looking tired and pale, but he didn't seem to be in any pain.

"Cakewalk!" he said as soon as he saw me.

"Hey, Mitch. How ya doing?"

"Well, I have to stay lying down or I tip over. Weighted heavy to the right now."

"Shit, you're joking about it?" I asked.

He gave me a little shrug. "I'm deflecting. But I'm also alive. Not so very long ago, I was facing the very real fact of my imminent death. Either that shit that crazy Juliet injected into me was going to kill everything that was me or you guys were going to have to."

"What was it like?" I couldn't help asking. He waited while a nurse came in and injected something into his IV line. He smiled at her, ignoring the hypodermic in favor of her pretty face. I, however, read the label and noted it was a mild sedative.

"This will help you rest," she said, plumping his pillow with an answering smile of her own. Then she left, and once his eyes stopped watching her butt as she walked out, he finally answered.

"It hurt when she stuck me with that silver pen, which now,

obviously, wasn't really a pen. It throbbed and ached while we were setting up for the entry, and I was getting these weird shooting sensations up my arm, but I ignored them. Then we made entry and we were going down the stairs. You three were shooting the dogs and I didn't have a clear field of fire, so I was checking our six while waiting to step in when someone ran dry. But my left arm just suddenly moved, all on its own, like it wasn't mine. It yanked forward just as I was bringing my rifle up to take Agent Jay's arc of fire. My finger was just slipping into the trigger guard when it did, causing the shot that hit Jay. After that, my hand and forearm went crazy and pains were moving up my arm. At that point, I *knew* what it was... knew it was that nano shit that was in those crazy bastards you fought in the shipyard. I mean, it was suddenly clear as day. That shit was spreading up my arm and I wasn't going to be me for much longer. Then your Chinese pal chopped my arm off and it was all gone."

His smile had slipped away almost at his first words, a gradual horror taking over as he relived his arm becoming something else.

"Was it like that for you? You know? When they put those things inside you?" he asked.

I hadn't thought about that day in a long, long time. I'd been very little when the nanites were first introduced, and it had taken numerous upgrades and many additional treatments until the colonization and integration was successfully complete.

"It was cold. Like an injection of ice. And yeah, it did run through me. But it happened very fast, as fast as blood moved through my veins and arteries. It seems like it was a lot slower for you... like maybe the technology moved right through the muscle and flesh rather than the circulatory system."

"Thank God. If it had done the blood thing, I'd have been gone almost instantly," he said, his eyes blinking sleepily.

"That tech had enormous control of those bodies, both the men in black suits and the dogs. Perhaps it has to integrate at a much slower pace to get that degree of control and change?" I suggested.

"Yeah, you don't have things taking control of you, do you?"

"Only once. Locked up all my muscles."

"What happened?'

"A friend made it so that it couldn't happen ever again," I said.

"Oh," Mitch said, thinking about that. Then the light dawned. "Oh! Your friend with the voodoo?"

"Yeah. He's got lots of that," I agreed.

"Well, you should thank him when you think of it. I only lost control of my arm and hand, but that was horrible. Losing your whole self would be unimaginable." His eyes fluttered. "But I'm just glad your new boyfriend showed up when he did. Never thought I'd be happy to have someone cut off my arm."

"Fan is my enemy, not my boyfriend," I said.

"Yeah, well, he sure watches you pretty closely," Mitch said, yawning.

"Yes, because I am the most dangerous opponent near him. We fought with knives!"

"Shit, that's like your version of flirting," he said with a snort, immediately yawning again. "Just glad he showed up."

"Yeah, me too."

He nodded, eyes now closed, and then he was out—sound asleep.

Good. And actually a really good idea. I can go a long time

without sleep; a factor of my genetics, my nanites, and my training. But I was feeling pretty tired and one thing my instructors had hammered into me was to always grab sleep when I can.

Twenty-two minutes later, I was back at the hotel, in my bed, and falling fast asleep as my head hit the pillow.

CHAPTER 38

My power nap lasted four hours, then I was back up, showered, changed, and rearmed, ready to go. In the suite's common room, I found Seth and Chana eating room service breakfast and watching the news.

"We got lots, knowing how you eat," Seth said, cutting a pancake with the side of his fork while thumbing over his shoulder with the other hand. My stomach rumbled at the sight of the hotel trolley cart stationed behind their sofa, filled with dishes of eggs, pancakes, hash browns, stacks of toast, piles of bacon, not to mention the big carafe of coffee.

I filled a plate while scanning the television, recognizing the images of the navy shipyard. The banner at the bottom was rolling past and every other word seemed to be *alien, Vorsook, spacecraft,* or *dogfight.*

"*—Breaking news. We have new footage, cell phone video taken from across the Delaware River on the shore front in New Jersey,*" the blonde anchor announced. Immediately the screen filled with a fairly clear picture, showing the black expanse of the nighttime river with flares of light and explosions flashing in the sky above it.

"*—what the f**bleep is that?*" a voice said.

"**bleep* if I know,*" a second answered.

The camera shook a bit then suddenly zoomed in, the area across the river leaping forward to fill the screen. The silver image of the Vorsook craft zipped into the center, white and red flashes flaring out the camera resolution, dark round objects moving at crazy speeds around the silver one.

*"S*bleep, Dude, it's a real as F dogfight! That UFO thing is fighting those black drones!"*

"Those are the computer's drones—Omega's!"

An explosion flared bright, whiting out the screen for a second, then the image came back and resolved to clarity just in time for a blast of power to strike at the ground. It never made it. Instead, an arched dome illuminated and figures became visible on the darkened ground.

*"Sh*bleep! There are people down there!"*

Instantly, two fast pulses of intense energy lit up the silver ship, flaring up a partial dome in mid-air, rocking the ship where it hovered.

I knew the next part by heart but seeing it on some guy's camera phone was surreal. The Vorsook ship went sideways, faster than the eye could follow, stopping instantly like it didn't have to obey any laws of physics. Then came the two shots of its primary energy weapon, both blasting straight down. They lit up a perfect half dome of white so bright it, again, flared out the camera. The camera corrected as the power coursing across the dome disappeared, the light lifting smoothly like some kind of curtain before vanishing completely.

A dark figure on the ground directly under that awesome display of frightening power raised an arm and the hottest, brightest, most visually painful beam of light in the whole fight shot from its upraised hand and struck the spacecraft, blasting completely through it like a red-hot poker shoved though a thin pane of ice.

The alien ship came apart in a thunderous explosion that shook the videographers and sent rippling waves out in expanding arcs across the surface of the river.

"We've asked retired Air Force pilot Major Christine Estrades to help us understand what we're seeing. Major?"

"Ah, Susan, I've never seen any aerial combat like this before. No fighter plane on earth could make those maneuvers inside an operational envelope that small. This looks to be Vorsook against the Omega computer. Look at those energy weapons, and that has to be some kind of forcefield."

"Then who is that on the ground?" Susan asked.

"Susan, you should probably have brought in Bristol Chatterjee for this one, as I think this is right in her wheelhouse. That said, is it my imagination or is one of those figures on the ground much taller and bigger than the others, and covered all in white fur?"

"Oh my God, you are right! That has got to be Stacia Reynolds, Major!"

"I think so, Susan. Which I think means that the fella with the raised arm would likely be..."

"The Warlock!"

"That's actually really clear footage," Seth Harwood said. "Whoever took that just got their fifteen seconds of fame."

"Yeah, this angle is actually better than what we could see from way back in the shipyard," Chana said, using the remote control to lower the volume on the television as the talking heads started to get really wound up.

On screen, the image was being enhanced and artificially expanded, a blurry Declan frozen right at the moment he fired off his spell, his palm just beginning to glow.

Chana raised the volume as the pilot turned to the anchor. *"I think that pretty much answers the question about the Warlock's abilities, Susan."*

"That, Major Estrades, is the understatement of the year."

"How the hell can he do that?" Seth asked as the scene replayed for like the eighth time in five minutes.

"He redirects the energy," I said.

"But he didn't do it instantly," Seth argued. "He absorbed one shot, then the two really big ones, then took his sweet time before blasting it all back out in one giant bolt of power. What the hell does he do with it in the meantime?"

"I don't really know. Most witches work from energy that they pull from their personal well of, for lack of a better term, magic. Declan can do that too, but he almost always *borrows* energy from other sources and recycles it. I've listened to him try to explain it to other witches, but even they don't really follow it. I once asked his aunt if he was as good as his mother, and she just snorted. Said that what he does on an instinctive level, no other witch has ever done," I said. "Even the best of the Irish Circle he's descended from."

"You just hung around with all of them? Like it was normal?" Seth asked, incredulous.

"To us, it *was* normal. You have to admit that I'm not a very normal kind of girl, yet at that school, with those kids, I wasn't all that odd."

"Well, we're really glad you decided to join the Bureau and this team," Chana said. "And I know that Lois was very excited to be named SAC of this group."

"She came from Oracle originally, right?" I asked.

"Yup. She's half Native American on her father's side," Chana said. "Apparently, her ancestors, particularly the females, were considered to be very sensitive. Had some kind of version of the Sight. Let them feel if an area was good, bad, or neutral. The tribe prospered when it listened to these women, and fell on hard times when it didn't."

"And SAC Jay has it?" I asked.

"She's never said. But I will tell you that Nathan Stewart was extremely unhappy when she left Oracle, and they don't generally recruit people who don't have some kind of gift or edge," Chana said.

"Speaking of the boss, what are we supposed to be doing?" I asked.

Seth held up his plate. "This. We've been ordered to stay in the suite and wait for additional orders. They've benched us."

"So Caeco," Chana began, looking at me intently. "How are you? You know... with everything that happened?"

"Oh, I'm fine," I said. She looked at me dubiously, glancing once at Seth, who just shrugged.

"You sure? With all that..."

"Listen, I'm over it," I said. "In fact, I think we're still kind of friends even. The girls at Arcane always said it was damned near impossible to be friends after going out, but I think we are. It was a bit messy when we broke up and I think *he* could have handled *that* better, but then *I* didn't behave all that great in Italy, so you know. But I don't think I feel that way about him anymore... not really. In fact, I'm kind of glad he ended up with Stacia because the whole imbalance thing won't matter to her."

Now they were staring at me with a bit of shock before exchanging another glance, eyes a little wide.

"Ah, Caeco, we were asking about you being captured by indestructible men after finding another soldier like you, then getting caught in the middle of a War of the Worlds laser battle before fighting off giant mutant dogs and having to kill a sentient being from another galaxy," Chana said. "Not about how you were feeling about your ex-boyfriend."

"Oh," was all I could come up with. Damned mysterious social cues. "Um, yeah, that stuff is fine."

"What did you mean by an imbalance?" Seth asked.

"Yeah, sorry about that. Didn't mean to dump that on you."

"No it's fine. We asked how you were and you answered about the thing most worrying you," Chana said. "That's cool. But, yeah, what did you mean she would be okay with an imbalance?"

"Well..." I started, pausing to stall for time while thinking of my answer. "I think, and the girls at school agree, that big power imbalances make for awkward or short-lived relationships. When I first met Declan, he had these cool abilities with machines and computers and I knew he could do some sort of magic or something, but I didn't really know what or how much. I was impressed when he blew a vehicle all to shit with a lightning bolt, but it seemed like having a thunderstorm handy wasn't really a thing. Then at school, we started all this survival training and magic was forbidden. They wanted to teach us the skills I already knew. So I got kind of held up as an example. And I wasn't a freak among werewolves and witches. They separated us physical kids from the ones who used powers of the mind, so I didn't really see what they all got up to. Some shit went down in survival class and Declan got hurt really bad, beat up by an Alpha werewolf. I didn't react as well as I should have. Not my finest moment. Without going into the details, I got a bit confused. When he showed his true abilities, the ones he'd been taught to conceal all his life, it was a bit... shocking. Kid was like a one-man armored tank brigade for destructive ability. So I went from thinking my skills were all that to watching him shoot lasers out of his hands and throw cars around with his mind. Now he's way,

way worse. But Stacia is a werewolf, and her wolf has chosen him. And while she's kind of a poster child for what a were should be capable of, he's like… well, you saw," I said, pointing at the television. "But the wolf wants what it wants—at least that's how the kids at school talk about it. All the boy wolves mooned after Stacia but when she chose Declan, they got over it like she was dead or something. Anyway, it won't matter whether he can blow up a moon or barely feed himself. Her wolf won't care either way."

Neither of them said anything for like ten seconds. Nine-point-four, according to my internal clock.

"Well. Okay, I guess that makes some sense," Seth said.

"Hey, look, they just cut to the press conference," Chana said, pointing at the screen, like she was glad for the change of topic.

I moved around the end of the sofa, aiming for the lone chair on the side, but Chana and Seth moved apart, automatically, without taking their eyes from the screen. I froze for a split second. Chana glanced at me and patted the seat between them, eyes flicking back to the conference.

Oddly touched, I sat between them and started to eat while watching.

"—so I can say, as your mayor, that I have been unequivocally reassured that there is no danger. The threat has been contained. Now, as to the particulars of last night's events, here is FBI Director Tyson to explain."

"Thanks Eric. I am Tucker Tyson, Director of the FBI. Last night, my agents successfully neutralized a national threat," the big man began, fully puffed up. SAC Richards stood next to him, looking pretty self-important.

"Director Tyson, is it true it was a Vorsook? Here—in Philly?"

a reporter yelled out from the front row. Tyson frowned at being interrupted, but the sheer eagerness of the press seemed to give him some pause. He opened his mouth to speak, but sudden motion stopped him. Three small Omega orbs shot out above the podium area and came to one of those sudden, complete stops. They were spaced out in a triangle, one in front, two equidistant to the rear. Light flickered and suddenly President Polner was standing there, right next to the FBI director.

Tyson, Richards, the mayor, and the Philly Police chief all jumped or stepped back, totally taken off guard, and the press corps got loud with startled shouts. President Polner looked a little dazed, himself, but then a dazzling smile lit up his face as he looked around. He held up both hands in a calming gesture.

"My friends, my apologies for the theatrics. But I so wanted to be there in person and the responsibilities of state were keeping me here in Washington, so when Omega offered to project me holographically, well, I'm sure you all understand." The press laughed, a bit nervously.

"Mr. President, are you saying you are just a hologram?" the same reporter asked.

"Yes, exactly. Tucker, my apologies for upstaging you, but this is a vital moment and your victory deserves complete recognition. My friends, Director Tyson is likely far too modest to give you the best and most complete explanation of the role he and his agents have played in this war between worlds.

"Director Tyson had the enormous foresight and wisdom to create a special task force, back when he was appointed by my predecessor. This task force, the Special Threat Response Team, was designed from the ground up to give the Bureau a well-equipped tool to handle the threats of our post-emergence world. And that same team has, under Tucker's guidance, handled multiple events with skill and excellence. But what they've accomplished here is nothing

short of brilliant. To detect, through rigorous but largely old-school investigative work, an alien threat right here in one of our oldest cities, then neutralize that threat without harm to civilians and with minimal collateral damage is absolutely outstanding."

"Mr. President, wasn't the aerial battle handled by the Omega and the Warlock?"

"Jerry? Wow, you got here from the DC bureau faster than I did, and I'm working at the speed of light!" Polner joked, getting another laugh, even from the reporter.

"The answer is... of course! You think even our best-equipped law enforcement are ready to fight space battles? Hell no. You find yourself facing dinosaurs with a pea shooter, you call in heavy artillery! Tucker's team, through their interface with Omega, requested very special aid, and they got it. But, and this is no mean feat, they handled the actual Vorsook, itself, by themselves!"

"Where are they, sir? They don't seem to be here?" another reporter asked.

"No, they're not. Some are recovering from wounds received in battle and some are just keeping low, on Tucker's orders. There is, at least for now, more to be gained by keeping them anonymous than giving them their much-earned limelight," Polner said. *"I predict that you will meet them in the not-too-distant future, but for now, they are staying low."*

"Sir, there are those who say foreign agents were involved?"

"Mike, you must be as fast as Jerry here. Yes, I can say that some aid was offered by our Chinese allies, very specialized aid that was extremely vital. That's all I will say as, again, I don't want to endanger our assets or theirs. Here is the story in a nutshell: Special Threat Response, on their own, discovered an anomaly that led them here to Philadelphia. Further investigation revealed the likelihood of Vorsook operations to subvert part of our national will to fight. Operations conducted by the team resulted in flushing out the alien

and its weapons platform. That platform was destroyed, as you all know, by the efforts of Omega and Mr. O'Carroll, who, while still recovering from the events in the Aleutians, still rose to the challenge. I have spoken to Mr. O'Carroll, not an hour ago, and thanked him for his service and was reassured that he is none the worse for the experience." The president shook his head with a disbelieving smile. *"That young man could give lessons in modesty. But I digress. After the successful elimination of the aerial weapon, which some of you are calling the Vorsook Saucer of Doom... it wasn't even saucer shaped? Nonetheless, once it was defeated, the Special Threat team assaulted the actual Vorsook entity responsible, in its hiding place, and not only survived the confrontation but defeated it. The alien was killed during the firefight and three of the team, including the team leader, sustained severe injuries. All are currently out of danger and beginning the recovery process. Tucker, again, my compliments on your extraordinary team."*

"Ah, thank you, Mr. President. Very kind of you to say. Now, I think the president has summarized events throughly, so I will take questions, although it seems he was answering them all along."

The Q and A that followed covered all kinds of rumors, most of them flat wrong, but a few containing kernels of truth. Mostly questions about the extent of the damage, the operations the alien was conducting, and the follow-up investigations, all of which Tyson handled smoothly. A few reporters pushed for more information on the STRT but Tyson deflected everything thrown his way. The president's hologram stayed beside him, but Polner referred any questions thrown his way back to Tyson, except one.

"Mr. President, it has been said that numerous violations of foreign airspace and FAA regulations have been committed by the Omega computer. What is being done about that, sir?"

"I can't answer for other countries, Simon, but I am assured by the head of the FAA that Omega is filing all appropriate flight plans

prior to flying. As Omega has access to virtually every flight system and air controller network on Earth, I would say it is uniquely suited to fly its vehicles through inhabited air space. In fact, I'll let you know a little tidbit you might not have heard... since Omega's own emergence, there has not been a single flight accident related to air traffic control. And several incidences involving mechanical issues were solved by Omega's attention to our airspace."

You could tell that the reporter wanted more, but Tyson called on a different journalist, who asked about human accomplices to the alien, and all attention shifted to that topic.

Finally, after about ten minutes more, Tyson thanked the press, the president thanked the press, the mayor, and Tyson, then blinked out, the three Omega drones zipping away too fast to follow.

Seth turned down the volume with the remote and turned our way. "Well, that was a surprise," he said.

Chana snorted. "No one was more surprised than Tyson... except maybe SAC Richards. Why *he* was even there, I don't know. He lost Caeco's Chinese friend *twice.*"

"Oh? Fan disappeared?" I asked.

"Yeah, but I wouldn't worry. I have a feeling you'll be hearing from that man again," Chana said.

"I'll say!" Eve's voice said through the suite's speaker phone.

"Eve? You've been on the line? All this time?"

"Yup. Morris too. It was... enlightening. Thought you knew," she said.

"Oh," I said, mentally reviewing everything I had said earlier. "Wait. Why do you think Fan will be back? Assassination? He's welcome to try."

"Ah, no. His expressions are muted, but I'm a pretty good student of human body language. Let's just say that I think you might be his type," Chana said with a smile.

"Type? Are you kidding me?" I asked. I've gotten a lot better at back and forth banter, but I still miss things from time to time.

"Yeah. Kickass bioengineered soldier assassin who looks great in fitted tactical gear," Chana said.

"You think he's... attracted to me?" I asked.

"Your mouth is actually hanging open," Seth pointed out in a helpful manner. I closed the offending mandible, eyes still on Chana Mazar and her Cheshire Cat smile. I always thought that was a funny phrase, but Talon gets it when he drops a fat chipmunk or mouse on my living room floor, and my teammate absolutely had one now.

"We almost killed each other with knives," I protested. Wait... hadn't I said the same thing to Mitch?

"That's like speed dating for you uber combat types," Eve said. Damn. Was everybody that blind?

"Incoming call from Agent Jay," Omega said.

"Good morning, team. Did any of you happen to catch the news conference?" Agent Jay asked over the speakerphone.

"Yes, pretty much all five of us," Seth said.

"So you'll understand that we are done with this mission as of now. Follow-up interviews and investigations will be conducted by the Philadelphia field office."

"Wait... they get to take over our case? They didn't do anything... except lose that Chinese spy," Seth protested.

"Yes, and they are being punished by doing the tedious cleanup work on a case that we have already resolved. Our mission will be to

track Agent Fan and recapture him if he's still in country, or make sure he's out, if that's the case. As we are at less than full strength until Alice and Mitch fully recover, this will keep our hands full."

"*How are they?*" Eve asked.

"Since you've most likely already hacked the hospital's medical systems, you probably know that Alice is out of ICU. She's awake and mostly lucid. She has multiple fractures that will take time to heal, but otherwise she'll make a full recovery. Mitch is weak from blood loss, but his stump is clear of infection and the pain is well under control. Both are slated to be released today, as additional hospital stay will not provide any additional benefit. So... today you all will pack up our gear and prep for travel back to DC. Caeco, you will pick me up with your personal vehicle and the two of us will proceed back to headquarters. Eve and Morris, work with Omega on tracking Fan. Build out a full workup on him and his movements. Chana and Seth, after you pack up the suite, you'll use the Suburban to transport Mitch and Alice back home. Tomorrow we start our hunt."

"He'll have had almost thirty-six hours' head start. *I'd* be out of the country if I had that much of a lead," I said. "We need to start the hunt now!"

"At the request of the president, Director Tyson has ordered us to begin the hunt tomorrow, and no sooner. Computer work not included in that prohibition. Understand?"

"The president is letting him get out?" I guessed.

"Exactly. But if he chooses to remain in country, we'll find him. Either he leaves on his own or we recapture him and this time hold him. Chana, what do you think he'll do?"

"Standard doctrine would call for escape, evasion, and egress. However, I will point out that I believe he is mildly fascinated with our own enhanced operator," Chana said, smirking at me.

"I concur. Caeco, what do you think?"

"He'll egress. Either he'll slip out of the country as invisibly as possible or, if Chana is right, he'll make intentional slips to create a trail," I said.

"A trail that you could follow? One that might lead you out of the country and somewhere he could better approach you?" Jay asked.

"Yeah, something like that," I said.

"Okay. Eve and Morris, you know what to do. My guess is he'll leave plenty of sign showing his trail. The rest of you have your orders. Caeco, I'll be ready to check out in forty-five minutes. Please be out front."

"Yes ma'am," I said.

The phone disconnected and both Seth and Chana laughed.

"What?" I asked, because it was clear that *I* was what was amusing them.

"You kind of come to attention when she gives you an order," Seth said. "It's kind of funny."

"Well, if you grew up getting beaten or tasered if you *didn't* come to attention, you might do it too," I said.

"Ouch. Sorry," he said with a wince.

"Let's pack," I said, waving it all away.

CHAPTER 39

My cat greeted me at the door when I got home. He let me feed him but wasn't about to let me pet him. He does this every time I'm away. Punishment for abandonment. It lasts about fifteen minutes and then he's usually in my lap, my lesson hopefully well learned. Today was no different.

So I was sitting in my living room, lap full of cat, when I heard the very slightest sound on the balcony. Talon heard it too, as he jumped off me and faced the sliding glass door, tail puffed up.

"Come in. It's unlocked," I said, my hand wrapped around the grip of my personal pistol, a Sigarms P320 9mm. The gun was tucked between the arm of my chair and the seat cushion.

A second ticked by and then the door slid open, revealing Fan dressed in the ubiquitous name-brand type of athletic clothing that many of my young neighbors wore on a regular basis, as did I.

"You are unsurprised?"

"Doctrine would call for rapid departure. But you don't strike me as the type to follow the predictable path. I wasn't sure, but I thought it a possibility, which is why the door was unlocked."

"You aren't going to attempt to capture me?" he asked, head tilted in slight bewilderment.

"We've been ordered to stand down from the hunt until tomorrow," I said, watching him. He could easily pass for any young professional, although a highly athletic one, and he was… cute. Girls would certainly notice him.

"You will not need that weapon," he said, nodding at my hand.

"In that case, you can push that knife back up your sleeve," I said, giving him a chin point of my own, my hand still on the Sig.

His fingers twisted and the little bit of hilt I had seen disappeared from his hand, which he held up, along with the other one, to show me they were empty.

"Have a seat," I said, taking my hand off the pistol and pointing at the sofa ten feet away.

He took a step in the direction of the couch and Talon hissed at him sharply, freezing him in place, his hands moving in ways I didn't like.

"You hurt my cat and I'll shoot you where you stand."

"*That's* a cat? I thought it was a small orange leopard," he said, hands falling away from hidden weapons. Then he took a careful step forward. Talon hissed again, jumping up on a side table that left the huge cat well within leaping distance of the intruder.

"He is trained to attack?" Fan asked me, serious.

I shook my head. "No, but he's a street cat."

"Close enough to attack, but from a different angle, forcing me to divide my attention. Exactly what a trained animal should do," he said, watching Talon, who watched him back.

"So. My cat's combat assessment aside, what do you want?" I asked.

He turned his dark eyes back on me for a second, then gave me a single small nod. "Yes. I sought you out, as we should not be adversaries. Our common enemy is the being that died in that underground dwelling in Philadelphia."

"The old enemy of my enemy is my friend trope?"

"Essentially. Although we are not friends. Yet. I think at this point we are potential associates with very complementary skills and abilities. My commander feels the future may require us to work together to protect our planet."

"So this is what? An assassin meet and greet?"

"Such colorful expressions. Yes. It is a meet and greet. Our last two encounters were perhaps too *busy* for casual conversation."

"Hmm. Okay, Fan... what do you use for a last name? Group number? Personal identifier code?"

"I don't use those," he said, a flicker of something like pain flashing through his eyes.

Something, perhaps the intuition Jetta and Ashley always talked about, told me the reason. "At least *you* have a sister. None of my siblings made it."

"At least *you* have a parent," he shot back, eyes narrowed.

I stared at him for a second, then burst out laughing. His expression turned to confusion.

"My *mother* is the least motherly person on the planet. If your sister is as focused and disciplined as you are, then she is still ten times more emotional than Dr. Abigail Jensen."

His head tilted again. It was kind of cute. "Our intelligence indicates that your mother was raised by a normal husband and wife couple. How would she be as emotionally stunted as individuals brought up in a combat training facility?"

"It's just how she is. I never got to meet my grandparents, but I think they must have been very confused by having a child as un-childlike as I think she was. But even combat instructors show emotion, if mainly anger, disgust, and disappointment. They usually also exhibit humor, sarcasm, and, occasionally, minor approval."

"I see. So this, here, this exchange we are having now, is exactly what is potentially helpful. It provides some level of understanding."

"Sure. When can I meet your sister? What's her name?"

"Her name is Daiyu. When can *we* meet your mother?"

"Black Jade? Hmm. Pretty name. My mom? Um, I'll take you to my mom anytime you want, but only if you acknowledge, in writing, that you do so of your own free will and not under any coercion."

He frowned outright, perhaps the most emotion I had seen yet. "You are not afraid I would kidnap her and smuggle her to China?"

I laughed. "You are funny, Fan. All full of yourself with your augmented strength, speed, senses, intelligence. She'd eat you for breakfast. In fact, it would be all I could do to keep her from locking you away for permanent study."

He frowned even deeper, opening his mouth to speak but closing it again, clearly at a loss for words.

"Fan, my mother raised *me* in a lab facility. She oversaw every aspect of my care, training, and development. She knew every capability, every advantage that I had, and had planned ahead with quintuple redundancy to contain me. If she, herself, hadn't led the escape, I would still be in that lab. I would love nothing better than to drop you on her unexpectedly and watch the fun, but I wouldn't do that to my worst enemy."

"But she is only human?"

"Hah! There's prejudice for you. You think because you were carefully designed by science that nature couldn't create your match on its own? Like, say, werewolves? Vampires, at least older ones; the newbies are pathetic. Mother is *not* your physical match. But do not delude yourself into believing that you are *her* mental match, no matter what they did to your IQ. She was born with a unique mixture of ruthless sociopathic genius that you can't comprehend."

He was taken aback. Clearly our conversation wasn't going in the direction he had envisioned.

"You make her out to be some kind of villain?"

"If that's what she'd chosen for a path then yes, she'd be a supervillain. But luckily, she is fully focused on the pursuit of knowledge. Power, money, prestige—none of that means dirt to her. Knowledge. That's what she wants. That's what she hoards."

He looked at me, deep in thought, processing what I had said. Then he glanced at the clock on my wall.

"You will pursue me to the best of your abilities?" It was more statement than question.

"Yes. Of course. I've been ordered to."

He nodded. "As I thought. Then I will take my leave and make use of my remaining hours to ensure you do not catch me. This has been... informative. We will have to reassess our profile on your mother."

"Yes. Do. If she *let* you kidnap her, then it would be because she wanted to penetrate your own programs."

"You are truly that confident in her?"

"She has had more than a year with almost unlimited Demidova funding to prepare her lab. It is undoubtedly a deathtrap. In fact, she likely designed its protections with Chris Gordon and Tanya Demidova in mind. Now *that* would be cool to watch."

"She would prevail against even them?" he asked, incredulous.

"Actually, I don't think so. But it would be a hell of a fight. She can only surmise so much about them; they haven't shown the world everything about themselves. She is very wary about them."

"What about your ex-romantic interest?"

"Declan?" It was my turn to be incredulous.

"Yes. Would she capture him?"

"She wouldn't try. Like Chris and Tanya, there are far, far too many unknowns with him. You saw yourself, at the shipyard."

"He was not invulnerable."

"No, he wasn't. But I'm not sure how Omega would react to a conflict between my mother and the dynamic duo. I *know* damned well how he'd react to a threat to Declan."

He looked thoughtful. "You have been very insightful, Caeco Jensen. I hope to meet with you again. I would like to introduce you to Daiyu should opportunity present itself. But for now, I will take my leave," he said, giving me a little bow, eyes locked on mine. Then he stepped backward, graceful and sure-footed, back out the door and then, with a little jump, he was gone.

I couldn't help myself, rushing the balcony to see what I could see. Outside, it was early evening, nowhere near dark enough to hide from my eyes. I saw nothing below me on the most obvious path down, the one I might take in an emergency, like a fire. Looking up, I saw just a trace of motion at the corner of the roof, near the end of the building. Then a face peered over the side of the roofline, giving me a small wave before disappearing.

Interesting.

CHAPTER 40

"You allowed him to escape." It was an accusation.

"Yes, Mother." We were in her lab, me on a stool, her bent over the results of her tests on the latest batch of Declan's blood. She hadn't told me it was his, but I could smell it.

"The reason?"

"He is correct. We need allies more than we need additional enemies."

"You were impressed with this Vorsook." A statement.

"Yes."

"And you allowed them to just spirit it away?"

I reached into my coat pocket and pulled out a vial of green fluid, setting it carefully on her lab counter.

"Ah. You attempt to beguile me with a present?"

"Is it working?"

She picked up the vial and studied it, eyes glittering. "Yes. Clever girl."

"How is the Declan project going?" I asked, waving a hand at her test papers.

She raised one carefully groomed eyebrow.

I knew without a word what she wanted. "Smell."

"Excellent. Both to your senses and the project itself. His centrioles are almost fully recovered and the structure of them has enlarged."

"Meaning what? Enhanced ability to move energy?"

"That is my theory. Your observations during the battle support that. In addition, Stacia has told me that his physical condition is improving steadily. This is the last sample I will be getting, as he has refused more. But this alone advances my understanding of what he does immensely."

"Could you design it into a person?"

"At this moment? No. But by the time you provide me with grandchildren, perhaps."

"You believe that I will allow you to engineer my children, should I ever choose to have any?"

"Ah, dear heart. You most certainly *will* have children."

It hit me in a flash. "You designed something into me, didn't you?"

"Let's just say it will be very difficult for you to circumvent your own nature."

I stared at her. The concept wasn't shocking. This was, after all, my mother. Still, I hadn't expected it and it caught me off guard. But the prime directive of my childhood was in full effect—never show weakness in front of mother.

"In fact, I had hopes for the witch, but you ruined that yourself. Now, between the wolf and the computer, it would be very difficult to obtain his sperm."

"It's good that you acknowledge that, Doctor Jensen," Omega said over the lab speakers.

"Just facts and odds, that's all," Mother said with a shrug. "But there is a new contender."

"Fan is merely a fellow soldier."

"Hmm," she said, then held out her hand, palm up. I looked at it, then back up at her. Triumph gleamed in her eyes. With a sigh, I pulled the second vial from my pocket. This one had only a tiny drop of fluid, but it was red rather than green.

"That's all?"

"I managed to get the tip of my knife into his hand. That's all that was on it."

"Hmm, sloppy of him. Did he, by chance, get any off you?"

I shook my head.

She smiled. "Good girl. He may not be ideal after all. Although he did elude the government, yes?"

"Yup. Very smooth. Hardly any trail at all. We think he hid in a tractor trailer and then went over the Southern border. Pretty easy for someone with enhanced senses, although they're starting to include weres on the border patrol. That'll make it harder."

"Well, are you ready to leave that ridiculous agency and come work with me?"

"No. Absolutely not. I'd go crazy in a lab, plus I make an actual difference out there. Remember, we *did* flush out an alien and kill it."

"Hmm, true. Plus, you obtain such interesting samples for me," she said, acquiescing too easily.

"You knew I wasn't going to leave... why ask?"

"Just because *I* know something doesn't mean you know it too," she said. "I like to hear conviction in your voice. If the world is going to benefit from *my* life's work, then *you,* at least, better be happy with it."

I sat back and watched her label the samples, answering her questions as she added dates, times (because my onboard system could provide exquisite detail), and other information pertinent to her studies. But while I watched and even, at some level, recorded her motions, my mind was on her words.

After a moment, I smiled. "I love you too, Mom."

She snorted, not even looking up. But there was no lecture on useless emotion, no warnings of ill logic, no diatribes against biologically induced states of mind. Hmm. Mom was getting soft in her old age.

AUTHOR'S NOTES:

Caeco arrived as a character way back in *Fallen Stars*. Unfortunately, she slipped out of the main storyline as her path veered away from Declan's. But I always liked Caeco and I was a little shocked at how much fans ended up hating her. After all she is just a very young adult when we first meet her and she was raised in an extremely harsh and unforgiving environment. Today, almost everyone can use a little therapy to help them through the trials and tribulations of life. I shudder to think how much Caeco would need. And as a father of two daughters, I'm very, very aware that young love is much more about learning than it is about long-term permanence. So it never occurred to me that she and Declan could be a forever couple like Chris and Tanya. And breakups, being full of pain, are usually a bit messy. When a fan wondered what she was up to, I did too. This is the result. I hope it answers a few questions.

As usual, thanks to Gareth Otton for spot on artwork and thanks to my editor, Susan Gottfried, for trying to teach me how to use the English language more goodly. Thank you to Aikido of Maine for an excellent introduction to a wonderful martial art. And thanks to my nephew, Trooper Ryan Mousaw for help with law enforcement protocol. Any and all errors made in either of these areas are entirely my own.

Demon Accords will continue on, even as I prepare to end the Zone War Trilogy and ramp up for a full high fantasy series that's been crowding my brain lately – remember the word Thandarra. But no worries, there is much story left to tell in the universe of Chris, Tanya and company.

Finally, thanks to my amazing family for all they do to support me and prop me up. And thanks to you, my fans, for continuing the journey that began over ten years ago.